He passed the boulder that marked his last checkpoint. He was only five minutes from the stone jaguars.

As he approached the two effigies, the sound came rumbling down the canyon like low thunder. Conrad was confused. There wasn't a cloud in the sky.

The noise came again, louder, more guttural.

Conrad looked up at the valley ahead of him. In the distance the beam of a flashlight bounced erratically. He could hear the muffled sound of running feet and a man gasping for breath.

The roar shattered the night, reverberating off the canyon walls. A second later a man screamed, a piercing, blood-chilling scream.

The beam of the flashlight disappeared as the night air filled with the vicious sounds of an enraged animal.

Conrad stood frozen, knowing if he dared move, he would be next. . . .

Dell Books by Micah S. Hackler

COYOTE RETURNS
LEGEND OF THE DEAD
THE SHADOWCATCHER
THE DARK CANYON

THE
DARK CANYON

◄ A SHERIFF CLIFF LANSING MYSTERY ►

MICAH S. HACKLER

A DELL BOOK

Published by
Dell Publishing
a division of
Bantam Doubleday Dell Publishing Group, Inc.
1540 Broadway
New York, New York 10036

The trademark Dell is registered in the U.S. Patent and Trademark Office.

ISBN: 0-440-22358-X

Printed in the United States of America

Published simultaneously in Canada

November 1997

10 9 8 7 6 5 4 3 2 1

WCD

Acknowledgments

Continued thanks to George Sewell and Dan Baldwin. The FACTORY really works.

To my wife, Suzie, who says watching me finish a book is like watching a woman give birth, thanks for putting up with the long nights, short weekends, and general chaos.

I want to give special thanks to Jim Krestalude and Dr. Linda Welden, old and dear friends who've provided both encouragement and inspiration over the years.

To Bobette Apple, a special woman and a special friend, thank you for telling me you loved anything I ever wrote.

As always, thanks to my agent, Nancy Love, and her assistant, Sherri. Also to Jacob Hoye, my editor, and the usual suspects at Dell.

IT WAS IN THE DAYS BEFORE THE LONG WALK, BEFORE we were driven from Cañon de Chelly. It was when we still called Eagle Chief Carson our brother. It was during the time when the white men fought their great war to the east.

Star Chief Carleton came to our land with two thousand Pony Soldiers. There were no Gray Coats for him to fight, so he waged war on us, the Dinneh. He wanted all that the red man had, our ponies, our cattle, our land. He wanted our gold and silver, but we had no such riches.

In his greed and madness he learned of Cañon de San Carlos, the place we call Chaco, and the great ruins there. We told him this place was built long ago by the Anasazi. We said there was nothing there but the ghosts of the dead and evil. But he did not believe. He said it was built by Montezuma. He said it held great treasures of gold and so he sent his soldiers. When they found nothing there they captured a Dinneh shepherd boy. They tortured him and said his sheep would die if he did not take them to where Montezuma hid his gold.

The boy could think of only one place. His grandfather had spoken of it. But it was a place of evil, where no man should walk. Still he led them to the mountains, to the valley of the stone lions. The soldiers saw many mounds of earth, the graves of the Anasazi. They began to dig wildly with their knives and their hands as if they had gone crazy.

In the Great Mound they found their gold, as well as turquoise, and jade, and a strange stone of green, carved in the image of a demon lion. The bones of the dead were tossed aside and trampled, the soldiers not caring about the evil they had done.

To keep the canyon their secret the soldiers chose to kill the boy. One man in their midst stopped them, turning him loose. This angered the other soldiers and they turned against him. He was tied to a piñon tree and left for the *zopilotes*, the buzzards.

That night, though, the demon of the valley walked. Angered that the souls of the Anasazi had been awaked, the demon went on a rampage, killing the horses and destroying the men in the most terrible ways. The only one spared was the man who showed kindness to the shepherd boy.

The lone survivor returned to Star Chief Carleton. He told the story of what had happened, but he was not believed. He was cast from the society of white men and he went to his grave a forgotten man. And until the day he died, he never again mentioned the night when the demon walked.

But across the high desert, even on the stillest of days, you will sometimes see a lone cloud of dust chasing phantom riders. We call this *niyol bééhoozin da*, the Wind of the Lost. The dust is all that remains of the Pony Soldiers who dared to wake the dead from their sleep, doomed to ride forever in search of the Tombs of the Anasazi.

—Navajo legend

MATTHEW VICINTI SAT ON A SMALL BOULDER, SUR-
veying his flock of sheep in the dim moonlight. Before
the sun had gone down he'd made one last count.
There were still 251.

He took a deep breath, trying to appreciate the
fresh mountain air and trying to stay awake. He had
251 head. A week earlier there had been 255. He
had lost four sheep in as many days. He couldn't
afford to spend the night in the cabin. He had to keep
watch. He was going to have hell to pay as it was.
Four sheep in four days.

He was almost glad this would be his last summer
in the pastures. He would be turning sixteen in another
month. That meant next year he would have to get a
real job. The task of watching the family flock would
pass on to Michael, his younger cousin. Michael would
be thirteen by then, the same age Matthew was when
he began minding the flock in the summer pastures.

Matthew shifted the carbine on his lap. Four
sheep in four days. The numbers kept running through
his mind. Two, three sheep in a summer season. That
was acceptable. There were lots of predators in the
mountains: coyotes, bears, mountain lions. Sometimes

even an eagle would carry away a lamb. He had lost two sheep early in the summer. That was to be expected. But things had gone well for the last five weeks. Now, suddenly, four sheep in four days. How was he going to explain that?

The Vicinti brothers, Abraham and Jacob, didn't keep the largest flock on the Jicarilla Apache Reservation. At 250 head it barely represented three percent of the tribe's total. But the wool and the spring lambs the flock provided accounted for a sizable portion of the family income. The Vicinti brothers weren't herdsmen or farmers. They were tribal policemen. Matthew was proud of the fact that his father, Abraham—or Bram, as he liked to be called—had been promoted to chief of the tribal police.

Being tribal policemen, however, didn't allow much time for second jobs, so the brothers maintained a flock of sheep to supplement their wages. Keeping the flock was a family affair.

Matthew's grandfather had been a sheepherder his entire life. When he was younger, Matthew spent his summers helping in the mountain pastures. After his grandfather died, it was only natural for the Vicinti family to continue herding and it made sense for Matthew to maintain the flocks.

A deep sigh came from the ground next to Matthew's boulder. Boss, his lead dog, was trying to get comfortable for a short nap. Tico, Boss's mate, sat on the opposite side of the rock watching and listening, just like her master.

Matthew crossed and uncrossed his legs, trying to find a more comfortable position. Even though he been there for seven weeks, these highland pastures were unfamiliar to him. The herdsmen drew lots to see which mountain meadows they would use for summer grazing. The Vicinti brothers were assigned pastures on the southwestern slopes of the reservation.

For Matthew it was unfamiliar territory. He was twenty miles from the nearest highway and sixty miles from his home in Dulce. His living quarters were a small, one-room cabin at the edge of the pasture. He had no electricity. He drew his water from a well, using a hand pump. He used a kerosene lamp at night and cooked on a kerosene stove. Once a week his father or some other family member showed up with supplies.

Except for those brief visits his only companionship was the two sheepdogs.

The next visit wasn't for two more days.

He had no idea how he was going to explain the loss of four head. He had looked for tracks but there were none. He had looked for splotches of blood where the animals had been attacked but couldn't find any.

Boss and Tico slept outside. They always raised the alarm when they sensed the presence of a predator. For the last four nights they had been silent.

Matthew began to suspect the sheep were being rustled, but it didn't make any sense. Why take only one sheep at a time? Why not six or a dozen?

He had reasoned his way out of any plausible explanation. The best he could do now was make sure no more sheep disappeared, even if it meant a twenty-four-hour watch. His father would expect that of him.

All of the disappearances happened at night. He figured if he could stay awake till morning, he could always catch a few winks during the day.

He had debated whether or not to light his

lantern. If it was lit, the predator would probably stay away and the flock would be safe. But Matthew wanted to catch the culprit. He wanted to be able to explain what had taken his sheep. So he sat in darkness at the edge of the pasture, waiting.

Sometime past midnight a ewe at the far side of the flock gave a nervous bleat. A handful of others joined in.

Matthew jerked awake. He had been dozing, but the sound of the anxious flock roused him. To his side Boss emitted a low growl.

The quarter moon, though high overhead, gave little light.

More plaintive bleats joined the first ones and the flock began to shift nervously. Tico gave one sharp bark and looked from her master to the restless sheep.

"Go on, girl," Matthew instructed. "Go get 'em!"

He was on his feet now, straining his eyes to see anything. Tico took off running, followed by Boss. Both dogs ran for the center of the flock, barking viciously. The sheep scattered to let them through.

Matthew ran after them, bolting a shell into his carbine as he did.

The dogs ran through the flock toward the far end of the pasture, disappearing into the woods beyond. As Matthew got closer he could hear the savage yips and snarls of animal combat.

He slowed his pace. The woods were dark. The battle was close. He didn't know what to expect. One of the dogs let out a terrifying yelp and the commotion in the darkness was decreased by half.

Matthew recognized Boss's bark as the animal pressed his attack. The boy stood frozen. He didn't know if he should follow, fire blindly into the darkness, or run.

The mountain pasture filled with the unearthly scream of a wounded animal.

Boss let out one final yelp.

Knowing he wouldn't be harming his dogs now, Matthew put the carbine to his shoulder and began firing, hoping he would hit something.

Two, three, four shots. He fired as quickly as he could chamber the next round.

From the corner of his eye he saw darkness move within darkness. He wheeled around as the air was shattered by the creature's roar.

Before Matthew could chamber the next round a great claw came crashing down on him, ripping the rifle from his hands. A second claw swiped at his head, knocking him to the ground. Before he could scream, powerful jaws crushed his windpipe and snapped the vertebrae in his neck.

Death was mercifully quick.

During the height of the melee the flock stampeded, trying to find safety as far away as possible. Three sheep were killed, a dozen others injured. The rest scattered into the mountains.

It would be two days before anyone discovered the tragedy.

2

JOEL CONRAD PULLED HIS TRUCK TO A STOP IN FRONT of the Carson Trading Post, waving the dust away as it billowed through the open window. "One day," he promised himself, "one day when I'm rich, I'm going to have a car with air conditioning."

It took him two tries to unlatch the driver's door so it would open. "And I'm going to have a truck with doors that work."

He stepped from the cab and stretched. The thought of buying new shock absorbers also raced through his mind. It was quickly followed by the thought of a cold beer.

He went around to the walk-in camper shell at the back of his truck and opened the door. A medium-sized ice chest sat on the floor. He was pretty sure it was empty, but he checked it just the same. He was right. No beer.

Pulling the chest from the truck, he stomped the dust from his boots before pushing open the door and going inside. The cool air wafted over him and he stopped and closed his eyes, truly appreciating the modern, decadent convenience.

Harvey Sparks looked up from his paper. He was

perched behind his counter on a padded chrome lounge stool he had rescued from a junk heap. A man in his mid-sixties, he had a full head of white hair, leathery, weather-beaten skin, and piercing blue eyes. He looked as though he spent more time scrambling through the high desert than sitting inside an air-conditioned store. "Well, if it isn't my favorite grad student."

"I told you, Harvey. I'm a Ph.D. candidate now."

"If you're still going to school, you're a student." Sparks snorted.

"And as far as being your favorite!" Conrad smiled. "I'll bet I'm the only graduate student you know."

"Don't flatter yourself, Professor. They've had summer excavations over in Chaco every year since I've been here. That's over forty years. You graduate students are slave labor. Hell, I remember when your Doc Vencel came through the first time. He was your age."

"He was never my age." Conrad grunted. "He was born forty years old." He walked over and set his ice chest down in front of the beer cooler.

Legend had it that the Carson Trading Post was named after Kit Carson, the famed Indian fighter and mountain man. In fact, he was supposedly the original proprietor. The remnants of an adobe house stood behind the present store. The ruins represented what was left of the original establishment. At least that's what the plaque in front of the ruins said.

The Trading Post served as a filling station, grocery and general mercantile store, tourist trinket emporium, and trading station. Many of Sparks's Navajo, Pueblo, and Apache customers bartered handcrafted goods for a fill-up or a bag of groceries. He managed to stay afloat by selling their handiwork to tourists and the occasional art dealer. A third of the single-roomed store was dedicated to Indian crafts.

"You and the doc still bumping heads?"

"Only for ten more days. That's when the dig's officially over and we get to go back to school."

"So what brings you over here in the middle of the afternoon? Shouldn't you be in the canyon gluing pottery back together?"

"I won the toss. I got to go get the beer this time."

"Nageezi's a lot closer to the canyon. And the beer's cheaper."

"You don't want my business?"

"I was just curious. The trading post is ten miles out of your way."

"Would you believe me if I told you I stopped by because I missed you?" Conrad asked as he loaded his ice chest with cans of Budweiser.

"No."

He picked up the chest and lugged it over to the counter. "Actually, I've been doing some scrounging in the desert around here. A little independent research."

"Looking for anything in particular?"

"No, not really," Conrad admitted. "But crawling around on your hands and knees all day scraping away tons of sand with a dental pick gets old. And we're working on a site Wetherill probably found a hundred years ago. There's no challenge. Just tedium."

"It's called paying your dues, kid. You're not supposed to play National Geographic Explorer till you get that string of letters behind your name."

"You sound like Vencel." He reached inside his

shirt pocket and pulled out a black plastic film-roll container. "I need to get some pictures developed. If I dropped them off today, how long before you'd get them back?"

Sparks thought for a moment. "Let's see. Today's Wednesday. I can get it up to Bloomfield and back by noon on Friday."

"That sounds good."

Sparks reached under his counter and retrieved a film processing envelope. "Here."

Conrad started filling in the blank spaces on the envelope. "Can I use your address here?"

"Yeah. Just put Carson Trading Post. They'll know where it goes."

Conrad finished the address, then stuffed the film inside. "Harvey, you're the local historian around here."

"Yeah. Sort of."

"What does this look like to you?" Conrad reached into his pants pocket and produced a round brass object. He set it on the counter.

Sparks picked it up for closer examination. It was a button. Stamped into it was a tiny eagle with spread wings behind a federal shield. It was still shiny, as if it had been freshly polished. The proprietor's mouth was set in a pondering frown as he studied the piece. "Where'd you get it?"

"Just out there. On the desert," Conrad said vaguely. "Do you recognize it?"

"U.S. Regular Army. Cavalry, most likely. Civil War era. Could be from an officer's tunic."

"You sure it's Civil War era?"

"I'd bet you that case of beer you're buying that it is. I have a book in the back that can prove it."

"No, I'll take your word for it." A smile crept across Conrad's face. It was the kind of smile that said he knew a secret no one else in the world knew.

"Is this what you were out looking for?"

"Not exactly." He studied the button for a moment. "Have you ever heard of Carleton's Lost Patrol?"

"Who in these parts hasn't?"

"I thought I might have found a trace of it."

"Why? Do you have more of these?"

"No. Just the one. But if this is really from the time of the Civil War . . ."

"Just where did you say you found that?"

"You know, I can't even remember," Conrad said, putting the button back in his pocket. "It was just lying on top of the ground. When you're looking for dull brown pottery shards, something like that really grabs your eye."

"So you weren't looking for the Lost Patrol?"

Conrad shook his head. "That didn't even cross my mind until I was halfway here." He reached for his wallet. "I have four six-packs and I need a bag of ice."

"I'll make you an even trade," Sparks offered. "The beer for that brass button."

Conrad didn't think twice about the suggestion. "I don't think so, Harvey."

"That's twice as good a deal as you'll get with a dealer down in Santa Fe."

"How much for the beer?"

Sparks rang up the total on his register. "You know where the ice is outside. Anything else?"

"No. That's it." He paid for the beer and ice and picked up the ice chest. "See you Friday, Harvey."

"Yeah. See ya, kid."

Sparks watched as Conrad drove around the trading post to the dirt road leading to Chaco Canyon. Closing the register, he picked up the phone and dialed. A woman answered on the other end.

"Yeah, this is Sparks. Can you watch the trading post for a while? I want to take a run to the desert. Thanks. I'll see you in about ten."

Sparks walked to the back room, his living quarters. On one wall hung a large geographic survey map. The chart was well worn, with hundreds of annotations Sparks had made over the years. Conrad had arrived at the trading post by way of Highway 44. He had probably found the button somewhere to the south and east.

That helps a lot, Sparks thought. *Most of New Mexico is south and east of the trading post.*

3

INITIALLY, THE SOUTHERN APPROACH TO CHACO Canyon Monument is confusing. One mile short of the turnoff on Highway 57 is a brown national park sign signaling the approaching road. At the turnoff is another sign pointing up a dirt road. The marker indicates twenty-one miles to the visitors' center. There is no other sign of civilization. Visitors are easily convinced they are on the wrong road.

After winding past a few private ranch buildings the road climbs up a short hill to the top of the south plateau. The dirt-and-gravel road was designed to carry two-lane traffic. However, during the monsoon season portions of the road will be washed out or turned into mud bogs. Brave tourists in four-wheel-drive vehicles accept the challenge, sometimes blazing new paths in the sagebrush around the bogs, sometimes simply plunging through the mud, leaving ruts a foot deep. When the rains depart, the mud ruts bake as hard as adobe brick in the desert sun, leaving deep gouges in the road that even a Caterpillar can't eradicate. At places like this the road is not much more than a path, barely wide enough for one car.

Visitors are sometimes forced to retreat a quarter of a mile to let oncoming traffic through.

After the first hill of the plateau the vista is blocked by another hill a mile or two farther north. The expected view on top of the next hill is blocked by yet another. Not until the road has pushed nearly ten miles to the north does it reach the edge of the plateau.

From there a vast valley of sage and scrub brush opens up. The plateau to the east marks the Continental Divide. To the west is the drainage basin for the San Juan River. To the north are the three Chacra Mesas and Fajada Butte, marking the southern edge of Chaco Canyon, one of the richest archaeological sites in the Americas.

Conrad made his approach to the canyon from the north, the back door, as he liked to call it. The view from that direction was far less dramatic. The Chaco Plateau ended at the northern rim of the canyon. The gently rolling hills of the plateau blocked any grand vistas, so that the canyon itself didn't appear until the road began its descent to the canyon floor two hundred feet below.

Once he reached the canyon floor, Conrad turned his truck toward the west, away from Pueblo Bonito, Chetro Ketl, and the other restored sites. The Museum of the Americas was sponsoring their dig at Kin Escavada, an ancient pueblo site at the western edge of the monument. Buried for over eight hundred years, it had only come to light six years earlier during summer flooding.

Conrad had found the excavation work routine and boring and for the ten weeks of the dig had made himself as scarce as possible.

*   *   *

"Yeow!" Renee shrieked as she jumped up, grabbing the back of her neck. She wheeled around to face her tormentor.

Conrad stood with an aluminum can in each hand and a grin on his face. "It's just a cold beer."

"Sometimes you're a real pain in the butt. You know that, Joel?"

Three undergraduate students looked up from their trowels and dust brushes to see what the commotion was. When they saw it was only Joel Conrad, they went back to their tedious work, seemingly oblivious to the rest of the world around them.

"The sun's past the yardarms. It's cocktail hour."

"You wish." Renee grabbed one of the beers and popped the tab. "While you were out playing the prodigal son I cleared away three grids. You get to stay up tonight and classify the shards. I have four trays waiting for you."

Conrad surveyed the ruins as he opened the remaining can. Kin Escavada barely covered a quarter of an acre and less than a third of the site had been excavated. Preliminary studies revealed it was one of the older ruins in the canyon, probably abandoned before Pueblo Bonito and the other more elaborate palaces were even started. "Are all the shards from the same level?"

Renee took a sip from her can. "Yes."

"It'll take two minutes. Same stratum, same pottery."

"I think Dr. Vencel would like to see a little more detail in your analysis. We're looking at a transition layer. We have both Pueblo One and Early Pueblo Two pottery."

"I know. He expects me to separate Chaco shards from imported ceramics. I did that for my master's thesis. I'm a Ph.D. candidate. There are other things I want to work on."

"You signed on for this summer dig. It pays your bills."

"Barely."

"Considering the amount of time you've actually spent on-site, you should be grateful they're paying you at all."

Conrad studied his associate as he took another sip of beer. Renee Garland was a first-year graduate student. She was petite and sandy haired with skin that bronzed a golden brown in the summer sun. She straddled the fence between pretty and cute, a feature Conrad found almost unattractive. She tried too hard at sounding intelligent so people would take her seriously. She worked overly hard and long hours to gain the respect of Dr. Baron Vencel, her sponsor, and the other students in the department.

He could almost guess what would happen to her: summer digs; winter classes, either as a student or an instructor; a doctorate in archaeology by the time she was thirty; a department head by the time she was fifty; all the time trying to prove she was more than a cheerleader and at the same time missing out on everything else the world had to offer.

"Lighten up, Renee," Conrad said. "It really doesn't matter if the pottery gets classified tonight or not. Tomorrow Vencel's going to realize we have nine days left before we close down for the season. From here on out we'll be boxing up everything so we can haul it down to the university for the winter. That's when he'll worry about classifications." He glanced around. "Speaking of the master, where is he?"

"Santa Fe. He said he was late with a report to the museum staff."

"Couldn't he fax it from the visitors' center?"

"He said he tried, but the machine was down. He decided to take it himself. I guess he'll be back in the morning."

"All the more reason not to worry about his precious pottery pieces." Conrad finished off the rest of his beer in one long gulp.

4

IT WAS RENEE'S TURN TO SIZE UP HER ASSOCIATE. JOEL Conrad was average in height with a slim build. But he carried himself with a confidence that made him seem taller and older than his twenty-seven years. She'd had a crush on him for three years, ever since she had taken Introduction to Archaeology.

He was a master's candidate then and Arch 101 was one of the courses graduate students were allowed to teach. It was partly because of her crush and partly because she found archaeology so fascinating that she ended up in the field.

Renee knew she was attractive. She had been popular in high school. She had been popular as an undergraduate. She knew it had to do with her looks and the fact that she didn't abuse her advantage. She'd had her share of dates and proposals and had gotten plenty of propositions from graduate instructors and full professors.

But Conrad had been an enigma. He'd never made a pass. She'd seen him out on plenty of dates, so his masculinity wasn't in question. He just didn't seem to be interested in her. When she heard he was going to be the senior assistant on the Chaco Canyon dig that summer, she jumped at the chance to be the undergraduate coordinator. She was in charge of Huey, Dewey, and Louie. If she couldn't interest him sexually, maybe she had a shot at rousing his intellectual curiosity.

So far that had been a bust.

Almost as disappointing as his lack of interest in her was his near disdain for their work. He wasn't the meticulous, dust-chewing type. He spent as little time as possible on his hands and knees brushing away a millennium of dirt from buried pots and bones.

"There are the diggers and there are the discoverers," Conrad would say. "The diggers are content with gluing a few pottery pieces together and thinking that they've accomplished something. The discoverers have a vision of civilization, where it's been, where it's going. They're the ones who know how to find the hidden secrets of the past."

Dr. Vencel had referred to Conrad's views as the "Indiana Jones School of Archaeology." "He'd tear down five-thousand-year-old pyramid to recover a five-dollar scarab," Vencel had said, "and be damned with the architecture and technology it took to build the edifice."

Renee wasn't sure Joel Conrad was as bad as all that. He had rocked the foundations of North American archaeology with his master's thesis. Pundits in the field were still trying to disprove his theory, but after three years, they couldn't. He was backed up by dendrochronology, computer modeling, and a mound of pottery shards that had accumulated over three hundred years.

She knew Vencel resented his work, but Conrad had a protector, Dr. Elmo Giancarlo, director of the

Department of Archaeology at the University of New Mexico. Giancarlo not only held tight control over his department, he was the reigning Olympian in southwestern archaeology.

He had fought for years trying to push back the dates for man in the Americas. Up until the 1950s the deans of American anthropology ruled that Homo sapiens first crossed the Bering landbridge during the last ice age. He had been in the Americas no earlier than 10,000 B.C.E., Before the Common Era. Giancarlo led a small band of young Turks who believed otherwise. As their proof built and the old hard-liners died off, the dates of man in North America had been pushed back by ten, twenty, possibly forty thousand years.

The terms C.E. and B.C.E. were another contribution Giancarlo had helped establish. For years there were a lot of non-Christian historians and archaeologists who took offense over the Western use of "Before Christ" and "Anno Domini," the Year of Our Lord, as a dating system. Giancarlo was one of the senior members on the international committee that changed the nomenclature. A.D. was now C.E., the Common Era. Anything prior to that was considered B.C.E., Before the Common Era.

Because he had never backed down in any of his beliefs, the aging archaeologist had been unofficially anointed by his fellow North American scholars as their leader.

Giancarlo liked being king. He also liked nurturing the young minds coming up in the field, especially those that bucked convention. Joel Conrad had just one of those minds. The young Ph.D. candidate could do no wrong in the old man's eyes.

Renee could tell there was mutual dislike between Vencel and Conrad, though neither criticized the other openly. She thought Conrad's problem was that he didn't like authority figures. She suspected Vencel resented Conrad for being in Giancarlo's favor. Of course, Conrad didn't help his case. He was constantly out wandering the hills when he should have been digging in the trenches.

"How about another beer?"

Renee sloshed her can. She was nearly finished. "Sure. Why not?" She followed him to the back of his truck as he retrieved two more.

"So, let me guess," she said, sitting on his dusty rear bumper as she opened her beer. "You couldn't be bothered with Kin Escavada because you're busy doing research for your dissertation."

Conrad, who always had a flip response to almost any statement, seemed strangely quiet. Renee looked up to see him studying her intently. The expression on his face said, *How did you know?*

"Have you spent much time down at Bandelier?"

"I've climbed around there a few times," Renee admitted. "Why?"

"Did you ever go up to the Shrine of the Stone Lions?"

"Yeah. Once."

"The two statues were carved out of volcanic ash about seven hundred years ago. They're so eroded and weather beaten, you can hardly tell they're supposed to be lions."

"I remember."

"The story always went that the Pueblo people carved them so that they could pray to the lion spirits before they went on hunts. At least that's what the modern Pueblos say."

"So?"

"So maybe that's not what they were for." Conrad set his beer down and began pacing back and forth in front of Renee as he sculpted his theory with his hands. "Twenty years ago they thought they found a drainage canal on the Chaco Plateau leading from Pueblo Alto to Chetro Ketl. As they started looking around they found a few more of these canals. It dawned on them, these weren't canals. They were roads."

Joel Conrad had fallen in love with Chaco Canyon when he was fifteen, during a family camping trip. Even though the Conrads lived in Denver, he had managed to spend his summers working one job or another at the canyon just so he could ponder its mysteries.

Chaco Canyon had always been one of the lesser-known treasures of the American West. It didn't draw crowds like Yellowstone, Yosemite, or the Grand Canyon. It didn't enjoy the popularity of Mesa Verde or Santa Fe. Yet, despite its low profile, it had been designated by the United Nations as one of the ten most archaeologically significant regions in the entire world. In an area of less than thirty square miles over 9,500 separate archaeological sites had been identified.

Completely abandoned by the year 1200 C.E., the canyon had remained forgotten for over six hundred years. The Spanish first wrote of visiting the canyon in 1804 where a passing reference was made to the ruins. The first known American encounter occurred in 1849 when a detachment of U.S. Cavalry happened on the canyon while chasing marauding Navajos.

Scientific inquiry into the origins of the canyon ruins and the people who built them didn't start in earnest until the 1890s. Richard Wetherill, a cattle rancher and the man who discovered the great cliff dwellings of Mesa Verde, was the first white man to attempt systematic excavations of the sites. Despite the fact that he was considered a plunderer and an amateur by most archaeologists of the day, he assigned classifications to the different strata he studied that were still being used a hundred years later.

Over the hundred years of study Chaco Canyon had proved to be a giant onion. Every ten or twenty years, a new discovery was made, peeling back another layer of the great mystery called Chaco. In the twenties and thirties archaeologists identified ruins similar in design to the ones in Chaco Canyon. But these ruins were found as much as a hundred miles away. It was assumed they were built by a similar culture, but the scientists couldn't prove a direct link with the Chaco people. It wasn't until 1972 that archaeologists began to correlate aerial photographs of the area with markings on the ground. A large area of the Chaco Mesa had been cleared for what had formerly been presumed to be irrigation canals. The aerial photos show differently. The supposed canals were actually roads, roads that went on for miles. Some roads were direct links to ruins that had been discovered fifty years earlier. A couple of tracks actually led to the discovery of new ruins. And yet other roads led nowhere.

The largest ruin in Chaco Canyon was Pueblo Bonito. Shaped like a half-moon, at its zenith it was five stories high and contained five hundred separate rooms. Pueblo Bonito was the center of the Chaco culture. Its influence radiated a hundred miles in every direction. In antiquity it was said, in Europe, that all roads led to Rome. The same was true in the American Southwest five hundred years later, except that the roads led to Chaco Canyon and Pueblo Bonito.

However, despite everything that had been discovered about the Chaco Canyon and its people, the Anasazi, every answer only revealed more questions. Why was this dry canyon in the middle of a desert the center of a thriving culture for nearly four hundred years? Why had they come there to begin with? What drove them away? Who exactly were their descendants? Could the fall of the Chaco culture be a warning to the rest of the world?

Conrad was in love with the mysteries of Chaco, and Renee could feel his enthusiasm every time he talked about his mistress.

"I'm familiar with the Chaco road system, Joel. They've found over two hundred miles of roads. They go as far north as Aztec."

"And the theory is that they all lead to Pueblo Alto and funnel in to Pueblo Bonito."

"That's the foundation of your master's thesis."

"And it's accurate, as far as it goes."

"You mean, there's more?"

"What if there was a road system leading away from Chaco Canyon?"

"Well, they all lead away—"

"I mean, it leads to a place no one has seen for eight hundred years."

"In this day and age I'd say you're nuts. The Cliff

Palace they found over on the Anasazi Strip will probably be the last great find of this century. Maybe ever again."

"All right, then. People probably have been to this spot before, they just didn't realize what it was."

"I still don't know what you're talking about."

Conrad knelt in front of her. "Can you keep a secret?"

"I don't know. For how long?"

"Just till the end of the dig. I'll have my photographs back by then. I'll have more artifacts."

"What have you found?"

"In Frijoles Canyon, just beyond the Shrine of the Stone Lions, are dozens of burial sites. It was always assumed that was sacred ground because of the lions. What if it was the other way around? Maybe the Stone Lions were placed there to guard the graves."

"I know you don't like using the term *Anasazi* for the pre-Pueblo people, but I'm going to use it now. From everything we've ever found, the Anasazi didn't seem to place much significance in the afterlife. They buried their dead in shallow graves, sometimes inside their own homes, without a lot of pomp and circumstance. Except for a few rare occasions like Frijoles Canyon, there are no burial grounds, no burial mounds, nothing."

"Yeah, and what if we've been wrong all these years?" He gave her the most earnest look he could muster. "Promise me. You have to keep this under your hat until I'm ready to go public."

"Okay. I promise."

"What would you say if I told you I found two more stone lions, larger and better preserved than the ones at Bandelier?"

"I'd say you found something remarkable. Where are they?"

"You'll find out soon enough. Everyone will. But take a look at this." He reached under his shirt and pulled out a small green stone. The stone dangled from a leather shoelace that hung around his neck. He placed it in Renee's hand.

Renee studied it closely. The stone was really a cube, nearly an inch on a side, with a figure etched into it. As she looked more closely she realized the stone had been fashioned into a tiny human skull. It was creepy and fascinating at the same time. "This doesn't look Anasazi. And this can't be turquoise."

"No, it's not turquoise. It's jade. And it's not Anasazi. It's Mayan." He took the cube from Renee's hand and stuck it back under his shirt. "And for right now, it's our secret."

As he stood Conrad had the uneasy feeling he was being watched. On the mesa above them nearly a mile away a lone figure stood surveying the canyon below with binoculars. Conrad watched the man for a moment.

The binoculars seemed to focus on the tiny dig at Kin Escavada, then began to pan slowly along the canyon floor, as if looking for nothing in particular. After a few minutes the visitor appeared satisfied with the view and disappeared beyond the mesa rim.

Conrad shrugged the man off, embarrassed at his own paranoia. It was just another tourist. They saw dozens every day. He turned his attention back to the beer he had just started.

5

Tyope sat at the bar, nursing a tonic with a twist. The first time he'd ordered the drink the bartender gave him a strange look. Hector's Saloon was not the kind of place where red men came to sip gentle drinks. It was a place where they came to get drunk. After three days of Tyope sitting at the same spot and ordering the same drink, the man behind the bar quit thinking it was strange. But he was curious.

Hector's was like a half-dozen other bars in Albuquerque that catered only to "Indians." It was an unwritten policy, to be sure, but it was a fact just the same. Whites weren't welcome. Most of the time neither were Hispanics. Of course, the owners couldn't enforce the policy. They had to serve anyone who came in. It was the patrons who made it clear only their kind was welcome.

Even the Albuquerque police knew better than to send in a couple of white cops to break up a brawl. They were even less welcome than their civilian counterparts. The officers had better be of Apache or Navajo heritage or they didn't go in. If no Native American officers were available, the police waited outside until reinforcements showed up or until the brawlers rolled through the doorway onto the street.

It had been fairly quiet for the three nights that Tyope had huddled at the bar. But they had also been weeknights. Things would be different when Friday rolled around.

"You sure you don't want anything a little stronger?" the bartender asked above the din of the country music coming from the jukebox.

Tyope glanced at the name tag and shook his head for the hundredth time. "No, thanks, Sam. I'm okay."

Sam glanced down the bar. Even for a Wednesday night it was slow. "I take it you're not from Albuquerque," he observed, trying alleviate his boredom.

Tyope shook his head, not bothering to look up.

"So, you down here visiting?"

"Looking for work, like everybody else."

"Oh," Sam said knowingly. "That's why you gotta stay sober."

"Yeah. Gotta stay sober."

"Name's Sam Chico," the bartender offered. "Mescalero."

"I'm called Tyope."

"You down from one of the pueblos?"

"Yeah."

"Which one?"

"Does it matter?" Tyope raised his head and gave Sam a look that said the interview was over.

"Just trying to be friendly, bud. That's all." Sam wandered down the bar looking for other ears to bend. He wasn't offended by Tyope's demand for privacy. A lot of his customers were the sullen, brooding type.

Tyope, the customer thought. Badger. Keres for

"Badger." A deception within a deception. He was Pueblo, yes. Tewa Pueblo. Not Keres. He knew there were reasons he couldn't use his own name. Still, why not Miguel or Esteban? They were common enough names among the Pueblo people. But the leaders of the moiety had given him the name. It would be for a short time only. While he was in Albuquerque. Until his business was finished.

He wondered why he had been the chosen one. He knew the society was small. Among the nineteen pueblos there were only forty members. But he was in his mid-forties. There had to be men younger than him who could take care of this business, though he wasn't positive. Even though he had belonged to the society for twelve years, he had met only a handful of the others face to face.

Unlike the shaman and koshare societies that performed their duties in public, their moiety was secret and sacred. Most of their pueblo brethren didn't know they even existed.

It was just as well.

Tyope poked at the twist of lime floating in his drink. He resented the fact that he had been told to wait at a bar. It was a tough environment for him. He hadn't had a drink in ten months and it was a battle he fought every day. Now he sat across from a display of a dozen different hard liquors. He could taste each one in his mind: the smoky scent of bourbon, the tart bite of gin, the thick sweetness of rum.

He knew he hadn't licked his demon. But there were other demons he feared even more. At the moment that was how he managed to stay sober.

The phone behind the bar rang. Sam picked up the receiver and, after a moment, frowned in Tyope's direction. He said something into the phone, then laid it on the bar.

"For future reference," Sam yelled above Waylon Jennings as he signaled his customer, "this phone ain't for personal calls."

"Yeah. Okay." Tyope nodded as he picked up the phone. He turned so that he faced away from the bartender. "Tyope." He glanced at his watch while he listened to the instruction. After a while he finally said, "Yeah, I got it."

He returned the phone to its cradle and slapped a five-dollar bill on the bar. Without another word he headed out the door.

"Thanks," Sam yelled, stuffing the bill into his tip jar. He glanced at another one of his patrons. "That one's a strange coyote."

"Yeah?" the customer grunted. "So what's normal in this place?"

Sam turned away in frustration. The malcontents seemed to be taking over the world.

It was after twelve when Sam pushed his third drunk of the night out the front door. There was no sign of the previous two. They had managed to crawl off somewhere to sleep off their indulgences.

As Sam turned to go back in, a figure stumbled around the corner. In the dim streetlight he could just make out the features. It was a customer from earlier in the night.

Tyope pushed past the bartender and grabbed the first stool he came to. Sam followed him in, taking his station behind the bar.

"You drunk?"

Tyope shook his head. "No," he said hoarsely. "Not yet." He looked up to study the array of liquor bottles. "Gimme a bourbon."

"Got any money?"

Tyope reached into his pocket and pulled out a twenty-dollar bill. He slapped it on the counter. "Yeah. I got money."

Sam retrieved a shot glass and a bottle. He studied his customer as he downed the booze and signaled for a refill. Tyope had been reasonably presentable earlier in the evening. While he was out he had undergone a considerable change. His clothes were disheveled, his face and hands were streaked and filthy, his hair was matted with sweat.

Sam guessed there had been a fight. "You in some sort of trouble?" he asked, filling the shot glass for a third time.

"I didn't do nothin'!" Tyope growled. He emptied the glass again and pushed the twenty toward the bartender. "I need some change for a call."

Sam took the bill and rang up the charges on his register. He returned with $7.50 in change.

Tyope took one of the quarters and hurried to the pay phone at the far end of the bar. A few moments later he was talking to someone. Despite his best efforts Sam couldn't pick up any of the words over the noise from the jukebox.

The conversation was short, and Tyope quickly returned to his stool. He glanced around the bar. There were only two other customers, and they were consumed with studying their own drinks. "How much for the rest of the bottle?"

"I can only sell by the drink."

"Come on," Tyope protested. "All the liquor stores are closed. I can't get a bottle anywhere else."

Sam glanced toward the door, as if to make sure no cops were watching. "Give me another twenty, I'll let you have a new bottle."

Tyope dug into his pocket and produced two tens. "Here."

The bartender produced an unopened bottle from behind the counter. "Stick it under your shirt and get the hell out of here."

"Thanks, man," Tyope said, quickly unbuttoning his shirt and stuffing the bottle under his arm. He started for the door.

"Hey!" Sam warned. "If the cops stop you, I never seen you before. Understand? Where you got that booze is your problem."

"Yeah. No sweat."

Tyope pushed the door open and disappeared into the night.

6

JOEL CONRAD BACKED OUT OF HIS PARKING SPACE AT the motel and flipped on his headlights. It was still dark but he was getting used to the long days. By starting a few hours before work began at the dig and continuing a few hours after the dig closed down, he had managed to dedicate almost eight hours a day to his independent research. He didn't have the money to spend an entire year away from a paying job. He figured by taking the assistant position on the Chaco job that summer he could get most of his survey work done. He had been more successful than he'd dared hope. With what he now had in hand he was certain he would qualify for a research grant. His money woes would be over.

He turned southeast on Highway 44. Halfway through Counselor he turned northeast, taking the gravel road that pointed him toward the western slopes of the Rocky Mountains.

He was so engrossed in his thoughts about what he wanted to accomplish that morning that he didn't notice the car that pulled out from the motel parking lot behind him. The headlights did catch his attention when they left town on the gravel road. That time of morning there were few stray vehicles wandering around. Five minutes outside of town, however, the lights behind him disappeared. In a way he was disappointed. The high desert seemed that much more lonely.

There was no way for Conrad to know the driver behind him was still following with his headlights off.

Conrad came to a stop in front of the cattle gate and got out, leaving his truck in park with the engine idling. The sun had yet to pull itself above the eastern mountains, though pale highlights in the sky indicated it wouldn't be much longer.

The chilly desert air sent a shiver through Conrad as he walked over and unlatched the gate, pushing it wide open. He almost wished he had worn something a little heavier than a windbreaker, but he knew the cool temperatures were only temporary. It was forty-five degrees now. By eight o'clock it would be seventy. By noon the August sun would push the temperature past one hundred.

Of course, he had no intention of climbing around the foothills until noon. Vencel would expect to see him at the dig in Chaco Canyon no later than nine. Conrad enjoyed pushing the older archaeologist's patience every chance he got. He truly hated the man. But he also knew there were limits. The Ph.D. candidate had blown off his assignment from the night before. He hadn't cataloged a single shard. Showing up late for work wasn't a good idea. He knew he couldn't get away with two major transgressions two days in a row.

He looked at the hills above him. The small

valley that had yielded the jade skull was poorly marked on every map he had seen. For some strange reason even the topographical maps based on satellite imaging failed to render an accurate size or location for the wash.

But the valley was there, its entrance guarded by two stone lions that had been hidden in a landslide. He had found them almost by accident. One of the heads had become partially exposed as he scrambled over the debris from the slide.

Conrad knew he had found something extraordinary.

The valley itself was not remarkable. Well-worn paths told him that sheep, cattle, probably even humans, had been passing through the basin for years. It was just that no one had recognized it for what it was.

That morning he wanted to do one last assessment. He had brought a hundred-foot surveyor's tape to get measurements and he wanted to make one final count. He was sure there were over one hundred separate mounds, though they had been severely eroded and masked by the falling debris of the surrounding cliffs.

But that all stood to reason. The valley had been abandoned over seven hundred years earlier, the same time Chaco Canyon had been deserted.

If he was correct in his theory, and he knew he was, he would make his mark in archaeological history alongside of the greats: Schliemann and Troy, Howard Carter and Tutankhamen, Richard Wetherill and the Mesa Verde cliff dwellings. His future would be secure.

As he got back into the cab of his truck, a thought

rushed through his head. Vencel had just published a paper on the linguistic ties between the Hopi language and the modern Mayan dialect of the Yucatán. His theory was that the great ruins at Casa Grande in Mexico had been the trade center between the two cultures, where both language and goods were exchanged. At best Vencel was merely rehashing the same ideas other archaeologists had accepted as fact for years.

Conrad suddenly had a clear vision of his objective. His evolving theory was much more radical than anything Vencel would ever dare to propose. Conrad wanted to prove that the Chaco Canyon culture had been directly influenced by migrating Mayans escaping a wartorn Yucatán Peninsula.

Turning on the overhead light, he grabbed his ever-present notebook and began jotting down his thoughts. One thought led to the next. He began to visualize the end of the Golden Age of the Mayan Empire in the year 900 of the Common Era and the first structures being erected in Chaco. He correlated the emerging Chaco culture with the expanding influence of the Mississippian Mound Builders, another group with suspected Mayan links.

Wrapped up in his thoughts, Conrad was oblivious to his surroundings. It wasn't until the last second that he noticed the movement from the corner of his eye. He turned his head to face the great black shape just outside his door.

Before his brain could comprehend the situation the glass window shattered in his face, the force of the blow knocking him backward and unconscious.

7

VIRGIL AENEAS LANSING

November 5, 1871

I have never been a man of words. Nor have I been a consistent and faithful correspondent when replying to the letters of my friends. It is almost with some surprise to myself that I am undertaking this endeavor.

I am writing this history in the small adobe home my generous relatives and friends from Burnt Mesa helped me construct. In the spring I will finish a proper house for my wife, Kele, and our son, Samuel.

I am now in my fiftieth year. And even though I am starting my life anew in this land I have come to know and love, I am cognizant of the fact I have lived a lifetime already. God has smiled on me and my small family in granting this opportunity.

When he is old enough to understand, I will tell Samuel my story, but as I write these words I realize they are not for my son to read. Nor do I write them for his son, or his son's son. It may be strange to say, but I hope no one has to read these words. And if these pages are found, I pray the reader accepts this history as fact and will understand his obligations.

I was born on August 14, 1821, the fourth child and second son to William and Elizabeth Marion Lansing, not far from Richmond, Virginia. My father was a successful tobacco planter and from my recollections had a stable of some forty slaves. I say, by my recollections, because I was sent away to school at a relatively young age. It was the custom in those days, much as it was with English gentry, that the eldest son stood to inherit the family estates and the bulk of the fortune. My older brother, William, eight years my senior and a person I never really knew, was groomed in the manner suitable to a plantation owner. It was my family's intention that I should, at least, be given a proper education so that I could pursue an acceptable profession in either medicine or law.

Although my father professed a great disdain for the British, having rallied Virginia militia against those soldiers during the War of 1812, he still sent my brother to England for his education. I presume that would have been my course had I not been rather unruly. When I was very young my playmates had been the Negro children from the slave quarters. It was many years before I understood why I and my friends were punished for keeping each other's company. It wasn't because we did wrong. Fraternization simply wasn't allowed.

I can only think of my youth in terms of bitterness and resentment. My father was stern and obdurate, my mother, cool and aloof. I felt nothing but gratitude when I was sent away to Mount Washington Military Preparatory Academy at the age of twelve. I found the school a haven and I avoided lengthy holidays on the plantation as often as I could.

When the question arose about my college education I

had already made my resolve. I believe my father was even relieved when I announced my intentions to attend the Military Academy at West Point. I don't think he necessarily approved my choice of a career. In those days professional soldiers were considered slackers and drunks. I'm sure he expected me to gain my commission and be assigned to some frontier post a thousand miles away, far from his sight.

When I think back on my West Point days, I can . . .

[NEXT SEVERAL PAGES UNUSABLE]

8

LANSING REFILLED HIS COFFEE CUP AND SAT BACK DOWN at the small kitchen table. He had read the first few pages of the journal a dozen times. He was fascinated. This was family history he knew nothing about.

As he sipped his coffee he reread the cover sheet to the fax transmittal he had received the previous day. The header announced the fax was from the University of New Mexico. The handwritten "From" block said: Department of Archaeology, Research Lab, Dr. Mary Ann Gill.

The next page was a short letter addressed to Clifford A. Lansing, Sheriff, Las Palmas, NM.

Dear Sheriff Lansing,

Two weeks ago my office received the leather-bound book you found on your property. Dr. Elmo Giancarlo, our department head, requested our assistance in deciphering its contents. Unfortunately, the journal is in very bad condition. Many of the pages have melted together in a natural "gluing" process and simply cannot be separated. The paper we can work with is mildewed and discolored, rendering the script unreadable by the naked eye.

However, we are having some success using the same chemical bath process first used on the Diyarbakir Scrolls found in Turkey. The chemicals bond with the carbon black of the ink. The writing can then be seen using a low-frequency blue light and a yellow filter. As you can imagine, the process is slow and time consuming.

I must admit as an anthropologist and historian I am finding the journal quite interesting. As an academic I am excited at being the first to work with an original document. I will send you transcripts of the journal pages as quickly as possible. Attached you will find a copy of the first few pages. Please contact me or Dr. Giancarlo if you have any questions.

Folding the pages to take with him, Lansing finished his cup of coffee. It was time to go to work.

Lansing stepped from the bunkhouse as he put on his Stetson. For years he had promised himself that he was going to convert the bunkhouse into guest quarters, though he wasn't sure why. He never had so many visitors that they couldn't stay in the main ranch house. Still, he was amazed at how quickly things changed when necessity reared its ugly head.

Across the ranch grounds, separated from the "guest" house, the barn, and the other outbuildings, stood the shell of his ranch house. The blackened stone walls, two feet thick on the exterior, stood as a monument to his great-great-grandfather's engineering skills. Three different architects had examined what was left after the arson fire. All three agreed, the house could be rebuilt using the original stonework.

There was no way the stones could be cleaned. They would stay blackened forever. However, they could be plastered over with stucco, giving the place a clean white surface inside and out.

After spending a month trying to recover what he could from the ashes, Lansing had to admit he was tired of anything black. He was glad the structure could be rebuilt according to the original design and he was ecstatic at the prospect of coming home to a clean white home.

In the interim he couldn't afford to live in a motel room. That's how the bunkhouse was finally converted. It now had two bedrooms, new plumbing, and a new kitchen. Once he was living at his ranch again, he began restoring the main house.

Lansing walked over to the black edifice and peered at the interior. Everything had been stripped away and carted off. All that was left were the stone walls and the dirt. He wished construction would go a little faster. So far only the pipes for the underground plumbing had been laid.

It was when they were digging the trench for the pipes that the workers stumbled upon the small, stone-lined crypt. At first they thought they had hit another boulder. The valley along the Rio Questa had at one time been a broad riverbed. The ground beneath the topsoil was littered with boulders and stones washed down from the mountains.

As the diggers tried to clear the dirt from around the obstacle, the foreman realized the stone had been fashioned into a square. There was a possibility they had stumbled onto an ancient Pueblo site, and he called a halt to the digging until Lansing could take a look.

Lansing watched as the workmen cleared away the dirt and gravel. The capstone was two feet square and almost three inches thick. When it was removed, it revealed a chamber only slightly smaller than the capstone and barely a foot deep. The bottom and sides of the hole were lined with rock to prevent collapse.

Initially, the mystery was a disappointment. The only thing inside was a rotting leather saddlebag. Whoever had buried it had been unaware of the fluctuating water table this close to the river. The carefully designed crypt, presumed waterproof, had been flooded time and time again, nearly destroying the contents.

Lansing himself lifted the saddlebag out of the shallow well. Stamped into the leather and still legible were the letters V LANS. The bag, he presumed, must have belonged to his great-great-grandfather, Virgil Lansing, the builder of the original homestead.

The leather of the bag was brittle and rotting. The tie strings that held the flaps closed broke as he tried to undo them. On one side of the bag he found what appeared to be a book, carefully wrapped in oilcloth for added protection. As he unwrapped the cloth he realized the book had suffered extensive damage. Its leather binding had rotted as badly as the saddlebag, and several of the pages began to crumble when he tried to open it. He decided to set it aside for the moment and inspect the other contents.

In the opposite side of the bag he found another oilcloth wrapped around a smaller item. As the foreman and the three diggers watched over his shoulder, Lansing unfolded the cloth. In his hand was a deep-green, almost translucent, emerald, nearly the size of a softball. The stone had been meticulously sculpted to resemble what Lansing thought was a mountain lion. The beast was fierce looking, with exposed teeth. And the stone itself, even in the middle of the day, seemed to radiate its own light.

The stone-lined crypt was still there as Lansing studied the interior of the building. The capstone lay to one side, out of the way of the newly laid plumbing.

He could only wonder. There had been no stories handed down about buried treasure on their land. Whatever wealth his family had accumulated over the years had been through ranching and just plain hard work.

Having no idea where the items originated from, or indeed, what they actually were, Lansing had contacted the University of New Mexico in Albuquerque. His old archaeology professor, Dr. Giancarlo, agreed to look at the articles.

That had been two weeks earlier.

Giancarlo had passed the book on to his research lab. Lansing was finally getting the results of their efforts.

The emerald was a different matter. Spectrum analysis revealed the stone was probably from mines in northern South America. The "fetish," as Giancarlo called it, appeared to be pre-Columbian. Possibly Aztec. More likely Mayan. And it wasn't a mountain lion. It was a jaguar.

A few days after Lansing discovered the saddlebags the news broke in the Albuquerque paper. No one seemed interested in the book, but there was a great deal of fascination and speculation about the emerald, especially its worth.

By carat weight alone the stone was valued at over one hundred thousand dollars. There was no accurate way to estimate its worth as a work of art or historical treasure. Five times its carat weight? Ten times its carat weight? Giancarlo guessed it would be whatever the market would bear, provided Lansing wanted to sell.

That wasn't a decision Lansing was ready to make. Before he did anything he wanted to find out why it had been there to begin with. For his own peace of mind, though, he allowed Giancarlo to keep the stone securely locked away in the university museum safe. Eventually he would make a decision.

In the meantime he had a county to watch over and a big battle on the horizon. He'd heard a rumor that county commissioners were getting ready to strip him of his budget, and he wasn't sure there was much he could do about it.

As he climbed into his Jeep, he hoped he could at least get the plumbers back out to finish their work.

9

THE COUNTY COMMISSIONERS' PRIVATE CHAMBER WAS almost crowded. In attendance were the five commissioners, their recorder, Lansing, Thomas Esquierdo, the county attorney, and Michael Dawson, the representative of U.S. Security. Dawson had come equipped with an overhead projector, flip charts, and dozens of fancy pamphlets printed on glossy paper. The presentation had taken over an hour.

"You have the five proposals in front of you," Dawson said as he concluded. "By far the least expensive will be number three. The biggest advantage, aside from the cost, is the fact that number three allows for expansion in the future, provided you've planned ahead with adequate land."

"Land is not a problem," Roger Kellim, the newest commissioner, commented. The other four commissioners nodded in agreement. "As one of the biggest ranchers in the county, I can assure you, there will be plenty of land available."

I'll bet you can, Lansing thought to himself. *And if you make a tidy little profit on the side, that's just coincidence.*

Lansing had said nothing during the presentation.

He knew that he was being railroaded but he hadn't figured out just how. San Phillipe County had outgrown its two-cell jail years earlier. Both he and his predecessor, Bill Fulton, had fought to build a new jail, apart from the courthouse, possibly on the outside of town.

Peter Alvarez, the president of the county commissioners, and his predecessors had fought just as hard to prevent that from happening. There was always an excuse: the land was too expensive; the building costs were prohibitive; or they couldn't afford the additional manpower. In the short run it was cheaper to house prisoners in neighboring counties. The trouble was, Sandoval, Los Alamos, and Santa Fe were running out of room for their own clients. San Phillipe had been put on notice that they would have to look somewhere else for accommodations.

The twenty-first century was staring them in the face and the idea of operating a jail facility for profit had captured the corporate imagination of the commissioners. They were going to build a state-of-the-art prison and rent out cell space.

Kellim had obviously solved the land problem. Michael Dawson and his corporation, U.S. Security, Incorporated, would privately operate the jail. But there was still the problem of funding for the construction and the payroll.

"Excuse me for asking," Lansing interrupted, "but how much will it cost to operate this place?"

Dawson smiled like a used-car salesman who had just hooked a customer. "A hundred-bed facility would cost approximately sixty thousand dollars a month. A two-hundred-bed operation would be only slightly higher. Since you are using prefabricated, stainless steel cells, there is virtually no maintenance. You don't have to figure in upkeep in your long-term costs."

Lansing looked at Alvarez. "Where is the county going to get that kind of money?"

"Sheriff Lansing, the operation pays for itself," Dawson continued. "All you need is sixty-percent occupancy. At a thousand dollars per unit, per month, San Phillipe County will have no problem meeting expenses. If all one hundred beds are filled, the county and U.S. Security will split a monthly profit of forty thousand dollars. That's almost a half million dollars a year."

"It all sounds well and good on paper." Lansing snorted. "Where are we going to get the money to build it?"

"Matching funds," Alvarez said. "We put up a little, the state and federal governments put up a lot, and we have a new jail."

In his late fifties, Peter Alvarez was perhaps the most influential man in the county. Descended from one of the first Spanish families to settle in San Phillipe County, he ranched land that had been granted to his ancestors by King Carlos II in 1696. He had been a county commissioner for over twenty years and was now on his second term as president. An honest, though shrewd, politician, he had a solid voting base in the Hispanic and Native American communities. On the whole he and Lansing got along. But Lansing had also learned over the years, when Alvarez made up his mind, there was little anyone could do to change it.

"When you say 'a little,' how 'little' are we talking about?" Lansing asked.

"Two hundred and fifty thousand dollars," Alvarez said. "That's hardly anything when we're looking at a three-million-dollar tab."

"I guess I'm going to have to ask again. Where are *we* getting the money? New county bonds?"

"We don't have time to put the issue to a vote," Kellim said. "The federal government has cut loose funds with the stipulation that it's spent by year's end. It's already the middle of August. We have to break ground within a month."

"You're beating around the bush, Roger," Lansing said.

"All right, Cliff," Alvarez interrupted. "We'll put it right on the line. The money's coming out of your equipment budget."

That was exactly what Lansing was afraid of hearing. "Dammit, Peter, that's a bunch of bull. I've been on my knees begging you guys for those funds for three years. I need new Jeeps. I need to upgrade our computer system. I need new radios, not to mention the remote transmitters you promised me."

"We understand your problems, Cliff," Alvarez said, trying to soothe him. "We honestly do. But this is a fiscal matter that involves the entire county."

"Let me explain something to you, Lansing," Kellim interrupted. "In simple terms. Your office eats up almost a third of the county budget. Half of that expense is spent housing our county prisoners in other county jails. It costs us twenty-five to thirty dollars a day for each prisoner. In the last two years we've averaged ten to twelve prisoners in jail every month. That comes out to a hundred thousand dollars a year just to pay for someone else to take care of our prisoners.

"If we build our own jail, that hundred thousand

dollars will be spent in our own county. If we build a large jail where we can accommodate the overflow from Taos and Santa Fe, we can turn around and charge them enough to cover our costs and make a little profit on the side.

"That profit can be plowed back into the county treasury. Higher salaries for county employees. Better equipment for your office. Better roads."

Lansing was fully aware of the benefits San Phillipe would derive from having its own jail. He had argued for a new one for years. He resented Kellim's condescending attitude, but this meeting was not the time to lock horns.

"We wouldn't be pushing this project if we didn't think your office would benefit in the long run," Alvarez pointed out. "Besides, we're not asking you to go without anything. Just use what you already have for a little longer."

Lansing had to admit that if all of the promises that U.S. Security had made came true, the county would benefit handsomely. But he also believed in the adage If something sounds too good to be true, it probably is. "I don't suppose I have any say-so in this."

"Actually, no, Cliff. You don't," Alvarez said. "We've already notified the county treasurer to cancel any orders your office has placed. Like Roger said, we're on the fast track with this project."

"Then why am I here? Why didn't you just send me a memo?"

"We want you to understand how important this new jail is going to be," Alvarez said. "Eighteen months from now we will have all the money you want for upgrading your hardware. New Jeeps. New radios. Whatever you need."

"Obviously, you've thought this thing through," Lansing said, trying to sound sarcastic.

"Completely." Kellim snapped.

"If U.S. Security is managing this operation, how far does my jurisdiction extend?"

"The county has the ultimate responsibility for controlling the jail," Esquierdo explained. "We are creating a separate department of corrections that will be headed up by a county jailer, a civil service position. What we don't want around here is another elected official."

"So you're saying I'll have no jurisdiction over the jail."

"That shouldn't bother you," Kellim said. "You're always complaining about being spread too thin. This will be one less headache for you."

"Yeah, until something goes wrong."

"Sheriff Lansing, U.S. Security's record is unblemished," Dawson pointed out. "We operate thirty facilities nationwide. We have had no escapes, no riots, and our staff receives the same training as federal prison guards. In short, we're professionals and we're proud of the service we provide."

"I guess we don't have anything else to discuss, then," Lansing said, standing.

"Thomas will drop off a copy of the U.S. Security contract and the charter for the jail operations," Alvarez said. "We would like you to look them over, make sure we don't miss anything."

"Absolutely. I can tell my input is vital to this whole project." Lansing turned and left the meeting room.

10

RENEE LOOKED UP FROM THE FRAGMENT OF POTTERY she was coaxing from the earth as Dr. Vencel pulled his red pickup truck to a stop. Huey, Dewey, and Louie were busy working their own grids, hoping to impress their mentor with how earnestly they took their jobs. As the dig supervisor approached, Renee couldn't help but notice he didn't look very happy.

Dr. Baron Vencel was a tall, imposing figure with salt-and-pepper hair. He had a deep, booming voice that commanded attention whether he was at a cocktail party or in a classroom. A dedicated archaeologist, he seemed to be more comfortable in khaki than academic tweed. But he also made no effort to hide his ambitions. It was assumed that one day he was going to be the chairman of the Archaeology Department. To that end he sponsored two major symposiums a year, headed up one archaeological dig annually, and chaired the graduate studies review committee. Much of his spare time was spent playing tennis or swimming to maintain his physique. Divorced for over ten years, he seemed to relish his freedom. Whenever he was seen away from campus, it was always in the company of an attractive woman.

"I don't see Mr. Conrad anywhere."

Renee stood, brushing the sand from her knees. "He was gone this morning before we ever left the motel."

"What time was that?"

"Seven o'clock. The same time we always leave." She glanced at her watch. It was ten o'clock. She knew there was no excuse for Joel not being there. "You made pretty good time getting back from Santa Fe," she said, hoping to change the subject. She had spent the past ten weeks making excuses for Conrad.

"I left early," Vencel said off-handedly as he looked around their excavation. "Did he classify the shards we had set aside?"

"Actually, he thought we were getting too close to the end of the dig. He said we should start boxing up everything so it can get shipped to Albuquerque for evaluation."

"Humph." Vencel grunted. "That was hardly his call to make. Do you have any idea where he went?"

"No. I think he was doing some preliminary research for another project."

"Oh? On what?"

"I'm not really sure. He said he was having some film developed, but I have no idea what he's been taking pictures of. Or where."

Vencel studied the pretty, young graduate assistant for a moment. Renee couldn't tell if he was buying her story or not.

"Well, if our Ph.D. candidate does show up, please tell him to at least hang around until I get back. I would like to talk to him." Vencel turned and headed for his truck. "I'm going over to the visitors' center. I'll be back shortly."

"Yes, sir."

Renee, like most people, found Vencel intimidating. She honestly hoped Conrad would show up soon. Vencel had an unpredictable temper and she didn't want to see its bad side. She suspected she would if Conrad wasn't back by the time he had returned.

11

"HOW DID YOUR MEETING GO?" MARILYN ASKED, TRYING to sound cheerful.

Lansing stopped and looked at his receptionist. Her forced smile told him she knew a lot more than she let on. "So how long have you known about the new jail?"

"I didn't hear about it until last night," she confessed. "Honest. But I was sworn to secrecy. I would have said something if I had heard about it sooner."

"Who did you hear it from?"

"Helen."

"Peter's secretary? How long have they been planning this?"

"She said they started looking into it a couple of months ago."

"That makes sense. I was wondering why they were dragging their feet about cutting money loose. They had no intention of letting me spend any of my funds." There was more frustration than anger in Lansing's voice. "Is there any coffee?"

"I just made a fresh pot."

Lansing disappeared into the dayroom to fill his

cup, reemerging a moment later. "Where are my deputies this morning?"

"Jack's taking the southern patrol around Espanola. Paul's cruising around Las Palmas. I had to dispatch Gabe to the west side of the county. We got some complaints about missing livestock."

"Let me know if Gabe calls in. I'd like a good excuse to get out of the office today."

"Oh, that reminds me," Marilyn said, reaching for a stack of papers behind her. "These faxes came in for you last night." She handed them through the window of her reception area.

Lansing took the paperwork. "Thanks. I'll be in my office."

When he sat down at his desk he realized he was holding more of the deciphered text from his great-great-grandfather's journal. Dr. Gill had scribbled a short note on the cover sheet.

Sheriff Lansing
Unable to separate several pages. Took some license with original text by guessing at a few of the missing words. Interesting material about the Mexican-American War. Mary Ann Gill

Lansing quickly turned to the next page.

12

JOURNAL OF VIRGIL LANSING (CONT.)

I was more than surprised when Sam Grant came riding up to our position. As quartermaster his orders, directly from General Taylor, were to maintain watch over the supplies and wagons as the bulk of our forces were directed against Monterrey. He admitted to me later he had heard the assault commence against the Citadel and he couldn't contain his curiosity.

I know for myself I could still taste the sweet victory we had experienced at Matamoros. I was game for more battle. I think old Sam was too. Why in Great Caesar's name he joined in the attack against La Tenería I'll never know. But he was in the thick of things when the 4th Infantry began the assault.

While Captain Stewart led the main force, I brought up the left flank with some thirty men. We were not prepared for the rain of fire the Mexicans poured upon us. A dozen of my own men fell on the first barrage. Captain Stewart easily lost thirty. And we had yet to cross half the distance to the barricades.

The Mexicans sent forth a second volley, shredding our ranks, and Captain Stewart called for our withdrawal. As we sought the safety of our lines, Stewart commandeered Lieutenant Grant's horse. Once he was in the saddle Captain Stewart set about gathering our men for a second attack. It was at this juncture that an enemy musket ball tore through his chest, mortally wounding him.

As I rallied what was left of my men, Captain Backus of the 1st Infantry ordered us to fall in with his men. Both of our units had been decimated by the enemy fire and we could barely muster a hundred soldiers for another assault. But we both knew Old Rough and Ready's penchant for pressing the attack once the business had begun and once we were formed up, Captain Backus ordered us forward.

Why the Mexican soldiers were not prepared for our second assault, I shall never know. We crossed the hundred yards with only minor losses and overran La Tenería, taking several of the enemy captive. From the roof of the building we found ourselves positioned behind the Mexican lines with full view of Fort Diablo.

When General Taylor ordered a frontal attack on the fort, we had already established a position that placed the Mexican army in a crossfire. As their sharpshooters mounted the parapets to drive back our soldiers, we were able to pick them off as soon as they were exposed. Our lack of knowledge as to the enemy strength proved to be our undoing. A well-concealed battery of riflemen opened up on General Butler and his Ohio Regiment as they crossed the canal in front of the fort. General Butler was killed and the Ohioans were forced to withdraw. We all spent a sleepless night in a chilling rain, tending to our wounded and bringing up supplies for a dawn assault.

The second day of the battle found Captain Backus, myself, and our troops holed up at La Tenería, keeping the Mexican soldiers pinned down at Fort Diablo. This was *the point where General Worth and his Texas Rangers brought up a twelve-pound howitzer and captured the Bishop's Palace. The palace had a commanding view of all of Monterrey, and soon three batteries of captured Mexican cannon were being directed against the Citadel and Fort Diablo.*

During the lull of battle on the second night General Ampudia ordered what remained of his troops to the central plaza of Monterrey for one last stand. His intentions most certainly must have been to ambush our soldiers from the rooftops as we worked our way through the streets. On our initial forays these tactics worked with a vengeance.

General Worth devised his own tactics to circumvent the sniper attacks. Using mortar shells with short fuses, he blew holes through the soft adobe interior walls of the buildings. Thus, house by house, his rangers worked their way to the plaza of the city without overly exposing themselves on the open streets.

I believe this tactic, which brought American troops to the very heart of Monterrey, as much as anything, forced General Ampudia to press for an armistice. We had hundreds of sick and wounded soldiers and were nearly out of ammunition. Had he known of our dire condition he might well have launched a counteroffensive and driven us from Mexican soil. General Taylor made a grand stand by playing the beneficent victor, allowing Ampudia and his troops to march out of Monterrey with their arms.

Although my taste for battle had been whetted momentarily, I quickly grew to dislike our situation. We were an army of occupation. The locals in Monterrey were barely tolerant of our presence and many of our men, so brilliant and steadfast in battle, degenerated into drunken ruffians. The senior officers, many of them commanders of state militias, urged General Taylor to press farther into Mexico.

Their volunteers had signed on for only one year of service and they were anxious to see a quick end to the hostilities.

Nearly all of us, officer and enlisted alike, had great respect for General Taylor. We didn't want to believe the rumors that he refused to push toward Mexico City for fear of losing a bid for the presidency. It was a rumor that ultimately proved to be correct.

As it turned out, though, Washington had devised other plans. After two months of occupation the majority of our army was ordered to withdraw to the coast. We were to join the invasion force being amassed by Winfield Scott, commanding general of the Army.

I arrived on Lobos Island, along with Lieutenant G. McClellan, on February first. Due to the disorderly conduct of many of the volunteer militias, Tampico had been placed under martial law. It was apparent that General Scott wanted to launch our invasion against Veracruz as quickly as possible, before the whole of our army was detained in the stockade. . . .

[NEXT SEVERAL PAGES UNREADABLE]

13

DEPUTY GABE HANNA TURNED HIS PATROL JEEP OFF the dusty dirt-and-gravel "main" road onto the equally dusty dirt-and-gravel ranch road. He had spent little time on the west side of San Phillipe, and the landmarks meant nothing to him. One dirt road looked just like the next one. He had to depend on his odometer reading to figure out where he was supposed to turn.

He had been working in San Phillipe County for eight months, and it still amazed him. It had a little bit of everything. Alpine mountains ran along the eastern county line and through the middle of the county. Between the two ranges ran the Rio Questa, a small river that eventually dumped into the Rio Grande. Toward the southern border were mysterious canyons butted up against the foothills. West of the Continental Divide, beyond the Jicarilla Apache Reservation, sat the rest of the county: high, parched desert. San Phillipe had three natural lakes and a reservoir, ski slopes on the reservation, forested mountains, portions of Carson National Forest, two Indian reservations, and very few people.

Sheriff Lansing had told him San Phillipe was

approximately half the size of Rhode Island with only one percent of that state's available law-enforcement personnel. Besides Lansing there were only six deputies. Patrolling the county was truly a full-time job, even with the help of the state police.

Gabe and his fellow deputies usually stuck to the paved highways, which accounted for less than half the roads in the county. To even get to the roads west of the divide, they had to drive all the way to San Juan County and backtrack. Lansing couldn't afford to send a daily patrol to that part of the county. Two or three times a week a patrol would pass through that area to check for broken-down vehicles; otherwise, they left it alone.

That is, unless someone called with a complaint.

Gabe pulled his Jeep to a stop in front of the ranch house. The building was by no means fancy. The weather-beaten exterior was unpainted wood that had turned a whitish-gray. In back were two sheds, a barn, and several corrals, made out of the same worn timber as the house. An ancient rusted windmill creaked under the slight breeze.

As Gabe got out of his Jeep an old Mexican dressed in blue jeans, a red flannel shirt, and a worn straw hat limped around the corner of the house.

"*Buenos días*, Señor Sanchez," Gabe called out.

The old man looked up, surprised at having a visitor. "*Hola.*"

"*¿Cómo está usted?*"

"*Bien.*" The old man eyed the deputy warily. "What brings the Sheriff's Department way out here?"

"I just left the Lopez place about ten miles back," Gabe explained. "They've had some problems with missing sheep. Since you don't have a phone, they thought I ought stop by. See if you've had any trouble."

Sanchez shook his head. "My nephew is keeping the flock for me in the high pasture. I go up every few days to bring him food. We have had no trouble.

"The Lopezes keep a big flock. The coyotes were bad in the spring. Are they still causing problems?"

"I don't know. Mr. Lopez doesn't think so. They've lost a half-dozen sheep in the last week or so, but they haven't found any carcasses. They think someone might be stealing them. You haven't seen any strangers around, have you?"

Sanchez shook his head as he thought. "No. No." He suddenly raised his finger as he remembered something. "There was a young man, some weeks ago. A gringo. He said he was a scientist of some sort. He asked permission to drive around my property."

"Did you let him?"

"Sí. ¿Porqué no?" the old man said, shrugging. "There's nothing here. He was in an old Chevy pick-up truck with a camper top. He didn't look like no rustler."

Gabe pulled out his notebook and started to make annotations. "What color was the truck?"

"Tan, I think."

"When was the last time you saw him?"

"Two, three, four weeks ago. All the days, they seem to go together."

"You said he was a white man. How old?"

"He was in his twenties, I think."

"You don't know what he was looking for?"

Sanchez shook his head. "He said he was with the university. He was a 'gist' of some kind."

"A 'gist'?"

"Sí. Like a geologist or a zoologist."

"Oh," Gabe said, smiling. "That kind of 'gist.' How long did he stay?"

"He came one day and left. Then he came back two more times, but he left each day after he looked around."

"Did he ever say what he was looking for?"

"No."

"Okay, then." Gabe slipped the notepad back into his breast pocket. "I guess that's all I need for now."

"You want to come in for some coffee? I don't get too many visitors. We can talk."

"Thanks for the offer, but I still have a lot of ground to cover. If you find out you've lost some of your flock, let us know."

"Then what will you do?"

Gabe wasn't prepared for the question. He had to think for a moment. "I guess go around and ask the same questions we're asking now."

"Ah." Sanchez nodded knowingly. "Then I indeed will let you know if I've lost any sheep."

Suddenly Gabe felt very stupid. "*Gracias, señor.*"

The rancher Lopez had been in touch with his neighbors to the north. None of them had suffered any losses. Sanchez didn't think he had lost any sheep, and there were no more ranch sites to the south of his spread. There was a lot more range land, however.

Gabe decided to take a casual drive through the southwest corner of the county. He doubted if he would find anything. But he was sure if he didn't, Lansing would end up asking why not.

It had taken a while, but Gabe was finally starting to understand why his Navajo forebears had settled in that country. There was a stark beauty to the high desert and a vastness that seemed to set the soul free. There were times he felt like standing on a hill and opening his arms to embrace landscape, pull it close to him, claim it as his own. He felt a sense of belonging. That was a feeling he had thought he would never know.

As he rumbled down the gravel road, he wondered why he didn't try to visit the western slopes of the county more often. He was starting to actually enjoy the bleak scenery.

Mounting a rise, he spotted the truck Sanchez had described earlier. It was pulled off the side of the road, parked in front of a metal gate. Barbed wire fence on either side of the gate stretched into the distance. Gabe was always curious why the ranchers even bothered to fence off the land. He suspected it was intended more to keep the curious out than keep their livestock contained. He had seen no sheep or cattle in the last ten miles.

He pulled his Jeep to a stop next to the truck. As he got out he noticed the gate had been unlatched and pushed open. He wondered why the truck's driver hadn't driven through.

He walked around to the driver's door.

The window to the door had been smashed open. Blood was smeared around the broken glass and down the side of the door. A host of flies cavorted around the red, sticky mess.

Gabe pulled his gun and cautiously looked through

the window. The cab was empty, save for the splattering of blood. He searched the ground around the truck. A spotty trail of blood led through the open gate and disappeared into the sagebrush beyond.

He began to follow the trail of blood through the maze of sage bushes. However, the pursuit didn't last long. A dozen yards into the undergrowth he heard the warning. It was the distinct rattle of a very large and, to Gabe's mind, very angry western diamondback.

He froze in his tracks. A few feet in front of him, hiding in the shade of one of the sages, was the biggest snake Gabe had ever seen without the benefit of a glass partition. With his pistol already drawn, his first inclination was to shoot the monster. Even though he was a fairly good shot, a second thought raced through his mind. If he only wounded the animal, would it come after him?

Slowly and cautiously, Gabe began to take a step backward.

The snake began to shake its rattle more violently.

Gabe stopped again.

The rattling suddenly stopped, as if the snake realized the hulking form just a few feet away, and well within striking distance, meant it no harm.

Gabe made a hasty retreat to the relative safety of the dirt road. He realized there had been some sort of accident and someone was injured. Although he was beginning to appreciate the great outdoors, he wasn't the cowboy type like Sheriff Lansing. It didn't make a lot of sense for him to wander off into the wilderness and get hurt. He figured the smartest thing he could do was get some backup.

He hurried back to his Jeep and picked up the

microphone to his radio. "San Phillipe dispatch. San Phillipe dispatch. This is patrol three. How copy?"

His question was greeted with static. He tried the call two more times with the same success. He knew the mountains were blocking his transmission. He could only shake his head, thankful at the thought they would soon be getting remote transmitters for their radio system.

He reached over and changed the channel on his radio. "New Mexico Highway Patrol. This is San Phillipe County sheriff's patrol on one-one-two point two. How copy?"

"San Phillipe sheriff's patrol, this is state patrol five-five. Do you read me?"

"Loud and clear, Marty," Gabe replied, realizing he had reached State Patrolman Marty Hernandez. "I need to relay some info to Las Palmas, and, if you have time, I need assistance."

"What you have?"

"I'm not sure. For right now let's call it a singular vehicular accident with possible injuries."

"What's your forty?"

Gabe quickly pulled out his county map and gave his best guess at his location.

"Ten-four, Gabe. I'll relay your info through my dispatch, then start heading in your direction. It'll be about half an hour."

"Ten-four."

14

LANSING LOOKED UP FROM THE FAX HE WAS READING when someone knocked at his door. "Come in."

Dr. Margarite Carerra pushed the door open and leaned against the jamb. She was dressing in her usual uniform of blue jeans and a western-style shirt. "Busy?"

He was surprised at seeing her. "I've been busier. What are you doing here?"

"I've been over at the clinic since seven this morning."

He noticed the haggard look on her face. "Something wrong?"

"Yeah. But I needed to take a break. Do you have time for breakfast?"

"I've eaten, but I can always squeeze in another cup of coffee."

"In that case it's my treat."

Lansing folded the fax report from the university. "I'll bring this along. You might find it interesting."

* * *

"So what brings you into town in the middle of the week?" Lansing asked as they walked from the courthouse to the Las Palmas Diner on the other side of the town square.

"Jonathan Akee."

"What? Some sort of accident?"

"Yeah, if you call getting drunk to the point of passing out an accident."

"Drunk! He's been on the wagon for a year."

"Well, he fell off and he fell hard. Susan called me at sunup. She was on her way to work when she found him stretched out on their front stoop. He had thrown up all over himself. She couldn't wake him. She could barely drag him into their house.

"When I got to him he was still out of it. We loaded him into my truck and I brought him down to the clinic. The only thing I could think of doing was put him on a saline drip, try to get some fluids back into him. "

"Couldn't you do that at the reservation?"

"We're waiting for our monthly supplies. Besides, I didn't have a bed or monitor to hook him to. His pupils responded okay, so I didn't see a need to ship him over to Farmington. I think he'll be all right if we get his electrolytes straight."

Lansing held the door of the diner open for her and they went in.

"Hello, Sheriff," Velma sang from behind the counter. "Hello, Dr. Carerra. Two coffees?"

"Yeah," Lansing, said, removing his Stetson. "We'll take them in the back." He followed Margarite to one of the booths along the far wall.

"I assume he's still at the clinic," he said, seating himself across the table from his companion.

Margarite nodded. "Susan's with him. John put him in one of the back rooms. I'll replace his saline bags when my supplies come in. He said there wouldn't be a charge as long as the county commissioners didn't find out about it."

"You'd better hope they don't. They've got a new pet project and they're trying to lay their hands on every spare cent in this county."

"What are you talking about?"

"The new county jail."

"Isn't that what you've been wanting?"

"Not like this." He filled her in on the morning meeting with Alvarez and his associates. His narration was interrupted briefly when Velma brought them coffee and took Margarite's order.

"So where do you think they'll put the new jailhouse?" Margarite asked when he was finished.

"I don't have the slightest idea." Lansing shrugged. "Probably on some chunk of property Roger Kellim owns and wants to get rid of."

"His spread is south of yours, isn't it?"

"Way past mine. He also has a few parcels not far from Espanola. If I was going to put in a jail and make it convenient for bringing in prisoners from other counties, that's where I'd put it."

Margarite nodded in agreement, more interested in the plate of food Velma had just delivered.

"Does Susan have any idea what set Jonathan off? I mean, he was doing so well."

"She said he had been gone for about four days. Initially she told me he was doing some business for the pueblo. But when we got to the clinic she told Dr. Tanner that he had been in Santa Fe looking for a job. I mean, it's no big deal one way or the other, but I asked her about it. She seemed a little hesitant, but she stuck with the story she had told Tanner. Jonathan was off looking for a job."

"Well, I guess if he wasn't having any luck, that could set him off."

"I suppose. It's strange, though. I hear about almost everything that goes on up at Burnt Mesa. Susan's been using their car to get to work. Jonathan would have had to catch a ride with someone. It's not unusual for a group of men to head south looking for work. Sometimes they even caravan down. It's always a big deal when they come back.

"But Jonathan took off by himself. Of course, he could have hitchhiked down, but he was in no condition to hitch a ride back. And whoever brought him back knew exactly where to dump him off."

"So he told his drinking buddies where he lived. It wouldn't have been the first time he sneaked off for a binge."

"It will be the first time in almost a year."

"Will he be all right?"

"I think so. But, boy, is he going to have a hangover when he wakes up."

"If that's the worst he's going to suffer, I guess he'll survive."

Margarite glanced up from her meal. "What are those papers you brought along?"

"Oh, those." Lansing had put the two sets of fax sheets aside, out of the way. He unfolded them and handed them to her. "They're from the book I found under my house. It turns out it was my great-great-grandfather's journal. The university is processing the paper so the writing can be read. This is what they've deciphered so far."

Margarite read the material as she finished her food. "That's really interesting," she admitted.

"I had no idea he had gone to West Point, let alone fought in the Mexican-American War. It wasn't one of those family stories that got handed down through the generations. All I knew was that he settled out here after the Civil War."

"It's kind of strange of him writing that he hoped no one would have to read his words."

"I know. It makes me wonder what's in the rest of his journal."

"Or why he wrote it to begin with."

"That too."

"Sheriff!" Kelly, the redheaded senior waitress called out. "Phone call."

Normally Lansing would have been annoyed at her yelling for him in the diner. Fortunately, it was midmorning and only one or two other customers were there.

"Excuse me," he said, getting up to answer the call.

He stayed behind the counter talking on the phone for only a minute before returning to the booth. "Sorry, Margarite. I have to run."

"Trouble?"

"I don't know. Gabe Hanna found an abandoned truck on the west side of the county. It sounds like someone might have gotten hurt. I may have to take a ride out that way."

"That's okay. I need to get back to the clinic."

Lansing bent over and gave her a quick peck on her cheek. "Thanks for the coffee."

15

"MARILYN, HOW DID GABE REACH YOU?" LANSING asked as he entered his offices. "It couldn't have been by radio."

"No. We got a relayed message from the state police dispatch in Bloomfield. Patrolman Hernandez sent it in. They said he's on his way to the accident site."

"Do you have that location?"

Marilyn held up a piece of paper. "Right here." She handed it over her reception counter.

Lansing took the scrawled directions. "Thanks. I'm going to make a quick phone call before I go."

Sitting at his desk in the inner office, he made a brief referral to the Rolodex, then punched in the numbers. There was one short ring at the opposite end before someone picked up.

"University of New Mexico, Department of Archaeology."

"Yes," Lansing responded. "I'd like to speak to Dr. Giancarlo, please."

There was a hesitant pause on the other end. "I— I'm sorry. Dr. Giancarlo isn't available."

"Oh." Lansing was disappointed. He wanted to

tell his old professor thanks for all the work being done on the journal. He thought for a moment, then remembered the fax he had been carrying around. He glanced at the cover sheet. "How about Dr. Mary Ann Gill?"

"Yes. One moment."

There was silence on the other end. A moment later a gravel-voiced woman answered. "Archaeology lab. Dr. Gill speaking."

"Dr. Mary Ann Gill?" Lansing asked. He was a bit taken aback. The thick, gravelly voice at the other end hardly fit his image of what a "Mary Ann" should sound like.

"Yes. Can I help you?"

"Yes. Dr. Gill; this is Sheriff Cliff Lansing in Las Palmas. I got your faxes. I wanted to call up and say thanks for all the work."

"Oh. Well . . . you're welcome." Dr. Gill sounded a little off guard about his call.

"I wanted to thank Doc Giancarlo, but he wasn't in. I'll try to get him later."

Gill cleared her throat. "I'm afraid you won't be able to do that." She sounded decidedly uncomfortable. "Uh, Dr. Giancarlo was killed last night."

"What?" Lansing couldn't believe the news.

"In his office, here at the university. He was always working late. Someone broke in. Tore up the whole place."

"What was it? A robbery?"

"I don't know. The police have his office taped off. I'm sure someone's taking an inventory."

"Do you know how he was killed?"

Gill cleared her throat again, as if she were having a hard time getting the words out. "Really,

Sheriff. I don't know anything and I'm rather upset. Maybe you should talk to the police."

"Yeah. Sure. I understand. Thank you for the information."

Lansing stared at his phone for a long moment after he hung it up. Deputy Hanna was at the site of a singular vehicular accident. The highway patrol was going to be there to provide assistance. There was really no reason for him to respond to the scene.

He flipped through his Rolodex until he found the listings for the Albuquerque police. He had left that department ten years earlier with a bad taste in his mouth, but he had never burned any bridges. He still knew a few people there who could fill him in on the Giancarlo case.

He picked up his phone and began dialing.

16

GABE FELT GENUINELY GUILTY ABOUT NOT FOLLOWING the blood trail any farther than he had. Someone had been hurt and was probably in need of medical attention. He tried to rationalize the fact that if he got hurt, there would be no one around to help either of them.

He tried to keep busy until Marty Hernandez arrived. He first checked the glove compartment for registration papers.

The truck belonged to a Joel S. Conrad of Albuquerque. When Hernandez arrived, Gabe would have him check and make sure the vehicle wasn't stolen.

The deputy continued to examine the cab of the truck. There was an ink pen on the floor, but no tablets or papers. The key was still in the ignition, in the off position. Glass on the seat and floor indicated the driver's side window had been broken from the outside. There was some blood in the interior, but not much.

He walked around to the back of the truck and opened the door to the camper shell. There was an ice chest just inside the door. The rest of the cramped accommodations were almost completely bare, as if someone had recently cleaned them out. There was nothing to indicate what kind of "gist" Conrad was: no tools, no rock samples or artifacts, no maps or other kind reference materials.

Gabe was just finishing with the notes he was jotting down when Marty Hernandez arrived.

"What do you have, Gabe?" Hernandez asked as he got out of his patrol car, slipping on his Smokey the Bear hat as he did.

"Basically, I've got an abandoned vehicle and a lot of blood," Gabe explained. He showed Hernandez the truck with the dried blood smeared down the side. "I need to find out if the truck's been reported stolen, though I doubt it. A rancher up the road said some scientist from the university has been looking around his place. I'm pretty sure this is the guy's truck."

Hernandez briefly inspected the truck, then noticed the drops of blood leading through the gate. "Did you see this?" He pointed at the trail.

"Yeah," Gabe said uncomfortably. "I followed it for a little ways. A big rattler decided I wasn't going to go any further."

"You let a snake chase you off?" Hernandez snapped. "Someone could be hurt out there."

Gabe was embarrassed now. He wanted to explain his excuse, but it suddenly seemed rather flimsy. "I just thought it would be better if I had a little backup. That's all."

Hernandez jotted down the license-plate number to the abandoned truck and went back to his car. Gabe kicked at loose gravel while the highway patrolman made a radio call. A few minutes later he emerged carrying his shotgun.

"The truck hasn't been reported stolen. It belongs to a Joel Conrad."

"Yeah, I got that from the registration papers." He nodded toward the shotgun. "What's that for?"

"In case we come across any more snakes. Come on."

Gabe fell behind Hernandez as he walked through the gate and into the sagebrush. He stayed a few paces behind, just in case they would both need some maneuvering room.

They reached the point where Gabe had made his retreat, but there was no sign of the snake.

"Just where is this reptile of yours?"

"I guess I must have scared him off," Gabe admitted. "He was right over there." He indicated a bush a few feet in front of them.

"You could have gone around him, you know." Hernandez said, sounding a little less perturbed. "You haven't been around snakes much, have you?"

Gabe shook his head. "No. Not really."

The two law-enforcement officers followed the bloody track for another twenty yards when it abruptly stopped. "Look around," Hernandez instructed. "See if it picks up again."

The two men began a close inspection of the ground, walking back and forth in ever widening patterns. The earth was made up of hard-packed sand and rocks and it was impossible to make out any footprints.

After nearly ten minutes Hernandez called a halt to their search. "I give up." He looked at Gabe. "I guess it really didn't matter if you followed the trail or not."

"Yeah, I suppose." Gabe wasn't sure that was

entirely true, but it was a moot point now. The two men turned back to their vehicles. "What do you think I should do now?"

"Well, you can leave the truck where it is with the keys in it. Maybe the owner's just out for a stroll. Then again, if you just leave it there, someone else might come along and steal it. Or you can impound it until this Conrad guy shows up. Of course, he may be a little ticked if he has to hitch a ride all the way to Las Palmas."

"There is one more option."

Gabe pulled the truck to a stop in front of the Sanchez ranch house. The old man emerged from his front door and gave the deputy a slight wave. He appeared a little confused as the highway patrol car stopped behind the truck.

"¿Qué pasa?" the old man asked.

Gabe got out of the truck with the keys in hand. "I'm not sure, but I think your 'gist' is lost in the foothills somewhere. This is his truck, isn't it?"

Sanchez looked the vehicle over. "Sí." He noticed the blood on the door. "What happened?"

"We're not sure. The man's name is Conrad. Joel Conrad."

"Sí. That's the name he told me. I remember now."

"I don't know if he's been hurt or what. He left his keys in the truck. I was afraid someone might drive off with it so I thought I'd drop it off here, if you don't mind."

"Sure. But how will he know it's here?"

"I'm going back and look for him. It's about ten

miles down the road. If I can't find him, I'll leave a note at the gate where he was parked. I know there's not very much traffic out this way, but if he does turn up, maybe he can hitch a ride here."

"Why is the highway patrol here?"

"Officer Hernandez is going to give me a ride. My Jeep's still parked back there." He handed the keys to Sanchez. "I'll stop back by this way. Is that offer for a cup of coffee still good?"

"Oh, *sí*." Sanchez beamed. "Anytime. Anytime."

"*Bien*," Gabe said. "I'll see you in a bit, then."

17

TRIBAL POLICE CHIEF VICINTI KNEW SOMETHING WAS wrong when he was still a mile from the mountain pasture. A half-dozen sheep were grazing along the side of the dirt road and there was no sign of the rest of the flock.

Vicinti stopped his Jeep to check the plastic ear tags that branded the animals. They were more skittish than usual, and it took him a few minutes to corral one. It was his sheep, all right. They probably all were.

Though he was a man of few words and a stern disciplinarian, Bram Vicinti wasn't thinking of a reprimand for his son. He knew something was wrong. Matthew had been raised to be responsible. He wouldn't have let a handful of sheep wander off like that. And even if the boy had been irresponsible, the dogs wouldn't have let anything like that happen.

Vicinti jumped back into his Jeep and sped down the road as quickly as the loose gravel would allow.

He skidded to a stop in front of the lowly cabin his son had called home for nearly three months.

"Matthew!" Vicinti yelled, leaping from his Jeep and running to the cabin. The one-roomed shack was empty. He turned his attention to the large tree-lined pasture behind the cabin. No more than two hundred sheep grazed idly on the brown grass. The rest of the flock was nowhere to be seen.

"Matthew!" he yelled again, cupping his hands to form a megaphone. His voice disappeared down the mountainside with no response.

Vicinti put his fingers to his mouth and let out a shrill whistle. If Matthew couldn't hear him, maybe the dogs could. He listened carefully for any sign that he had been heard, but there was none. He sounded his whistle again, then yelled, "Boss! Tico! Home now!"

There was still no response.

Vicinti got back into the Jeep and started across the pasture, honking as he drove toward the far end of the clearing. What was left of his flock scattered, terrified of both the sound and the approaching vehicle.

As he got closer to the line of trees that bracketed the far edge of the pasture, Vicinti noticed a dark shape stretched out in the short grass. He stopped his Jeep several yards short of the form and slowly got out.

He hoped his eyes were playing tricks on him. He told himself he was looking at a log. Or maybe even a sheep. Maybe it was Tico or Boss. He refused to let himself believe it could be anything else.

But as he got closer, Vicinti recognized the sheepskin coat he had given his son for Christmas. He broke into a run, nearly tripping over the carbine Matthew had wielded two nights earlier.

Vicinti stumbled to his knees as he grabbed for the still body in front of him. A cloud of dispassionate flies scattered at his intrusion.

The boy was facedown. The ground around him was brown and discolored from his blood.

Vicinti's hands were shaking as he turned the body over.

The face had been caved in on one side from the force of a tremendous blow. A wide gash exposed the larynx, and the jacket was in tatters as if shredded by razors.

Everything was matted in dried blood.

"No!" Vicinti bellowed, clutching his son to his chest. "God in heaven! NO!"

18

"CHIEF OF DETECTIVES," LANSING SAID INTO THE
receiver, "I can't believe it."

"Patience does have its merits," Detective Chet
Gonzalez said from the other end. "I moved over to
homicide not long after you left the force."

"Yeah, I knew about that," Lansing admitted.
"But chief of detectives? Kind of makes me feel old."

"You're getting there, Cliff. We both are."

It was nearly noon before Lansing was able to talk
to anyone working on the Giancarlo case. The
assigned detectives were still going over the crime
scene with the forensics unit when he first called. He
had asked that an investigator contact him at his ear-
liest convenience. He was surprised when one of his
classmates from the police academy returned his call.
Lansing and Chester "Chet" Gonzalez had worked
together on the Albuquerque police force for ten
years.

"Since homicide's been called into this case,"
Lansing continued, "I presume we're dealing with a
murder here."

"So it appears."

"How was he killed?"

"Just what is your big interest in this particular case, Cliff?"

"It's a little bit more than professional curiosity. I knew Dr. Giancarlo from my college days."

"Evidently everybody knew Elmo Giancarlo. And from what I can tell so far, everybody liked him. How did you hear about this way up there in San Phillipe? We made the press release less than an hour ago."

"I was trying to get in touch with him about a project his department was working on. Dr. Gill over in their research lab told me about it."

"Gill?" Gonzalez asked. "Is that G-I-L-L?"

"Yes." Lansing could tell from the detective's tone he was taking notes. "Dr. Mary Ann Gill."

"Just what sort of project are they working that you would be interested in?"

Lansing found it strange to be on the receiving end of an interrogation. He explained about the discovery of the saddlebags containing the emerald and the journal. Dr. Giancarlo and his staff were trying to decipher the book as well as analyze the possible origins of the ancient fetish he had found.

"Could you give me a description of the emerald?"

"I can fax you a photo if you want, Chet," Lansing said, getting a little tired of the inquest. "But why? What is it with all the questions?"

Gonzalez forced a chuckle. "Just being a cop. That's all."

"And?" Lansing waited for an explanation.

"It looks like we're dealing with a botched robbery here. At least that's what we're calling it right now. We've had Giancarlo's secretary try to make an inventory of everything in the office. See if anything's missing. It was kind of hard to tell because the whole place was torn up."

"I've seen her list and there's no mention of an emerald."

"I doubt if it was in his office. Doctor Giancarlo told me he was keeping it in a safe in the museum. I can't believe he would try to hide it in one of his desk drawers."

"You never know about these eggheads," Gonzalez observed. "They're not noted for their exceptional common sense."

"Yeah, I suppose. Do you mind telling me how he was killed?"

"It looks like someone went after him with a butcher knife. He was cut up pretty bad. But I don't think we're going to have a hard time finding the perp. There were bloody fingerprints near the body and they don't appear to belong to the victim. We'll run them through the FBI data bank. If our boy's been fingerprinted, we'll have his name within twenty-four hours."

"What about the emerald figurine? Do you still need a picture?"

"Yeah, fax me one. I'll also check with Giancarlo's secretary. If this totem of yours is so valuable, they may have a photo floating around too.

"Is there anything I can do for you, Cliff?"

"Not right now. I might give you a call in a day or so to see what's turned up."

"Feel free to call anytime. And if anyone gives you the runaround, just drop my name. I'll be anxious to see if it really pulls any weight around here."

"Sure thing, Chet. Thanks."

Lansing grabbed his coffee mug and headed for

the door. It was lunchtime, but he didn't feel much like eating. He had ten months to go in the fiscal year, with $250,000 less to operate on now. As much as he hated working with figures, he knew he had to come up with some creative bookkeeping if his budget was going to stretch till the end of the year. If he could have gotten someone else to do it for him, he would have been out the door in a second.

19

"JONATHAN? CAN YOU HEAR ME?" DR. MARGARITE Carerra asked as she shone the penlight into her patient's eye.

Akee managed a guttural, almost inaudible, "Um."

The pupils were still dilated but they were finally starting to respond to the light stimulus.

"Is he getting better, Doctor?" Susan Akee asked. Jonathan's wife hadn't moved from her chair for hours. She had sat with her pocketbook clasped to her chest, rocking back and forth and saying prayers.

"It looks like it," Margarite said reassuringly. "We probably need to keep this IV going till at least tomorrow morning."

"Will he stay here?"

"He's going to have to. I've already talked to Dr. Tanner."

"He doesn't mind?"

Margarite shook her head. "Dr. Tanner's a good man. He'll look out for you."

There was a slight rap on the door to the examining room and the receptionist stuck her head in. "Dr. Carerra, there's a call for you. It's the doctor at the Jicarilla reservation."

"Thank you. I'll be right there." She turned back to her patient's wife. "I don't think we have anything to worry about, Susan. He's starting to respond. All we have to do is keep pumping fluids into him."

Susan nodded grimly.

"This is Dr. Carerra," Margarite said into the receiver.

"Yes, Doctor," the voice on the other end responded. "Juan Velarde."

Juan Velarde was the new reservation doctor in Dulce. He had been one of the first Jicarilla Apache to get his medical degree and had just taken over their small ten-bed hospital. Margarite had met him twice before, but both encounters had been brief. However, they had talked several times on the phone. She had found him eager, though a little wet behind the ears. He at least knew his limitations and wasn't afraid to ask for advice.

"Yes, Doctor, what can I do for you?"

"I have a bit of a problem." He hesitated for a moment as if trying to phrase the words correctly. "How familiar are you with animal attacks?"

"What kind of animal?"

"You see, that's just it. I don't know what kind. I have a fifteen-year-old male who was killed up in the mountains. He had a severe trauma to his skull. His throat was slashed open and his clothes were torn . . . almost shredded."

"Was he mauled? Any bite marks?"

"The wound to the throat is so severe, it very well could have been from a bite. But I have no expertise in this kind of trauma and I'm afraid to attempt an autopsy. I don't want to destroy any clues as to what did this. Is there any way you could come up here and take a look?"

"I can be there in about forty-five minutes. How long ago did the attack take place?"

"From the state of the rigor, at least twenty-four hours. Maybe longer. The sooner you can get here, the better. Police Chief Vicinti is on a rampage. He's rounding up all the hunters and trackers in town. He plans on killing everything on that mountain."

"Is he afraid someone else is going to get hurt?"

"No. He just wants to destroy whatever it was that killed his son."

20

RENEE GARLAND SAT WITH HUEY, DEWEY, AND LOUIE under the ten-foot-by-ten-foot canopy, trying to choke down a soggy ham sandwich. The small covering provided their only escape from the midday sun. It did little to protect them from the gusts of sandy, hot wind or the swarms of flies that always showed up at mealtime.

She checked her watch for the fiftieth time that day. Vencel had run over to the visitors' center to make a phone call. That had been three hours earlier. He still wasn't back.

And Joel Conrad? He was missing in action somewhere. Renee could only shake her head. Boy, was he going to get his butt chewed when Vencel finally got hold of him.

She decided she couldn't take any more of the cold, wet bread. She folded the remaining half of the sandwich in plastic wrap and tossed it into a trash bag. She checked her watch again. "Five minutes, boys. Then it's back to work."

"Aw, come on, Renee," Huey protested. "What's the hurry? We've got a whole week to pack this stuff up."

"The sooner we get it packed, the sooner we get to go home and sleep in our own beds," she observed.

"That motel's better than any college dorm," Dewey said, leaning back in his lawn chair and pushing his ball cap over his eyes. "I think it's time for a nap."

Renee had discovered not everyone was cut out to be a field archaeologist. It was tedious, monotonous, often backbreaking work. It took a lot of dedication to sit bent over or prone on your stomach on hard, rocky ground for hours on end, equipped with nothing more than a dental pick and a soft-bristled brush, trying to extricate a thousand-year-old skull fragment or piece of flint from sun-baked clay as hard as bricks.

It was an occupation people took to or they didn't. There wasn't any middle ground.

All three of her undergraduate charges had started off the dig with great enthusiasm. After nine weeks only Louie displayed any real interest in the project.

Huey and Dewey treated their work with genuine disdain, unless Vencel or Joel was around. When a "real" authority figure was at the site, they were conscientious. It was enough to make her gag.

What they probably didn't realize was that Renee would be writing their evaluations. She suspected they would associate the word *bitch* with her name for the rest of their lives. She really didn't care.

"Come on, Louie—" Renee cut herself off in midsentence, a little embarrassed at revealing the pet name she had given him. "I mean, come on, Mark. Let's see what we can get packed up here."

Huey and Dewey continued to lounge in the shade for another twenty minutes. It would have been longer but they spotted Dr. Vencel's red truck approaching. Renee suddenly found herself with more help than she could handle. She didn't have to look around to see what had happened. She knew either Vencel or Joel had returned.

She stepped back and let her assistants take over their duties, carefully wrapping and labeling each pottery piece before it went into a crate.

Vencel got out of his truck, a scowl on his face. Renee could tell this would not be a pleasant afternoon.

"Still no sign of that damned Conrad?" Vencel growled.

"No, sir." She thought quickly, trying to engineer a reasonable excuse. "Dr. Vencel, I know Joel wanders off sometimes, but this just isn't like him. He must have been in some sort of accident."

"Then he'd better be in a hospital somewhere. Because if he isn't, he's finished at the University of New Mexico. I've been itching to get rid of him for three years."

Renee knew there was no love lost between Joel and Vencel. She also knew Joel had a guardian angel by the name of Elmo Giancarlo. There was no way Vencel could usurp the head of the department, though she knew she wouldn't dare say that to Vencel's face.

"This dig is officially over," Vencel said, brushing past the grad student to survey the site. "Everything has to be labeled and packed tonight. A truck will be here by noon tomorrow to pick up the crates."

"I thought we had another week," Renee protested cautiously.

"Not anymore. I've been called back to the university. I have to take over the department."

Renee wasn't prepared for that kind of news. "W-what happened to Dr. Giancarlo?"

"Somebody broke into his office last night," Vencel said grimly. "He was killed."

"Oh, my God," Renee whimpered.

"That's why I was gone so long. I was trying to make arrangements to get these artifacts picked up. Obviously I can't trust Conrad to get the job done, and it's beyond your scope of responsibility.

"That's all right. When I get back to Albuquerque, there are going to be a few changes made. I can guarantee you that."

He turned back to Renee. "Do you have everything you need to get this stuff packed?"

"Y-yes, I think so," she stammered, still shocked at the news.

"I'm going back to the motel, then. You can reach me there, but I expect everything to be packed before you leave here tonight."

"Yes, sir."

Vencel turned and headed for his truck, stopping halfway and turning back. "If Conrad shows up, get some work out of him. After you're finished you can tell him his affiliation with the university has been terminated."

As Vencel's truck disappeared in a cloud of dust, Renee was engulfed in a wave of nausea. She had taken a half-dozen courses from Giancarlo and really liked the man. She didn't know if she was ill from the thought of his death, whether it was Joel's impending dismissal, or if it was just the idea that Vencel would be taking over the department.

She stumbled over to the cooler to wash her face

with the water from melted ice. Suddenly she felt very alone. Suddenly she wished there were someone there who could hold her. She wished Joel were there to hold her.

"Joel," she whimpered to herself, "where the hell are you?"

21

BRAM VICINTI GRABBED HIS SHEEPSKIN COAT FROM THE peg along the wall and headed for the door. Six trucks and twenty men waited for him outside his office. A half-dozen dogs had been enlisted to assist in the tracking.

It was already midafternoon. It would take two hours to get back to the mountain pasture where he had found his son's body. That left them little daylight to work in. It didn't matter to Vicinti. He wasn't returning to Dulce until he found the animal that had killed his son.

"Chief!" the desk clerk yelled. "I've got a call for you."

Thinking it might be his wife or another volunteer, Vicinti grudgingly grabbed the phone. "Yeah?"

"Chief Vicinti, this is Sheriff Lansing. Dr. Carerra told me about your son. I'm awfully sorry. Is there anything my office can do to help?"

"We take care of our own, Sheriff."

"I know you do. But I think whatever you're tracking has been killing livestock outside the reservation. We've had complaints from ranchers on the west range."

"This is an Apache problem and we'll take care of it."

"Listen, Vicinti. I'm just trying to help. I understand how you feel, but I don't want to see my county all shot up. If you need help outside your boundaries, I want to know about it."

"I know how far my jurisdiction goes. I don't need some white man to tell me. If you don't have anything else to say, I've got people waiting for me, Sheriff. Good-bye."

Vicinti slammed the phone into its cradle before Lansing could say another word. Shoving his hat onto his head, he pushed the door open and went outside.

The men were gathered in small knots, talking in hushed tones, patiently waiting for some signal that it was time to go. They were all dressed in the garb of twentieth-century cowboys: Stetson hats, boots, blue jeans, cotton and flannel shirts. Nearly every man cradled a carbine or shotgun in his arms. A few had pistols strapped to their hips. And despite their calm exteriors there was blood lust in their eyes. A few of the younger men saw this as a rite of passage. Some had even made side bets on who would be the one to destroy this killer creature, whatever it was.

Vicinti didn't break his stride as he headed for his Jeep and shouted, "*Shil dah didoo-lwol!*"—the Apache equivalent of "Let's go!"

Men scrambled into the cabs and the backs of the trucks. As they sped down the highway behind their leader, several let out war whoops to let the town know they were off.

No one imagined how long a night it would be. Nor did anyone suspect that not all of them would return.

22

As the convoy headed south from Dulce, Margarite pulled into a parking spot in front of the Jicarilla Indian Hospital. As she got out of her truck, she wondered if she would be seeing Lansing anytime soon. She had called him from John Tanner's office and told him about the news from the reservation. He had said he would offer whatever assistance Vicinti needed.

Lansing had sounded antsy, as if he had something on his mind. She had come to learn that if Lansing sounded on edge, something was going on. The trouble was, getting him to talk was like trying to pull bent, rusty nails through a six-inch plank. Today, she didn't have time to play his stoic, silent-type game. She had to get to the reservation to see if there was something she could do to help.

She hoped she could identify what kind of animal had attacked before Vicinti headed back into the mountains. At least his trackers would know what to look for.

Dr. Velarde pulled the sheet down to expose the body. Margarite had seen traumas as bad or worse, but it never made the viewing any easier.

The body had already been disrobed. The majority of the wounds were located about the face and neck area. But there were also parallel scratch marks across the torso, where claws had ripped through a heavy jacket and a flannel shirt.

The most disturbing feature to Margarite was the face. The skull had suffered a severe blow from a wide, heavy object. It had been caved in from the side, almost halfway to the nose, leaving the left eye bulging from its socket.

"My first impression is that he was attacked by a bear," Margarite said, trying to sound dispassionate. She made a closer examination of the hair. "There are puncture marks in the scalp consistent with what an animal claw would leave."

She looked up at Velarde. Even hidden behind the surgical mask, he had, she could tell, a severe frown on his face. "Hopefully, this was the initial wound," she added. "If it was, he was dead before he ever hit the ground."

Velarde nodded but said nothing.

Margarite began to make a close examination of the neck wound. She paid particular attention to the edges of the tattered flesh. "Do you have a magnifying glass?" she asked without looking up.

"I have a jeweler's lamp for fine stitching," he said. "Just a minute, I'll get it."

A few minutes later he had the lamp positioned on the examining table.

Margarite studied the frayed edges of skin. Most of the flesh had simply been torn away. There were, however, two distinct, rounded entry wounds. "Calipers."

Velarde handed her the instrument.

Margarite took the measurement. "It appears I

have puncture wounds from incisors. Measurement is approximately twelve and a half centimeters."

"That's a big damned bear," Velarde wheezed. "That's five inches across at the snout."

"It couldn't have been a bear," Margarite said, shaking her head. "With a snout that wide, he'd have to be thirty feet tall."

"A mountain lion, then?"

"That would make more sense. A mountain lion would have the instinct to go for the throat. A bear just mauls its victims." She leaned back from the jeweler's lamp. "But we're still talking about a big damned animal. An eight-hundred-pound grizzly could crush a skull like that, but not a two-hundred-pound mountain lion."

"So what did this?"

"We need better expertise than mine."

"How long will that take?"

"Maybe only a couple of hours. I have a biologist friend over in Shiprock. Maybe she can help."

23

LANSING SWUNG THE DOOR OPEN TO HIS OFFICE A LITTLE harder than usual, banging it against the stop. Marilyn, their grandmotherly receptionist, looked up from the vase of flowers she was arranging. She noticed the sheriff had his empty coffee cup in hand.

"That's about your twelfth cup today, Cliff. You're starting to get a little hyper."

He ignored her remark. "Have we heard any more from Gabe?"

"He radioed in about fifteen minutes ago. Said he had just passed through Dulce and would come straight to the office."

Lansing looked at his watch. It would be at least another twenty minutes before his deputy got in. "Did he say if he found the driver to that truck?"

"No. Do you want me to radio him and ask?"

"It doesn't matter."

"What about you? Did you ever get hold of Chief Vicinti?"

Lansing stared at his empty cup, realizing he really couldn't handle any more coffee. "It's bad enough that SOB doesn't like white men in general. He's stubborn to boot. I'd bet he'd sooner drown than take a rope if I threw it to him."

"Didn't want our help, huh?"

"Worse than that. He made it sound like we'd better not get in his way." Lansing shook his head. "I'll tell you what. This has been a lousy damned day. I lose all the funding to my office, an old professor of mine gets murdered. I've got a bloodstained, abandoned truck, missing livestock, and a fifteen-year-old kid mauled by some wild animal. And all I can do is sit here and wait to see if there's something I can do."

"Why don't you go out on patrol?"

"What for? DeJesus and Rivera are already out cruising. With my budget cuts there probably isn't enough gas money for the rest of the week."

"Why don't you go to lunch, then? You've been cooped up in your office all day."

"I've been going over the budget, trying to figure out how we're supposed to make it through until next July."

"And?"

"How do you feel about volunteering your services for the next ten months?" Marilyn gave him a scowl that could have stopped a charging bull. "That's what I thought. I'll go back and massage the figures some more. Send Gabe in when he gets here."

It was another half hour before Deputy Hanna arrived at the office. Marilyn sent him directly to Lansing.

"So fill me in about this abandoned truck."

Gabe sat in one of the chairs in front of the sheriff's desk and pulled out his notebook. Referring to his notes periodically, he began to describe the events of the day. Lansing stared out his window, concentrating on Gabe's story, interrupting only occasionally to clarify one point or another.

"After I dropped the truck off at the Sanchez place, Marty Hernandez took me back to my Jeep. He and I both looked around for a while before he had to get back on patrol. I drove on through the gate and followed the road up into the foothills.

"I still couldn't find anything.

"After about an hour I gave up and went back to see Mr. Sanchez. Had a cup of coffee and came back to Las Palmas."

"I thought you didn't drink coffee."

Gabe shrugged, a little sheepish. "He didn't have any Cokes. Besides, he really enjoyed the company."

Lansing turned his seat around to face his deputy. "So we have an abandoned truck, not reported stolen. It's from Albuquerque. No sign of the owner but the keys are still in it. Bloodstains on the seat and down the door. But it wasn't an accident. And the owner is a 'gist' of some sort from the University of New Mexico."

Gabe nodded. "That's it in a nutshell."

"Plus we have complaints about missing sheep up in the mountain pastures."

"From at least two of the ranches. Mr. Sanchez doesn't know. He said he would go tomorrow and check up on his nephew."

"I'm starting to think we have a bigger problem than a few missing sheep and a deserted truck."

"What do you mean?"

Lansing explained what he knew about the tragedy on the Jicarilla reservation. "It sounds like we have a man-killer out there. It's already taken two lives and no telling how many sheep."

Gabe let out a soft whistle. "When was the Vicinti boy killed?"

"We don't know for sure. Dr. Carerra is at the reservation hospital doing an autopsy. But there are a lot of blanks we have to fill in. What was the name of the truck's owner again?"

"Conrad. Joel Conrad."

"We need to find out the last time anyone saw this Conrad. We need to find out when and where the Vicinti boy was killed. We need to correlate the times and locations of when the livestock turned up missing. Maybe we can figure out a pattern of movement."

"I thought you said Police Chief Vicinti was already tracking it down, whatever it is?"

"Yeah, and what if he comes up empty-handed? Let's get busy. It's not five o'clock yet. Call the university locator and see if you can find out where Conrad worked. Maybe they can give us a lead. I'll call Dr. Carerra and see if she's come up with anything."

"You got it." Gabe stood and headed for the door. "I'll tell you what. I sure will be glad when we get the new radio transmitters in. It's a real pain not being able to talk to the office when you need to."

"That's right. You haven't heard all the good news yet."

Gabe stopped at the door. "What do you mean?"

"Go make your calls. I'll fill you in later."

24

MARGARITE ALMOST DIDN'T RECOGNIZE KIMBERLY Tallmountain when she arrived at the hospital. She had abandoned her long, flowing black hair in favor of a close-cropped, boyish coiffure. It was not unattractive, but it was anything but traditional Navajo. Then again, Kim Tallmountain was anything but traditional Navajo.

While they'd been awaiting Kim's arrival, Margarite had explained to Dr. Velarde how the two women had come to meet. It had been that spring. It was while Sheriff Lansing and one of his deputies, Gabe Hanna, had been investigating the murder of Kim's father.

After her father's death, Kim took over as chief conservationist for the Shiprock District of the Navajo Reservation. From what Margarite could remember, Kim had "degrees in biology and chemistry or something of that sort." Her duties ranged from soil analysis to protecting endangered species.

Margarite was sure that if there was anyone around who could help identify their predator it would be Kimberly Tallmountain.

Kim approached the two doctors as they sat in the tiny coffee room/cafeteria. "Margarite?"

"Kim, you found us."

Dr. Velarde stood as Kim approached.

"Kim," Margarite continued, "this Dr. Juan Velarde, the chief resident here."

Velarde extended his hand. "That's a little misleading," he said, allowing himself a slight smile. "I'm the only resident. Thank you for coming on such short notice. Would you care for a cup of coffee?"

"No, thank you," she said, shaking hands. "It's a good thing you contacted me when you did. I was supposed to drive over to Cañon de Chelly this afternoon. If you had called five minutes later, you would have missed me. I don't mean to sound impatient, but I want to try and get home before dark. I don't care much for driving at night."

"I understand," Velarde said. "Please, come this way."

Matthew Vicinti's body was still in the surgical suite where the two doctors had conducted their examination. Before entering the room they each donned a surgical smock, mask, and latex gloves.

"Are you sure you're ready for this?" Margarite asked.

Kim took a deep breath. "I hope so."

They entered the room and positioned themselves next to the table. Margarite carefully pulled down the sheet, revealing the face and torso. Kim couldn't prevent an audible gasp.

Margarite had gotten used to the sight, but barely. "I've identified puncture wounds at the shoulder.

Probably from incisors. They measure twelve and a half centimeters apart."

"Let me see."

The two doctors rolled the body onto its side so that Kim could get a better look. "Definitely teeth marks." She nodded. "Was the boy wearing clothes when he was attacked?"

"Yes," Velarde said. "When the body was brought in he had on a T-shirt, a flannel shirt, and a heavy sheepskin jacket. Whatever made those marks bit through the clothing."

"You can put him back down," Kim said, starting to take a closer look at the rest of the damage. "I can see how a bear might have made the head wound. But bears aren't stalker-predators like mountain lions or wolves. They don't have the instinct to 'go for the jugular' like other hunters.

"If it's hungry enough, a mountain lion will attack an elk three times its size. It will clamp its teeth around the windpipe, suffocating its prey. Wolves and coyotes have a little less finesse, but they still go for the throat."

"Coyotes don't attack people, anyway," Velarde observed.

"That's not an absolute," Kim said, remembering an unexplained encounter she'd had once. "But this was no coyote or wolf attack. It wasn't a bear." She hesitated for a moment. "And I don't think it was a mountain lion."

The two doctors looked from one another, back to the biologist. "We're running out of options here, Kim. What are we left with? A rabid badger?"

"Where are the clothes he was wearing?" Kim asked, looking around the room.

"I threw them in a plastic bag," Velarde said. "I think it's in the other room. Just a minute." He returned a few seconds later with a large, clear bag. "Do you want me to dump it out?"

"No, no!" Kim insisted. "We need to leave everything in there. We need to get it down to the state crime lab as soon as possible. Especially the jacket. They can check it for blood, fibers, even saliva from the animal."

"How long will that take?" Velarde asked.

"If you can get it down there tonight and ask them to expedite everything, you might know something in another forty-eight hours."

"We don't have forty-eight hours." Velarde sighed. "Chief of Police Vicinti is already out looking for the animal. He said he wouldn't be back until he brought it in."

"But he doesn't know what he's looking for," Kim protested.

"Then I imagine he'll kill anything he can find up there. This is his son we're looking at."

25

LANSING HAD A SPLITTING HEADACHE. IT WAS ALMOST five o'clock, he hadn't eaten anything since breakfast, and he felt as though he hadn't accomplished a single thing all day. His desk was cluttered with page after page of computer printouts and scraps of paper scribbled full of figures and totals. As he emerged from his office, looking for an aspirin and a drink of water, Gabe came out of the dayroom.

"I think I finally tracked down Joel Conrad, Sheriff," Gabe said, notebook in hand.

"You know where he is?" Lansing asked, sounding tired.

"Well, not exactly. But at least I know why he was up this way."

"Go ahead," Lansing said, continuing past his deputy to the reception desk. "Marilyn, I need a couple of aspirin, please."

Marilyn started digging in a desk drawer as Gabe read from his notes. "Joel Conrad is a Ph.D. candidate in the Archaeology Department. It took me a while to find anyone to talk to at the department there. I guess somebody died or something."

"Yeah, I know about that," Lansing said, taking

the two aspirin Marilyn handed him. He walked over to the water cooler to fill a small paper cup. "Go on."

"Anyway, Conrad's supposed to be working at an archaeological site over in Chaco Canyon. I had to call around and finally got the number to the visitors' center there at the monument. They knew about Conrad and the work he was doing. But they said the site was at the other end of the canyon. Besides that, no one from the center had seen him in a few days."

"Is Conrad the only one working that site?"

"No. They've got a team there. In fact, they said one of the archaeologists, Dr. Vencel, was at the center that morning."

"Is this archaeology team staying at the canyon?"

"No. Evidently they spend the nights at a motel over in Counselor. I got the number and called. I guess no one's in their room right now."

"They're probably still at the site. Leave the number to the motel. I'll try it again later."

"Did you talk to Dr. Carerra?"

"She's supposed to call me back. The receptionist said that she and Dr. Velarde were still in the examining room. I can't believe they've been in there all this time. She got up there around two-thirty."

The console in front of Marilyn emitted a subdued ring as one of the buttons lit up. "San Phillipe Sheriff's Department," she said into her headpiece. She listened, then replied, "One moment." She looked at Lansing. "It's for you."

"That must be Margarite. I'll take it in my office."

*   *   *

"Sheriff Lansing."

"Yes, Sheriff, this is Dr. Mary Ann Gill. We talked this morning."

"Yes, with the lab."

"I apologize for being so abrupt this morning. I was a little upset."

"There's no need to apologize. I understood the circumstances."

"I'm afraid I do have something to apologize for. The reason I'm calling is about the journal my office is working on. I assigned two of my student assistants to work full time on the preparation of the pages. We were able to separate the last two thirds of the manuscript into two blocks of paper. We intended to soak the first batch in a formaldehyde base to moisten the sheets for separation. Unfortunately, our bottles got mixed up and an acid-based compound was used. We essentially dissolved a third of the book.

"I thought you should be notified. If you want us to discontinue our work and return what remains, I completely understand."

The news was surprising to Lansing but not necessarily upsetting. His own personal investment in the manuscript was minimal. What would have been absurd would be to insist the university return it. What in the world could he do with it without Dr. Gill's assistance?

"I appreciate your honesty, Dr. Gill. There's no doubt in my mind we're talking about an accident here. But what would I do with the rest of the journal? I'd just as soon you keep it and finish your work."

Gill's sigh of relief was audible over the phone. "Thank you for your understanding, Sheriff. If it's any compensation, my secretary is typing the first dozen or so pages of the final section. I would say it's more than a little interesting." She paused for a moment. "I was curious, do you have any other family papers, a family Bible, anything like that?"

"I'm afraid anything of that sort went up in flames a couple of months ago. If I hadn't had the house fire, I never would have found the journal."

"Oh, I see." There was silence on the other end for a moment. "Do you know much about Virgil Lansing?"

"Not a lot. He was my great-great-grandfather and homesteaded out here after the Civil War. I know that his wife was a Tewa Pueblo from Burnt Mesa. That's all I knew until the journal turned up. Now I know he went to West Point and fought in the Mexican-American War. Why?"

"From the fragments we've pieced together, and I'm talking about a sentence here and a word there, he spent his army career in the West. We've picked up references to California and the gold rush, the Santa Fe Trail, the Oregon Trail. Names like John C. Frémont and Kit Carson. I have to admit I've been surprised at what I've seen. I know we're going to be missing a major portion of his story. I hope there's enough continuity there for it to make sense.

"Like I said, my secretary is typing the last of the pages we were able to look at. If you want, I can fax it to you in just a few minutes."

"Thanks," Lansing said. "I'd like that." He paused for a moment. "Before I let you go, I was wondering. Do you know a student there by the name of Joel Conrad?"

"Absolutely. He's one of our best and brightest. Why?"

"I was just curious. We found his truck abandoned on the west side of the county. We know he's been doing some archaeological work over in Chaco Canyon. That's about thirty miles from where we found the truck."

"Has anything happened to him?"

"We're not sure. We're still looking. If you hear anything from him, I'd sure like a call."

"I certainly will."

"Thanks. I'll let you go. And I do appreciate all the work your office is doing."

"I think we're both benefiting from this experience." Dr. Gill said something away from the receiver, then spoke to Lansing again. "That was my secretary. I'll have her fax those pages to you now."

"Thanks."

Lansing walked to the outer office. Marilyn was gathering up her purse and the romance novel she was reading in her spare moments. Gabe casually leaned against the reception counter, finishing off a Coke. It was quitting time.

"There's a fax coming in, Sheriff," Marilyn said.

"Yeah, I was expecting it. Dr. Carerra didn't call from Dulce, did she?"

"Not yet. Deputy Peters did, though. He said he'd be in around five-thirty."

"That's okay. I can man the console till he gets in. I'll see you in the morning."

Marilyn let herself out of the receptionist area, then Lansing took her seat at the desk. He started looking over the fax sheets.

"Sheriff, if you don't have anything for me," Gabe said, "I guess I'll head out."

"Sure, Gabe. See you tomorrow." Lansing didn't even bother to look up. He was more interested in the newest installment from Virgil Lansing's journal.

26

JOURNAL OF VIRGIL LANSING (CONT.)

Although we counted the Battle of Cerro Gordo in late April a monumental victory against Santa Anna's army, it hardly improved our position to any great extent. Soon after the success, four thousand volunteers from Illinois, Georgia, Alabama, and Tennessee withdrew to return home, their enlistments being up.

As we moved forward to take the town of Puebla, our supply line to Veracruz became dangerously strained. We lacked sufficient oxen and wagons to keep our troops adequately armed and fed. And, even though we had defeated the regular Mexican army, our supply trains were constantly under attack from guerrilla units.

Compounding our supply problem was the fact that Commodore Perry had retired from the waters around Veracruz. His intent was to mount an offensive against the Mexican stronghold of Villahermosa, inland from the Bay of Campeche.

General Scott, suspecting the guerrilla attacks were being directed from Villahermosa, ordered that an expeditionary force be formed. The troops were to be sent

overland to join up with Perry's marines in a pincer move
against the enemy.

Major Marsden, my immediate superior, led the 4th
Infantry. I accompanied him as adjutant. Our force of 150
men was supplemented with two hundred volunteers from
the Mississippi Rifles and the Louisiana Tiger Brigade. The
logic to their inclusion was that once we reached Villahermosa, they could board ships and return home.

The estimated distance from Veracruz to Villahermosa was 250 miles. Unfamiliar though we were with the
terrain, Major Marsden concluded it would take us no
more than ten days to make the rendezvous with Perry.
We set out on June first.

The first four days the progress was . . .

[MATERIAL UNREADABLE]

. . . had gotten separated from the main force during our
reconnoiter. We could hear the sniper fire behind us and
both Captain Christmas and myself were resolved to rejoin
our units. By then the monsoon rain was driving so hard,
we were nearly blinded. The animal trail we had followed
was virtually obliterated and all we could do was seek
shelter beneath a ceiba tree and wait.

It was dawn before the weather lifted enough for us to
move. There was no more sound of battle, and to be perfectly honest, neither the captain nor myself knew in which
direction we should progress. We located what we thought
was the trail that had delivered us so deeply into the jungle
and we followed it for several hours.

It was during one of our rests that the canopy above
us erupted in a great commotion. The howler monkeys

proved to be great clarions against intruders into their domain. It was because of their alarm that the two of us hid, barely escaping the notice of two dozen Mexican soldiers.

The soldiers passed only inches from us. In my ten months in Mexico I had acquired a reasonable understanding of the language. As they sauntered along I could pick up pieces of their conversations. They were joining the rest of their army at a nearby Indian village. Captain Christmas and I decided to follow them, hoping they would eventually lead us to our own troops.

It was midafternoon when the soldiers entered a large clearing beneath two tall, conical hills. There were several huts in the clearing, obviously belonging to the Indian inhabitants. We estimated some sixty soldiers had already gathered there. They appeared to be in the process of plundering the huts, looking for, I presume, provisions.

Their actions reminded the two of us that we hadn't eaten since the previous day.

While several of the Mexican troops ransacked the hovels, the rest had the fifty villagers gathered in the center of their community, held at gunpoint. There was much shouting going on as the Mexican commander made demands of the elders. The man I picked out as the village chief stood shaking his head. This was not to the commander's liking. He directed his soldiers to pull a young man aside and had the poor creature executed on the spot.

The women of the village began to wail and three of them, along with a half dozen children, made a brave dash toward the jungle. They were all gunned down immediately as the soldiers laughed at their newfound sport.

I immediately jumped to my feet, my Colt revolver drawn. Captain Christmas grabbed me by the arm and pulled me down. He had no stomach for the massacre, either, but he insisted getting ourselves shot would not help the hapless natives.

The one small advantage we did have was that we were armed with the new Colt six-shooters and we had ample ammunition. One man could fire and reload more rapidly than six soldiers with single-shot rifles. Although we couldn't overwhelm the soldiers, we could at least draw them away from the village in hopes the Indians could escape.

Our plan was simple. We would begin firing at the edge of the village, then fade deeper into the jungle to draw the soldiers after us. Once we were sure they were chasing us, we would attempt to evade by circling around to the far side of the clearing.

I think we were both surprised at how well our tactic worked. We caught the Mexicans completely off guard. In their initial confusion they fired blindly into the jungle nearest their positions. Once they did focus on our position, we began a hasty retreat, continuing our fire. At best, we had hit only a few of the soldiers, but our intent had never been to overpower them. Simply cause confusion.

The Mexican commander must have been in a rage. Realizing they were being ambushed by only a few adversaries, he dispatched his entire brigade against us.

For our part, we retreated approximately a quarter of a mile into the jungle before we began a wide sweep through the undergrowth. The Mexican soldiers continued their blind firing into the foliage as they tried to overtake the unseen enemy. As we doubled back, we could hear the shouting and gunfire progress farther away from us and we knew our ruse had succeeded.

It was nearly dark by the time we reached the opposite side of the clearing. We mounted one of the cone hills to gain a better view of the village. The natives had grasped the opportunity we had afforded them and had disappeared into the jungle, taking the bodies of their dead with them.

It was at this juncture that I realized we had not positioned ourselves on a hill. We were on a great mound of rubble and stacked blocks. As I pulled the foliage away for a better look I could see intricately carved masonry, blocks of stone with strange human faces. There were mysterious Indian gargoyles and fantastic creatures, the like of which I've never seen.

Years earlier I had seen the drawings of Frederick Catherwood in Harper's Weekly. He had described the great fallen cities of Central America, built by an ancient people called the Maya. From what I could remember of his renderings, we were now standing on similar ruins. And the people we had just rescued must have been descendants of that once great civilization.

I must have expressed great amazement at our discovery, but Captain Christmas did not seem impressed. Though we had succeeded in freeing the village dwellers, he reminded me that we were still separated from our own forces and that we had not yet eaten that day.

With the village deserted and no sign of the enemy, we ventured into the clearing. The Mexican soldiers had conveniently piled a supply of maize and fresh fruits outside one of the huts. We each grabbed an armload of food and hurried back to the protection of the undergrowth. Our timing could not have been better. Just as we hid ourselves, the first of the Mexican soldiers began returning to the village. The pursuit had been called off and they were returning to recover the ill-gotten supplies.

We regained our position on the ruins overlooking the village to observe the activity. The commander directed that a half-dozen watch fires be built around the perimeter and guards posted for the bivouac. I had learned that, being so close to the equator, there was very little dusk. It became dark as soon as the sun set.

The captain and I were both exhausted. Not knowing which direction we should proceed, we decided to spend the night where we were. The jungle was confusing enough in the daylight. At night it would be impossible.

The only light in the world seemed to come from the fires in the village. And in the darkness the sounds of the jungle changed. The screeches of birds and howls of monkeys gave way to the grunts and snarls of animals we could only imagine.

That night, to keep ourselves alert, the two of us talked endlessly. It was strange how much we had in common, and how little. Captain Winfield Scott Christmas was from Louisiana. Despite his rank we were the same age. The state militias had a peculiar custom of electing their officers. Usually, the wealthier the individual, the higher the rank, and the Christmas family was reasonably well off. His enlistment was almost up, however, and he was anxious to return to the family cotton plantation outside Baton Rouge. I knew I would never return to my father's plantation, though I kept those thoughts to myself. I only admitted I had come to enjoy the army life and that I desired no other.

Despite the unnerving sounds of the jungle and our long conversation, we both dozed off. And it was with a start that we awoke. It was still night, yet even in that darkness we could see their figures. A half-dozen men armed with machetes and clubs encircled us. They spoke in whispers in a tongue I didn't understand. I reached for my pistol and found it had already been removed from its holster.

One of the men knelt in front of us. I recognized him as the village chief I had seen earlier. In a low voice he asked if we spoke Spanish. I answered in the affirmative, so it was me he addressed, though the conversation was somewhat difficult. I don't think his Spanish was much better than my own.

Somehow he knew it had been the two of us that had fired on the soldiers. He thanked us mightily for saving his people. He said word had come that soldiers from the sea had driven the Mexicans out of Villahermosa. That was the sign they had been waiting for. He told us the great war was about to begin and that all the Mexicans would be driven from the land of the Maya.

Years later I learned that the Indians very nearly succeeded. The Maya on the Yucatán rose up in rebellion and for four years killed every Mexican man, woman, and child they could lay their hands on. It wasn't until well after our war with Santa Anna was over that the Mexican government put down the insurrection.

That night we would hear, more than see, the initiation of that bloody revolt.

The chief produced items from a bag at his side. Around each of our necks he hung a strap. Each strap was threaded through a small square stone. In the darkness I could feel the totem. The stone had been fashioned into a figure of some type that I couldn't distinguish by touch.

The chief instructed us to keep the necklaces on and to stay where we were. We would be safe. I asked him what was this place where we were hiding. He called it El Templo del Tigre, the Temple of the Jaguar.

At that moment he produced an object from beneath his tunic and held it in his flat, upturned palms. It was a totem of some sort, a green stone that radiated its own light, a dull emerald glow. The stone, larger than the egg of a goose, had been fashioned to resemble a jaguar, the fierce predator of which we had been warned.

The chief raised his palms to the heavens. His warriors

fell to their knees at the sight of the stone and bowed their heads. The leader then began a chant in their strange tongue. It was a short verse, repeated four times, each time to a different direction. When he was finished, he returned the stone to its hiding place.

The chief signaled to one of his men and our pistols were immediately returned to us. He then gave us one last warning. No matter what we heard or saw, we were not to leave the safety of the temple.

Suddenly, Captain Christmas and I found ourselves alone. The Indians had simply disappeared into the darkness. Neither of us spoke, though I am certain as many questions raced through my companion's head as my own. Around us the jungle had become deathly quiet—an omen, I was sure.

Our eyes locked on the campfires below. There was no movement, save for the dancing shadows being cast by the dying flames. We watched for a very long time and I was almost to the point of believing nothing was going to happen.

Then came the roar. An unearthly animal scream that shredded the silence. A great black shadow launched itself into the center of the clearing. A creature on all fours, larger than a man and silhouetted by the surrounding fires, bellowed in defiance.

A sentry appeared. He fired his rifle almost point-blank at the beast, then charged with his fixed bayonet. The creature made a great swipe with its claw, decapitating the man on the spot.

The night began to fill with the muffled shouts of orders and screams of terror. Rifle shots exploded as soldiers fired helplessly at their attackers. I realized then that there were other dark shadows racing between the huts and sentry fires.

Some were dragging men from their bedrolls. Others were pulling soldiers to the ground as they attempted to reload their weapons. The scene was a blur of confusion and shadows.

Some of the soldiers tried to stand their ground. Many attempted to escape into the jungle, the creatures of the night close on their heels. However, none of their efforts seemed to matter. The melee in the clearing was over quickly. The sounds of pursuit and slaughter in the surrounding forest continued for several more minutes.

It wasn't long, though, until the silence of the night returned.

The heat and the humidity bore down on us in the darkness. My clothes were soaked in sweat. Yet I found myself shivering uncontrollably as the pall of death filled the air. I think my sanity only survived because I fixed my gaze on the dying fires below. They seemed to reassure me that dawn would soon visit us and we could remove ourselves from that field of destruction.

Morning broke with the warming calls of exotic birds. I think I was almost surprised we had survived the night. The look on Captain Christmas's face belied similar feelings, though he said nothing.

I noticed the leather strap around my companion's neck, then remembered the token the chief had left me the night before. I removed my own necklace and examined the pendant. It was jade stone, barely an inch on a side, fashioned to resemble a human skull. I could only guess at its antiquity, but I had no doubt regarding its purpose.

The chief had given us one each to protect us from the holy wrath loosed upon the soldiers. At the time I didn't honestly believe the charms held any special powers. However, I didn't doubt the power that had been wielded against the Mexicans.

As we left the ruins of the temple, we crossed the village clearing. Dozens of bodies, all belonging to soldiers, littered the ground. Their necks had been slashed, their chests ripped open. I thought of the machetes the Indians had carried the previous night and wondered if those weapons had caused the gore, or if, indeed, we had actually witnessed a rampage by wild beasts.

Whatever my curiosity demanded was overcome by a desire to be free of that place. What I did notice was there were no Indian bodies and no dead animals. Only soldiers. As we made our way past the village and into the jungle beyond, the carnage continued. We passed a dozen more mutilated bodies and I'm sure, in the surrounding undergrowth, there were victims we didn't see.

Though I had garnered no great love for our enemy, a part of my humanity ached at having seen them suffer such a horrific death. And all the time I thought of the jade skull dangling from my neck, wondering if it truly protected me. . . .

27

SPARKS SPREAD THE CONTOUR CHART ACROSS THE hood of his car. Next to it he laid a hand-drawn map. He studied both for several minutes, occasionally looking at the foothills above him, trying to correlate recognizable landmarks with the symbols on the papers.

It was already late afternoon. He didn't have much daylight to work with. He shook his head in frustration. He had tromped through those same hills a hundred times and had never found a thing. Then, after all those years that he'd spent looking, some snot-nosed college student accidentally finds the brass button from an army officer's tunic.

It was obvious to Sparks that Conrad had no idea what he had found. Or maybe he had. Maybe Conrad's claim that he was looking for Anasazi pottery was a ruse. Maybe he had been looking for Carleton's Lost Patrol all along and the smart-aleck was keeping the secret to himself.

Either way, it wasn't fair. Sparks had dedicated his life to finding the Lost Patrol. It was his right to possess the treasure. He had earned it.

And now it was only a matter of time. If he didn't

find it that day, he would find it the next. The day after at the latest. Other people were looking. He knew that. He couldn't waste a precious moment.

He folded up his maps and stuffed them into his backpack. He took a long gulp from his canteen, then stuck it in the pack as well. He knew he couldn't be out there all night. He had a trunkful of valuable information and he had a buyer. He would be more than compensated for whatever revenue he had lost that day from closing the trading post early.

He checked his flashlight to make sure it worked, then packed it along with his other provisions. He hoisted the pack onto his back. Grabbing his walking stick, he started toward the hills. For the first time in his nearly forty years of searching he felt confident that he would actually find what he was looking for.

28

THE TRACKING PARTY STARTED AT THE SPOT WHERE Vicinti had found his son. The six dogs, none of them bloodhounds, were shown the area. The animals had all been trained to work with sheep, and the new scent seemed to confuse them.

Two of the dogs began pulling at their leashes as if they were ready to track. Their owners followed them into the woods. The rest of the men crowded behind. In a few short minutes they had found the carcasses of Boss and Tico. The throats on both animals had been torn out.

The tracking dogs whimpered nervously as they sniffed the air for any hint of a predator.

"What now, Bram?" one of the men with dogs asked.

"We spread out. Follow the trails where you can. Look for spoor, dead sheep, anything. If we haven't found anything by dark, we return here. There are still two hundred sheep in the pasture. This thing will be back for an easy kill. We can destroy it then."

Vicinti pointed to George Atole, one of the men with a dog, to come with him. A moment later they were headed down an almost invisible animal trail.

The others split into pairs as well, some going back to the pasture to begin their search along the tree line, others simply melting into the woods, following Vicinti's example.

To an outsider the scene would have seemed eerily quiet. There was no crashing through the undergrowth. No whoops or war cries. There weren't even loud whispers.

Each two-man team knew they were tracking a wild beast. They had all been trained since young boyhood to be silent in the woods. It was a warrior tradition. It was a hunter tradition. It was part of their heritage that they handed down with great pride. What's more, the metal fittings on the dog collars had been taped, so there was no unnecessary jingling, and each animal had been trained to track as silently as its master.

Vicinti had taken point on the trail. Atole stayed several feet behind with the dog still on leash. They moved quickly but quietly down the path.

Abraham Vicinti had gone on his first hunting foray when he was only five. It had been with his grandfather. He could still remember some of the old man's instructions. "Let your feet feel the twigs before your weight snaps them." "Always keep the wind in your face, a man's scent carries far." "A bent blade of grass tells more than a broken branch."

They were the little things that made a difference. They were the same things Vicinti had taught his son.

Vicinti suddenly stopped and stiffened. A bolt of grief shot through his body as he thought of his dead son. The pain nearly dropped him to his knees, but he resisted.

"Bram," Atole asked in barely a whisper, "what is it?"

Vicinti shook his head, refusing to turn around. Now was not the time for mourning. There was a job to be done first. The grief could come later.

He had taken a few steps forward when he noticed a hair clinging to a twig about knee high. He knelt and examined it closely. It was a wool fiber. At least one of his sheep had wandered down that path.

With the slightest motion of his head he indicated to Atole that they should keep moving.

An uneventful hour passed. Vicinti, Atole, and the dog had worked their way to below the tree line. The two men kept a close eye on the undergrowth above them, looking for any movement. To their right, less than a hundred yards away, a branch rustled. Both men froze. Vicinti raised his rifle.

From behind a tree a dog appeared, followed by two men, another tracking team.

The police chief quickly lowered his weapon and nodded at the men. They gave the same silent response, then turned and reentered the woods. They were obviously having the same success as Vicinti and his partner.

The long afternoon grew into evening. Even though they were on the western slope of the range, the shadows were growing longer. And shadows could play tricks, tricks that fooled even the trained eye.

Vicinti's search had turned up nothing more than a few squirrels and a handful of elk. It was when he decided it was time to turn back toward the mountain pasture that he saw the creature.

Blending into the darkening shadows, the hulk was tearing flesh away from a carcass. To Vicinti it looked like the carcass of a sheep.

Atole's dog emitted a subdued whimper. It had caught the scent of the animal. Atole knelt and calmed his dog, not wanting to ruin this opportunity.

Vicinti signaled his partner to remain behind as he moved closer for a better look.

To Vicinti the bear looked huge. If it wasn't a grizzly, then it was the biggest black bear he had ever seen. The bear's muzzle and fur were smeared with blood, and it definitely was devouring what was left of a sheep.

Bears usually avoided the men and their flocks. When they didn't, they had to be tracked down and destroyed. As far as Vicinti was concerned, the bear had earned its death warrant. It would have been doubly satisfying to know for sure if this was the animal that had killed his son. For the moment, for Vicinti, it was.

He raised his rifle and took careful aim. Only thirty yards separated him from his quarry and it was a clear shot. A second later the tranquility of the mountain slope was shattered by the report.

Atole's dog began to bark anxiously as the bear bellowed in pain. Vicinti had had a broadside view. The bullet was intended for the chest, just behind the right foreleg. At the last moment the bear moved just enough to prevent a fatal wound.

The bullet lodged into the creature's right shoulder,

sending the animal into a rage of pain. The bear instinctively wheeled around toward the sound of the shot. As it did, Vicinti chambered a second round.

Atole wasn't sure if he should release his dog. He knew he couldn't fire his weapon. Vicinti was between him and the bear.

Vicinti hurried his second shot, missing the bear completely. He maintained his calm, chambering a third round.

The bear had already covered two thirds of the distance to his attacker when Vicinti raised his rifle once more. The animal was only fifteen feet away when it rose on its back haunches, ready to destroy its enemy.

This was the shot Vicinti wanted. He pulled the trigger, sending the bullet tearing into the animal's chest.

The bear stood frozen for a second, its huge paws poised in midair, ready to strike. There was enough energy left in the creature to allow one last bellow before it tumbled sideways, almost in slow motion, onto the ground, dead.

Vicinti cautiously approached the still animal. It was a male black bear, at least three hundred pounds. As with any man who grew up close to nature, a part of Vicinti grieved to have killed such a beautiful animal. But he also knew that in nature, there was no such thing as mercy. And there was no such thing as tolerance for man-killers. He had done what needed to be done.

Atole approached, his dog straining at his leash and yapping incessantly, wanting to be part of the action. Atole shook the animal around the collar to calm him down.

"We have no ropes," Atole said solemnly. "We'll have to come back in the morning for the carcass."

Vicinti nodded but said nothing. He had thought he would find some sort of satisfaction at having killed the animal. All he felt was more emptiness.

As the two men turned away from the dead bear, the mountains began to echo with the sounds of more rifle shots.

"What are those fools shooting at?" Vicinti growled. "We've already killed it!"

"Maybe they found another bear," Atole suggested.

"Then it's the wrong one."

"Either that, or this is the wrong one."

Vicinti shot his companion a shriveling look. Without another word he turned and hurried up the mountain slope. There didn't need to be any more killing. He had to bring it to a stop.

DURING THE HIKE BACK THE EVENING TWILIGHT HAD filled with gunshots. From what Vicinti could tell, the shots had come from three separate areas. Each time there was another volley, Vicinti quickened his pace.

It was almost dark when he and his partner reached the pasture. A dozen men had already beaten them there. They were engrossed in subdued but animated arguments.

On the ground, surrounded by the bickering hunters, were the carcasses of two dead mountain lions.

"Bram," one of the men called out. "Look what we have!"

Vicinti sadly walked over to view the slaughter. Atole followed, being pulled frantically by his dog.

"One of these has to be the killer," one of the younger hunters said. "I shot the one on the right. The big one there."

Two more men emerged from the darkening woods. "What the hell were all you people shooting at?" the one in front yelled. "We killed the bear about two miles back!"

"What are you talking about? It wasn't a bear,"

the young warrior snapped. "It was a mountain lion. I killed it. It's right there!"

"Then you killed the wrong animal, young one," the bear slayer declared.

"What do you know, old man?" the younger one snapped.

"Enough!" Vicinti shouted.

"What does he know, Bram?" the young hunter pressed. "A mountain lion tears throats, like we saw with the dogs."

"And a mountain lion would run from a man," the old hunter countered. "Bears have no respect."

Vicinti pointed his rifle into the air and fired. "Enough, I said!"

The arguing stopped immediately. All eyes turned to the police chief.

"We came for vengeance. I say, we have it! George Atole and I tracked down a bear. We killed it. We've killed two lions. Hector, you say you have killed a bear as well.

"My heart grieves for my son. I thought killing another creature would ease my pain, but it hasn't."

"You fed on my hate and now the air stinks with death. I blame myself. This should not have happened. I am ashamed."

The other men, proud men, proud hunters, also felt the shame. Whatever blood lust they had known that day melted at the sight of the two dead animals at their feet. Probably two innocent animals. And there were two more dead beasts rotting on the mountainsides.

Regret filled the air as thick as the heavy silence. The great hunters avoided each other's stares. Even the young warrior who claimed the larger of the two lions diverted his eyes.

A shriek shattered their solemn silence.

A man's shriek. A cry of pain and terror. From the woods, the dark woods, not far from where they stood.

Not more than a hundred yards away one of the hunters not yet gathered in the pasture began firing his rifle. One, two, three quick shots in succession. Then another scream of terror.

"George, Hector, the rest of you," Vicinti barked, "—turn loose the dogs."

The men with dogs released their leashes. The animals needed no instructions. They bolted for the sound of the commotion in the woods.

"Grab some flashlights," Vicinti yelled. "Come on! Let's go!"

Chambering a round, Vicinti began running after the dogs. Three men ran to their trucks to retrieve flashlights. The rest scrambled after their leader.

The meager twilight disappeared in the dark woods. Vicinti and his band had only the sound of the barking, yipping dogs to guide them, and the animals were far ahead.

It was Vicinti who found the first body, by accident, tripping over it.

"Bring a light!" he yelled. The other hunters crowded him, wanting to know what was it, who did he find, what had happened?

A man with a flashlight pushed his way to the front. The beam found its way to the kneeling Vicinti, then to the body on the ground. Simon Miles lay on his back, his eyes still wide with terror, his mouth contorted in a silent scream. His throat was a gaping slash with blood still oozing from torn arteries.

Another flashlight arrived. Ten feet away they found Miles's hunting partner, his face slashed, the chest cavity torn open.

The dogs had not stopped to inspect the carnage. They had captured the scent and continued in vicious pursuit. Far down the mountainside the quarry had been cornered. The distant sound of animal combat filled the night.

Vicinti grabbed the nearest flashlight and scrambled for the sound. A few were reluctant, but the entire posse followed dutifully.

The fight raged a half mile away, but as the pursuers grew closer the intensity diminished. Fewer and fewer yips and snarls filled the air. Finally, the last remaining dog let out a heart-rending yelp.

A second later Vicinti and two men stumbled into the small clearing. The bodies of the six dogs lay scattered on the ground, still bleeding. One dog, barely alive, whimpered pitifully.

Vicinti shone the light around, looking for whatever had done this. But there was only darkness. Darkness and fear.

30

ROBERTO SANCHEZ SELDOM HAD TROUBLE SLEEPING. As he grew older he discovered he didn't need as much sleep as in his younger days. But still, when he lay down for the night, oblivion usually came quickly.

That night it would not come at all.

He tossed and turned, punched his pillow, straightened the blanket on his bed a half-dozen times, but nothing made him comfortable. The old grandmother's trick of counting sheep made matters worse. He thought of his nephew, Antonio, in the mountain pasture. He wondered if the young man was all right.

At the time Deputy Hanna's visit hadn't bothered him much. He knew Antonio was resourceful and could take care of himself. Tomorrow would be soon enough to check and make sure his nephew was safe.

The deputy had left after a brief visit and a cup of coffee. When he was alone, Sanchez inspected Conrad's truck. He couldn't help but wonder what had broken the window and why there was blood smeared down the side of the truck. And what had happened to the "gist," Conrad.

Whenever he managed to push one questioning thought out of his mind, another one took its place. How many sheep did Deputy Hanna say had been killed? How many ranches had been hit? Was his own flock safe? Was Antonio safe?

Sanchez stared at the ceiling, acutely aware of all the night sounds that surrounded him. A cricket outside his window chirped a solitary chant. Between the chirps he heard the faint scratching patter of a mouse scurrying in the rafters. Far away a lone coyote called its mate.

From the dusty yard that surrounded the ranch house came an unmistakable *thump*. It was a hollow, metallic sound, as if something had fallen against Conrad's truck. But there was no breeze. Nothing would have blown over.

Sanchez held his breath, forcing all his concentration on the sound in the yard. There was the faint scrape of two footsteps on hard-packed sand. Something bumped against one of the support posts for his front porch.

Silently, Sanchez slipped from his bed and tiptoed to his bedroom door. The door was already open. He stepped into the living area. On the wall, next to the front door, was a series of pegs. An ancient six-shooter dangled in its holster from one of the pegs.

Stepping as quickly as he dared across the small room, Sanchez grabbed the pistol and gently cocked the hammer. With the weapon ready he placed his left hand on the doorknob and listened. From the other side of the door came the unmistakable sound of creaking floor boards.

Sanchez flung the door open. "*¡No te muevas!*" he shouted, clasping his pistol now with both hands.

On the edge of porch, framed by the open door, stood a dark, motionless form. One of its limbs was braced against one of the porch posts, as if for support. The dark shape made a guttural noise and began to raise its other limb.

"*¡No moverse!*" Sanchez screamed. The gun suddenly exploded in his hand. He hadn't meant to, but he had pulled the trigger.

The dark shape on the porch let out a yell as it stumbled backward and fell on the ground.

Sanchez flicked on his outside porch light and recocked his weapon. The form lay motionless on the ground a few steps from the porch.

The old man cautiously stepped beyond the safety of his front door. Still barefoot, he carefully approached the intruder. With the benefit of the porch light he could tell he had just shot a man.

The man's hair was matted with dirt and sweat. His clothes were torn. His face was streaked with dried blood. A new wound had been added. Fresh blood oozed from the man's scalp where the bullet had grazed him. Even in that unkempt condition Sanchez recognized the trespasser.

It was the "gist" from the university.

It was Joel Conrad.

31

THE WEST WIND MOTEL WAS COMPRISED OF TWO single-story cinder-block buildings that faced each other across a parking lot and a fenced-in swimming pool. Located on the outskirts of Counselor on Highway 44, it catered mostly to truckers, bikers, and highway-repair personnel working on remote jobs. It also fit well within the budget of the University of New Mexico Archaeology Department.

The walls of the rooms were either painted cement blocks or panels of cheap, dark pressboard veneer. The floors were all carpeted, although the colors depended on what had been on sale at a given time. Usually it was a coincidence if the carpeting matched the paint on the walls.

Heavy knit cotton spreads stretched over sagging double beds. Dripping faucets left perpetual rust stains in the chipped basins and worn tubs. Washcloths substituted for hand towels, and hand towels were reserved for drying off after a shower.

If Renee Garland was going to remember anything significant about the accommodations, she decided it was going to be the perpetual feel of grit. The rooms were anything but airtight. Sand constantly blew through the cracks around the window and doorjamb, getting into the carpet, the bedsheets, even the plastic ice bucket sitting next to the sink.

She performed the same ritual almost every night. Before showering she would strip the bed, take the sheets outside, and shake them out. Before making the bed she did her best to brush the sand off the mattress. After taking a shower she would remake the bed, then have to brush the sand off her feet before slipping them under the covers.

It was after midnight when she and her three subordinates got back to the motel. The good-nights were brief. They were all tired and ready for bed.

As she flipped on the light to her room, Renee realized she didn't feel like fighting the sheets again. This would be her last night in the room and she was exhausted. She didn't see a problem with saving her shower for the morning.

In her younger days she had considered herself a "clean freak." The thought of going to bed dirty would have been appalling to her. After three summers in the field she had come to realize getting a little dirty wouldn't kill her. Neither would one night without a bath. Besides, a morning shower would get rid of the residual grit she never managed to eliminate from the sheets.

Renee went into the bathroom. The least she could do was wash up a little and brush her teeth. After a day of eating dust, having a clean mouth was almost as refreshing as a sauna.

In the mirror her face looked dirty and sunburnt. Her hair looked as though she had brushed it with a cactus. She could understand why Joel Conrad hadn't found her attractive.

"Joel," she whispered. She hadn't thought about him in hours. She had been too busy ramrodding Huey, Dewey, and Louie, trying to get everything labeled, wrapped, and packed. She wanted to be back to the site by ten A.M. That would give them time to give the dig a final once-over, make sure they hadn't forgotten anything.

"We sure could have used your help today, Conrad," Renee said to the mirror, as if he were on the other side. They could have used Vencel's help as well.

She had thought about it at the time and she began wondering again. Why had Vencel left the site? He'd been all fired up to get everything packed. He'd insisted it had to get picked up by noon the next day. Then he'd just left, saying he was coming back to the motel. What could he have been doing at the motel for the last twelve hours?

As she finished washing her face she decided it was none of her business. Vencel was getting ready to take on a huge responsibility. He was probably making phone calls, setting up meetings, making arrangements for his ascent to power.

Renee dried her face, then rinsed out the ice bucket. She had gotten into the habit of having at least two glasses of ice water every night before going to bed. No matter how much liquid intake she had during the day, she always felt thirsty. To the uninitiated it was easy to become dehydrated and not even know it. The high, arid desert was tricky like that.

The ice machine was located in a breezeway that separated the office from the rental rooms. Renee had to walk past Vencel's room to get to the ice. As she went by his room she noticed the light was still on.

She wondered if he was expecting her to report their progress for the night.

She had almost stopped to knock on his door, when she realized the parking spot in front of the door was empty. Looking around she realized there was no sign of Vencel's red truck. She shrugged it off. He could have gone out for a snack or a late drink. Once again she convinced herself it was none of her business.

As she filled her ice bucket she heard the sound of tires crunching gravel. Looking toward the lot she saw Vencel's truck pass. For some reason he turned his headlights off as he pulled into the parking lot.

To Renee this was decidedly suspicious.

She left her ice bucket in the machine and quickly stepped to the corner of the breezeway. Peeking around the corner she had a clear view of the truck. Vencel had backed it into the parking spot.

Getting out of his truck, Vencel glanced up and down the parking lot, as if to make sure no one was watching. He quickly opened the door to his room, then began lifting boxes from the back end of his truck. He removed a total of three, pushing each one into the room before retrieving the next. Before closing his door he looked up and down the lot again to make sure he hadn't been seen.

Renee grabbed her plastic bucket from the ice machine. Making sure Vencel was still inside, she hurried past his door as quietly as possible.

Inside her own room, Renee couldn't help but wonder what the hell was going on. What was Vencel being so secretive about? Where could he have been that late at night? And what could have been in those boxes he hid so quickly in his room?

She drank her mandatory two glasses of water and crawled into bed. As tired as she was, sleep didn't come quickly. She kept trying to figure out what was going on with Vencel. And when she wasn't thinking about Vencel, she was worrying about Joel.

Eventually sleep did come. When it did, it was blessedly free of dreams.

32

"DISPATCH TO PATROL ONE."

Lansing picked up the microphone to his radio and responded, "Patrol One. What's up, Marilyn?"

"We just got a call from Albuquerque. A Lieutenant Gonzalez."

Lansing had spent the previous day cooped up in his office. He had no intention of being cornered there for another day. Leaving his ranch that morning he'd reported in, saying he was going to take a run to the south toward Espanola. He didn't have to explain why to Marilyn. He was the sheriff. He could do anything he wanted. At least he kidded himself that he could. "Oh? What did he have to say?"

"He said he's on his way to Burnt Mesa Pueblo with a federal marshal. He's got a warrant for Jonathan Akee."

Lansing let up on the gas to his Jeep and coasted to a stop on the shoulder of the road. "He's got a warrant for Akee? Did he say what for?"

"He said it had to do with the Giancarlo case."

"What are you talking about?"

"I'm just passing on what he said. They're not familiar with the pueblo. They plan on stopping by the office. I guess they want your help when they go up there."

"When are they getting to Las Palmas?"

"He said they should be pulling in around ten-thirty, maybe eleven o'clock. It depends on the traffic in Santa Fe."

Lansing looked at his watch. It was eight-thirty. "I'll be in the office in half an hour. Patrol One, out."

He checked the highway in both directions, then made a U-turn. He was back in the office in less than twenty minutes.

"Did Lieutenant Gonzalez say what the warrant was for?" Lansing asked as soon as he walked in.

Marilyn shook her head. "Isn't Giancarlo that professor of yours you were talking about yesterday?"

"Yea, the one that was murdered two nights ago. But why the hell would they be coming after Jonathan?"

"He wasn't in Albuquerque, was he?"

"No. At least I don't think so. Margarite said he had been in Santa Fe. I'd better give her a call."

Once inside his office, he dialed the number to the health clinic at Burnt Mesa. The receptionist said Dr. Carerra was with a patient, but she would have the doctor return the call as soon as she was available. For the moment there wasn't anything Lansing could do.

As soon as he hung up his phone Marilyn buzzed him.

"Yeah?"

"I have a call for Gabe, but he's taking the night

shift. It's a Roberto Sanchez. He's a rancher on the west slope. Do you want to take it?"

"Sure will." Lansing pushed the blinking button on his telephone. "Sheriff Lansing."

"*Sí*, Sheriff. I am calling about the truck Deputy Gabriel left at my ranch."

"Go ahead."

"I am sorry. Señor Conrad came to my house last night. I didn't know it was him. I was afraid and I shot him."

Lansing sat up straight in his chair. "Is he dead?"

"No, no. I think I am not so good a shot anymore. The bullet skinned his head. But I brought him to Esteban Rodriguez. His wife is a nurse and she bandaged him. He will be okay, I think."

"Where are you right now?"

"I am still at Esteban's. I do not have a phone."

"Is Mr. Conrad able to come to the phone?"

"No. He is still sleeping. Do you want me to wake him up?"

"No, that's all right. How about Mrs. Rodriguez? Is she around?"

"*Sí*, I will get her."

There was silence on the line for a moment, then a woman's voice said, "*¿Hola?*"

"Yes, Mrs. Rodriguez. This is Sheriff Lansing over in Las Palmas. I wanted to ask how Mr. Conrad is doing."

"He is sleeping for now, but he was awake earlier. Roberto's bullet grazed his scalp but the wound wasn't much more than a scratch. I put a bandage on it and cleaned up his other wounds."

"Other wounds? What do you mean?"

"Someone attacked him. He was scratched and bruised. His clothes were torn. I think he's also dehydrated. He is suffering much more from that than from the bullet."

"Did he say what had happened to him?"

"I asked. He said he didn't remember."

"Does he need to see a doctor?"

"I think that would be a good idea, just to make sure everything is all right."

"It may take a while, but I'll send one of my deputies over. I'll have them bring him into town." Lansing remembered that it was Esteban Rodriguez who had filed the report about missing livestock. "By the way. Have any more of your sheep turned up missing?"

"Not for two nights now. Esteban went out early this morning to check."

"Well, at least that's one bit of good news. Thanks for all your help, Mrs. Rodriguez. Like I said, one of my deputies will be by later."

Lansing pushed another button on his phone to buzz the reception desk. "Marilyn, I'm going to pull Gabe Hanna off night patrol. I need for him to drive over to Mr. Rodriguez's place and pick up this Joel Conrad. He needs to see a doctor."

"Couldn't one of the other deputies do that?"

"Gabe's already familiar with the case. I'd just as soon he see it through. If we can't find a replacement for Gabe tonight, I'll take the patrol."

"You're the sheriff. By the way, while you were on the phone, Dr. Carerra called."

Lansing hated playing telephone tag. "Thanks."

He dialed the number to the Burnt Mesa clinic. This time Margarite was available.

"What's going on?" she asked.

"I got a call from the Albuquerque police. They're on their way up. They have a warrant for Jonathan Akee."

"What for?"

Lansing realized he hadn't told her about the Giancarlo case. "Have you heard anything in the news about a college professor down in Albuquerque being murdered?"

"Yeah. There was a short blurb on radio last night."

"That was Elmo Giancarlo. He was that old college prof of mine that was looking into the stuff I found on the ranch."

"Oh, my God. I'm sorry."

"Somehow or other they have Jonathan linked to the case."

"How?"

"I don't know. They'll be here in a couple of hours. They have a warrant for his arrest. Didn't you say yesterday that he had been in Santa Fe?"

"That's what Susan Akee said. Of course, she had two different versions for why he had gone down there."

"I can't believe Jonathan had anything to do with murder. By the way, how's he doing?"

"I don't know. I need to call and check. He spent the night in the clinic in Las Palmas."

"You mean, he's still here in town?"

"As far as I know, he is. You might call over to the clinic and find out."

"Thanks. I'll do that."

*   *   *

"No. I'm sorry, Sheriff," Dr. John Tanner said over the phone. "He looked fine this morning when I came in. I went ahead and released him."

"So he's on his way back to the pueblo?"

"The Akees didn't have a car. Margarite Carerra must have driven them from the pueblo. I think they were going to walk over to the diner for something to eat, then see if they could hitch a ride back."

"Thanks, John. I'll see if I can catch them there."

Jonathan and Susan Akee were sitting in the back booth, away from all the other customers. Although Susan had tried to clean them as best she could in a clinic sink, Jonathan still wore the soiled clothes from his drinking bout.

To Lansing's way of thinking Jonathan still looked hungover. But the plate in front of him was empty, attesting to a healthy appetite.

The lawman tried to look casual as he sauntered across the diner and pulled up a chair, sitting at the end of the booth. "How ya feeling, Jonathan?"

"Um," Akee grunted. "Better than yesterday."

"Yeah. I heard," Lansing said, smiling. "I was surprised to hear it even happened. You were doing so damn well."

Akee shrugged. "Like they say in AA. It's a day at a time."

"Hope you don't mind my asking, but what set you off?"

"Guess I got tired of no work, no job, no one hirin'. Bottle of booze was just as cheap as buyin' a meal."

"You were off looking for work?" Lansing tried to sound casually surprised.

"Yeah," Akee said, diverting his eyes. He took a sip of coffee. "I was lookin' for work. Down in Santa Fe."

"I must have heard wrong. Someone told me you were taking care of pueblo business."

Akee shot his wife a piercing look. Susan physically withered in her seat. Lansing missed none of subtle language.

"No." Akee was emphatic. "I was lookin' for work."

"I guess they didn't know what the hell they were talking about. They said you were on pueblo business and all the way down in Albuquerque."

"We gotta go, Sheriff," Akee said abruptly, pushing his way out of the bench seat of the booth.

Susan slid out of her seat as well. She mumbled a good-bye to Lansing as she picked up the ticket for their breakfasts.

Lansing sat quietly at the booth, watching. As soon as Susan paid for the meals, Jonathan dragged her through the front door, onto the street. He gave her a slap and began yelling at her. Lansing regretted putting her into that situation, but he needed an excuse for his next move.

Seeing that he was attracting attention, Jonathan took his wife by the arm and began pulling her to the side of the building. Lansing jumped from his seat and headed for the lunch counter.

"Morning, Sheriff!" Velma smiled as she came out of the kitchen with a platter of food.

"Morning, Velma," Lansing said as he pushed past her and headed for the back door. He knew Jonathan wouldn't try anything more with Susan until they had reached the back of the building.

He was just stepping into the alley when the Akees came around the corner.

"I told no one!" Susan yelled as Jonathan pushed her to the ground.

"No one else knew!" Akee shouted, raising his hand threateningly.

"Hold it right there, Jonathan!" Lansing yelled.

Akee looked up to see the sheriff standing behind the diner, his gun drawn. "I ain't doin' nothin', Sheriff."

"I'm afraid you are, Jonathan. I've got you for battery."

Susan jumped up to stand between Lansing and her husband. "He wasn't doin' nothin'. I tripped."

"I saw him slap you in front of the diner."

"I'm not going to press charges," Susan protested.

"You don't have to. I'm a witness. I can press charges. Turn around, Jonathan. I'm going to have to cuff you."

"What are you doin' this for?" Akee growled as he turned to face the wall. "I didn't break no laws."

"We can talk about it at the courthouse," Lansing said as he holstered his gun and pulled out his cuffs.

"Why are you doing this, Sheriff?" Susan asked, almost in tears. "We were minding our own business. All we want to do is go back to the pueblo."

"Right now, Jonathan may be better off in one of my cells." He firmly clamped the cuffs around Akee's wrists, trying not to be too rough.

"What's so good about one of your cells?" Akee grumbled.

Lansing ignored the question for the moment, leading his charge from the alley to the courthouse across the town square.

33

MARILYN LOOKED UP FROM HER PAPERWORK TO SEE what the commotion was all about. She was more than a little surprised at seeing Lansing pushing Jonathan Akee through the door. Susan was close on their heels. "So you caught him in town, huh?"

Lansing quickly put his finger to his lips to silence her. "Call Judge Morales's office," he instructed. "See how soon we can get Jonathan on the docket. I just picked him up for battering his wife."

"What about—?"

"We can talk about that other business later," Lansing snapped. "Call the judge's secretary while I put Jonathan in a cell."

"Yes, sir," she said, totally confused.

Lansing guided his charge to the jail's two-cell lockup. It wasn't an unfamiliar place to Akee. He had been a frequent visitor during his drinking days. Akee stepped into the cell and waited patiently while Lansing removed the cuffs.

"I still don't know why you're doin' this, Sheriff. We were goin' home. We weren't botherin' nobody."

Lansing closed and locked the cell door. "If you

want to know the truth, Jonathan, I brought you in here because I wanted to ask you a few questions."

"Why didn't you ask me at the diner?"

"I started to, but you jumped up and left." There was another reason. Akee was taller than Lansing by an inch and outweighed him by thirty pounds. If they had ended up in a physical confrontation during questioning, someone very easily could have gotten hurt. They were both safer being separated by the cell bars.

"So if I answer your questions I can go?"

"Depends on your answers."

Akee sat on one of the bunks in the cell. "So ask."

"What were you doing in Albuquerque two nights ago?"

"I wasn't in Albuquerque. I was in Santa Fe. I told you. I went there lookin' for work."

"Okay. What do you know about a Dr. Elmo Giancarlo?"

"He's some sort of heart doctor, isn't he? Over in Texas somewhere."

"No. He's head of the Archaeology Department at the University of New Mexico. Let me correct that. He *was* head of the Archaeology Department. Someone killed him two nights ago."

"So what does that have to do with me?"

"I don't know. I was hoping you could tell me."

"I don't know nothin'. I never heard of him."

"Maybe I should go ask Susan. Maybe she's heard of him."

"She don't know nothin'. She was home at the pueblo."

"She was home when?"

"When"—Akee stumbled for his next words—

"when I was lookin' for work. Down in Santa Fe." He looked up at Lansing. "I answered all your damn questions. Can I go now?"

"I have one more. If you get this one right, I'll open the door. Why would the Albuquerque police have a warrant out for your arrest?"

"I don't know. Maybe I forgot to pay a parkin' ticket."

"The meter maids aren't after you. It's the homicide detectives. They say you were in Albuquerque two nights ago. They say you had something to do with Giancarlo's murder."

Akee jumped from his seat and grabbed the cell bars.

"That's bull. I didn't kill nobody."

"Why would they say something like that?"

"I don't know. They're liars. I didn't do nothin'."

"Come on, Jonathan. Of all the people in New Mexico they could choose from, why did they pick on you?"

"Mistaken identity. They do it all the time."

Lansing nodded thoughtfully. "Yeah, that's true. They do. Besides, it was late. There couldn't have been that many people on campus that time of night. No one saw you, did they?"

"No," Akee said, shaking his head. It took a moment for his own response to sink in. He shot Lansing a hateful look. "No," he growled. "No one saw me 'cause I wasn't there!"

"Believe it or not, Jonathan, I'm trying to help. We've known each other practically our entire lives. I don't believe you killed anybody. But there's a federal marshal and a police detective on their way up here, and they think differently."

"They're coming here to arrest me?"

"They'll be here in a couple hours."

"I didn't kill nobody. You gotta believe me, Cliff!"

The pueblo people were traditionalists. They accepted the rules of formality, especially with whites. Even though they had known each other since high school, since Lansing's return to San Phillipe County, Akee had always addressed him as "Deputy" or "Sheriff." For the Pueblo to use Lansing's given name spoke volumes. Akee wasn't lying. He hadn't killed anyone.

"I do believe you, Jonathan. But you have to be straight with me. What were you doing in Albuquerque?"

Akee sat back down on the bed and buried his face in his hands. "I can't tell you."

"You weren't down there looking for work, were you?"

Akee just shook his head.

"So it was pueblo business."

Akee shook his head again.

"All right, Jonathan. What was it, then?"

"I cannot say."

Lansing thought he had been so damned smart in getting Akee to admit he was in Albuquerque. His smugness was quickly being replaced by frustration. "Listen, Jonathan. I can help you if you let me. You were in Albuquerque for a reason, and it wasn't to kill Giancarlo. I'm sure there are people who can back up your story, whatever it is. But you need to talk to me."

Akee sat silently, his face still buried.

"I can buy us a couple of days, Jonathan, if you want. The Albuquerque police have a warrant on you.

As soon as they show up they can drag you back there, no questions asked. But I can hold you here until you're formally arraigned on battery charges. It will be a lot easier for me to help you while you're still under my custody."

Akee took a deep breath and let it out slowly. "Can I think about it?"

Lansing checked his watch. "It's nine-thirty. You've got an hour to decide."

34

"CHET, IT'S GOOD TO SEE YOU," LANSING SAID, COMING out of his office. The two lawmen shook hands.

"Same here, Cliff," Detective Gonzalez replied. He looked genuinely glad to see his old partner. "I'd like you to meet Tom Haggard. He's a marshal attached to the U.S. Attorney's office in Albuquerque."

Lansing shook the marshal's hand. "Nice meeting you."

"Same here, Sheriff."

The two big-city lawmen were dressed in suits and ties with highly polished shoes. By contrast Lansing wore his standard khaki uniform, no tie, and scuffed cowboy boots. The sheriff couldn't help but notice they seemed to exude an air of self-importance.

"Would either of you care for a cup of coffee?"

Gonzalez glanced at Haggard. "I don't think so, Cliff. We're going to make this short and sweet."

"Okay. Let's go into my office."

It had taken a great deal of persuasion, but Lansing finally managed to convince Susan Akee to go home. She was confused about Jonathan's arrest. Lansing didn't want to upset her further with the murder warrant. He assured her he would explain everything later. Deputy Rivera had picked her up just minutes before Gonzalez arrived.

Once inside the office Lansing sat behind his desk while his visitors took the two chairs in front.

"I guess you got our message earlier," Gonzalez began.

"Not until I got back here about an hour ago. I understand you have an arrest warrant for Jonathan Akee."

"Yeah. Do you know him?"

"Populationwise, this is a pretty small county. I know practically everybody. You told my receptionist this had to do with the Giancarlo case. You have witnesses or something?"

"Or something," Gonzalez admitted. "We found bloody fingerprints all over the place."

"Yeah, you told me that yesterday."

"We got a positive identification from the DOD data base. The prints we pulled matched up with a former Marine sergeant, one Jonathan Akee. Present residence, Burnt Mesa Pueblo."

"You're sure about that match?"

"It was convincing enough to get a warrant issued."

"Since this is your county," Haggard added, "we figured you would know your way around the pueblo and could probably help us track this Akee character down."

"Oh, there won't be any problem tracking him down. I know exactly where to find him. I just don't think you'll be able to take him back to Albuquerque anytime soon."

"What do you mean?" Gonzalez asked.

"I had to arrest Jonathan for felony wife battering

this morning. I have an arraignment hearing for him next Monday. That was the soonest I could get on the judge's docket."

"You mean you have him in jail here?" It was Haggard's turn to ask the question.

"Yes."

"That's great." The marshal smiled. "There's nothing worse than trying to arrest an Indian on their own reservation."

"I don't think I quite understand your statement, Cliff," Gonzalez interrupted. "Why can't we take him back to Albuquerque?"

"Oh, you can. But not until we're finished with him."

"We have a warrant for his arrest. You understand that."

"Certainly, and knowing that, I'm not about to turn him loose. But like I said, he's scheduled for arraignment Monday. That's four days away. As soon as we're finished with the arraignment I'll turn him over to you."

"We're talking about a capital murder case here, Cliff."

"I'm familiar with murder cases, Chet. I know how the process works. I also know that possession is nine points of the law. Right now, Jonathan Akee is under my jurisdiction. When I'm finished throwing the book at him, it'll be your turn."

Haggard shook his head. "You must really have it in for this guy."

"Something like that," Lansing said, frowning.

Gonzalez returned the frown. "I don't want somebody showing up and bailing him out."

"Bail won't even be set until the judge sees him.

And since there's another warrant out for him, he won't be going anywhere."

"Would you mind if I talked to him?" Gonzalez asked.

"Help yourself. As soon as Marilyn gave me the news you were coming, I tried to ask him a few questions. Couldn't get a thing out of him."

"Wish you hadn't done that," Gonzalez said, still frowning. "It's a lot easier to get information out of a suspect if you can spring a few surprises on them."

"And to be perfectly honest, Sheriff, you're screwing things up for us. If you release him to us, we can run lab tests to check for latent blood on his skin and clothes. We can check for carpet fibers and bloodstains in his car."

"First off, he doesn't own a car," Lansing said. "And if he was there, the clothes he was wearing are probably long gone. I don't see where I'm screwing anything up for you. And what happened to you using my first name?"

"We're working on a strictly professional basis from here on out," Gonzalez said, a hint of anger in his voice. "I've had to deal with country sheriffs before, and sometimes it's not like dealing with real law enforcement."

Lansing truly resented the inference, but he had to let the statement slide. He wanted Gonzalez to think he had turned into a backwoods sheriff. "All right, Lieutenant," Lansing said pleasantly. "However you want it. Would you like to talk to the prisoner now?"

"Yes."

*   *   *

Lansing wasn't surprised to see Gonzalez emerge from the cell area in a worse mood than when he'd entered.

"What time is his arraignment on Monday?" the detective asked.

"Were you able to get anything out of him?"

Gonzalez ignored the question. "I need to know what time I can pick Akee up."

"We should be finished around ten-thirty. I'll have him in shackles, ready to go."

"I'll see on Monday, then." Gonzalez motioned to Haggard and the two men started for the door.

"Listen, Chet. I'm really not trying to screw things up on your investigation."

"Don't worry about it," Gonzalez said flatly. "We'll straighten everything out when we get him down to Albuquerque." He thought for a moment. "I hope you realize you have a vested interest in all this."

"What do you mean?"

"The emerald figurine you sent to Giancarlo was being kept in the museum safe. He signed it out the afternoon before he was murdered. No one's seen it since. I heard it was worth quite a bit of money.

"It looks like we have a pretty solid case against Mr. Akee. Motive, opportunity, and proof that he was there.

"See you Monday."

The two men from Albuquerque left without another word, leaving Lansing to ponder the situation. He didn't believe Akee had killed anyone, but he certainly had been at the scene of the crime. Giancarlo had said he'd had an offer of $200,000 for the stone. Lansing knew men had been killed for a whole lot less.

A dozen questions started filtering through

Lansing's thoughts. For the moment the most important was why had Akee gone to Giancarlo's office?

Lansing went into the lockup. Akee was stretched out on the bed, feigning sleep.

"All right, Jonathan. We bought some time. Detective Gonzalez won't be back until Monday to take you to Albuquerque. You need to start answering some questions if I'm going to help you."

Akee opened his eyes and stared at Lansing.

"First off, why were you in Giancarlo's office the other night?"

The Pueblo sat up in his bunk and shook his head. "Before I can say anything I must speak to someone first."

"Who?"

"Querino Ortiz."

"Who's that? I never heard of him."

"He belongs to the Pojoaque Pueblo."

"How am I supposed to get in touch with him?"

"He works at the Casino. Sometimes he deals blackjack. You can ask for him there."

"What should I tell him?"

"Just tell him Tyope needs to speak with him."

"Will he come?"

"Oh, yes. He will come." With that Akee lay back on his bed and closed his eyes. There was nothing more to be said.

35

"Good morning, Mrs. Rodriguez," Gabe said when she answered the door. "I don't know if you remember me. I'm Deputy Hanna."

"Oh, *sí*. You were here yesterday. You talked with my husband."

"Yeah. It was about his missing sheep. Sheriff Lansing sent me over to take Joel Conrad into town."

"I'm sorry. He's not here."

"Where did he go?"

"He insisted he was all right. He had Roberto take him back to his ranch so he could get his truck."

"Is he in any condition to drive?"

"I think maybe he will be okay."

"When did they leave?"

"I don't think more than fifteen minutes ago. Maybe twenty."

"I'll see if I can catch up with him. *Buenos días*."

"*Buenos días*."

Gabe's interest was more than just Conrad's driving ability. He really wanted to know why the man had gone missing for an entire day. And with all the reports of missing sheep, he wanted to know what had attacked him as well.

* * *

Conrad stared at the empty space in the back of his truck. Nearly everything he had accumulated was missing. "Mr. Sanchez, did you clean out the back of my truck?"

"No," Sanchez said, walking around the side of the vehicle. "I have not touched it."

"Well, what happened to all my stuff?"

Sanchez shook his head. "I do not know. Deputy Hanna drove your truck here."

Conrad rushed to the cab. It was as bare as the back end. "Damn!" He swore. "All my maps. All my notes. Everything I found! It's gone! I can't believe it."

"Maybe the deputy knows."

"I've got to get in touch with him." There was a hint of desperation in his voice. "I need the keys to my truck."

"They're inside," Sanchez said, almost apologetically. "I will get them."

As Sanchez went into the house to retrieve the keys, Conrad slipped behind the steering wheel. He buried his face in his hands and took a deep breath, fighting off a wave of nausea. He wasn't sure if it was because of the trauma his body had suffered over the last twenty-four hours or because of the loss of his artifacts and maps.

He reached inside his shirt. The jade skull still hung on the strap around his neck. Ten weeks of work, ten weeks of scrambling over hills and valleys, dozens of pages of notes and hand-drawn maps, gone. Every spare moment he could squeeze out of a day every day for ten weeks, wasted. All he had to show for his efforts was the jade trinket he was wearing.

Sure, he thought, he could reconstruct most of the notes. The maps could be redrawn. The location of the valley was etched in his brain. But the artifacts he had uncovered, the brass buttons and buckles, the jade knife, the jade and turquoise beads, items he had systematically cataloged, their locations carefully marked on maps, were all gone.

His growing fear wasn't simply that they had been stolen. He hadn't just been scrounging artifacts. He had been developing an archaeological theory. As the theory evolved he had made copious notes in his field journals. Anyone reading those journals could piece together his ideas . . . and take credit for them.

Academia had one unrevokable rule: Publish or perish.

Conrad knew his find was groundbreaking. It was going to be the foundation for his dissertation, and he knew it would be published. He would be set for life in the field of archaeology.

But if someone else announced his discovery and took credit, he knew he would be screwed, both personally and professionally.

Sanchez emerged from the house, keys in hand. He went directly to the truck and handed them to Conrad.

"I'll go in a minute," Conrad said weakly, still fighting the nausea. "Would you mind if I got a drink of water first?"

"Come inside. You should rest before you go."

"No, I don't have time," Conrad protested. "I just need a drink of water."

"Come inside. I'll fix you an ice water."

Conrad nodded, getting out of the truck and following Sanchez into the house.

The archaeologist took his time sipping the water. When he wasn't drinking, he closed his eyes and gently rolled the cold glass across his forehead. He poured a little of the water into his hand and dampened the back of his neck. The nausea began to dissipate.

Sanchez sat across the kitchen table from his visitor, a worried look on his face. "How do you feel?"

"Better," Conrad admitted. "Much better."

"You should lie down for a while, I think."

"I think you think too much," Conrad said, trying to make a joke. He finished off the glass of water. "Would you mind fixing me some more?"

"*Sí.*" Sanchez filled the glass with ice from his freezer and added more water. As he handed the glass back to Conrad, someone knocked on his front door.

"Ah, Deputy Hanna," Sanchez said when he opened the door. "They sent you to pick up Señor Conrad?"

"Yes," Gabe said, removing his ball cap as he stepped inside. "I saw his truck was still out front. Is he here?"

"In the kitchen." Sanchez led the way to the back of the small house.

"Mr. Conrad," Gabe said, extending his hand. "I'm Deputy Gabe Hanna with the San Phillipe Sheriff's Department. I came by to give you a lift into town."

"What for?" Conrad asked, standing and shaking hands.

"We heard you needed to see a doctor."

"I'm fine." Conrad sat back down.

"Deputy Hanna is the one who found your truck and brought it here," Sanchez said.

"You are?" Conrad looked up at the deputy. "What happened to all my things?"

"All what things?"

"I had maps and notebooks, artifacts. My truck was full of stuff."

"I don't know what you're talking about," Gabe said, shaking his head. "There wasn't anything in it when I found it yesterday. Just the keys. That's why I drove your truck up here. So Mr. Sanchez could keep an eye on it."

"I guess I should be grateful. They didn't take my wallet and I still have my truck."

Gabe tried to make a quick assessment of Conrad's condition. There was the hint of a bruise on the left side of his face, along with several small scratches. There were two deep gashes on the left side of his neck just above the shoulder. At some point they had bled profusely, because Conrad's shirt had a large stain of dried blood. The shirt was torn at the left shoulder and the left sleeve was nearly shredded. Through the tears Gabe could see several more cuts and scratches.

Along his scalp, above the right temple, was a bandage. Gabe presumed this covered the graze from the bullet.

"Are you sure you're in any condition to drive?"

"I'm just a little dizzy from the gunshot. That's all."

"It looks to me like you might have lost a little blood too," Gabe observed. "I'm going to have to file a report. Would you mind telling me what happened?"

"I wish I could," Conrad said, shaking his head. "I can't remember a thing."

"What's the last thing you do remember?"

"I was in my truck yesterday morning, about ten miles south of here. I was getting ready to drive through a cattle gate when someone smashed in the driver's side window. The next thing I remember, I'm out in the middle of nowhere. I'm at the base of the foothills surrounded by miles and miles of sagebrush. I couldn't remember how I got there.

"I just started walking. Maybe stumbling's the better term. All I could think about was trying to find something to drink. It might have taken me ten minutes, it might have been two hours, but I finally remembered I had a truck parked somewhere.

"I tried to get my bearings straight but it didn't do much good. I finally ran into a barbed wire fence. I followed it west, toward the setting sun. I eventually reached the dirt road out there about the time it turned dark. I just followed it north.

"I kept going till I got here. Of course, I wasn't expecting Mr. Sanchez's little welcome surprise."

"I did not mean to shoot him," Sanchez apologized.

"Would you mind explaining what happened?" Gabe asked.

Sanchez described the events of the previous night. It was obvious from his tone and demeanor that he thought he was in a great deal of trouble. He concluded his story with a question. "Do I have to go to jail now?"

"I don't think so," Gabe said, giving the old man a reassuring smile. "You were only protecting yourself and your property, although next time you might turn on your porch light before you start shooting."

"Sí, I will do that." He appeared immensely relieved.

Gabe turned to Conrad. "Do you have any idea who did this to you?"

"No. But I think I know why. They were after my research material. That's what was in my truck. Almost three months' worth of work."

"You're an archaeologist, right?"

"Yes."

"How many people are there that would even be interested in your work?"

"Around here, several dozen. As soon as someone tries to publish anything based on my work, I'll know exactly who did it. Unfortunately, I won't have any proof that I did the original research. They took it all."

"Can't you go dig up some more pots or whatever it was you had?"

"That would be a partial solution. But I don't know when that would happen. I have to get back to my job. I've already missed a day and a half of work. And classes for the fall term start in another two weeks. It could be weeks before I get back up here. By then it might be too late."

Gabe shook his head. "I wish I could help."

"I'm afraid I'm beyond help," Conrad said, standing. "Thanks for the water, Mr. Sanchez. I need to get going."

"You're sure you don't want to see a doctor?" Gabe asked.

"No. I'll be all right." Conrad turned and headed for the door.

Gabe and Sanchez followed. Outside the three men said their good-byes.

The deputy stood in the ranch yard and watched as Conrad backed his truck around and drove off. He wanted to make sure the archaeologist was indeed capable of driving.

Gabe turned to Sanchez as he opened the door to his patrol Jeep. "By the way, have you talked to your nephew yet?"

Sanchez shook his head. "With all this?" He gave a slight shrug. "I go up there now. I prayed to Mother Mary to watch over him. He will be okay, I think."

The deputy glanced at the decrepit old truck Sanchez used for transportation. It didn't look as though it could make it out of the ranch yard, let alone up a mountain. "You're going up in that thing?"

"*Sí.*"

"How long does it take to get up to the meadows?"

"Less than an hour."

"Why don't we go up in my Jeep?" Gabe offered. "That way we'll both know everything's okay with your nephew."

Sanchez beamed. He motioned with his hands for the deputy to stay put. "I'll be right back. I need my hat."

36

A TOTAL OF FORTY-FIVE WOODEN CRATES HAD BEEN packed. The boxes were square, three feet on a side, and were designed to stack easily for storage or transport. When loaded into the back of the three-ton van, they would take up most of the available space.

Huey, Dewey, and Louie were in the process of making sure all the lids were securely fastened. The valuable relics were safely packed inside the containers. If one of the boxes was to fall, its contents would be reasonably safe. With the lids secure, chances were nothing would spill out during such an accident.

While they awaited the arrival of Dr. Vencel and the transport truck, Louie asked one of the more intelligent questions of the entire summer. "Renee, how long do you think this site was occupied?"

"It's hard to tell. Using the Pecos dating system, the top layers are definitely Early Pueblo Two, which started around 900 C.E. The lowest stratum we've seen indicates Basketmaker Three influence. That pushes the age of the site back to at least 750 C.E. We're looking at a site that was occupied for at least two hundred and fifty years."

"Where are all the skeletons, then?"

"You haven't taken the Chaco course yet, have you?"

"I'm taking it this fall."

"Well, you just asked the sixty-four-thousand-dollar question. No one knows where the Chaco people buried their dead."

"They've found skeletons here," Dewey protested. "They have displays down at the visitors' center."

"Did you bother to read the explanations next to the displays?" Renee quipped.

"I glanced at them."

"Maybe you three could use the short course. Humans began to occupy Chaco Canyon over two thousand years ago," Renee explained. "Most of the early sites that have been excavated were seasonal homes. The pre-Pueblos would stay in the valley during the rainy season, then move on when things started drying up in the early fall."

"The 'pre-Pueblos,'" Dewey interjected. "You mean the Anasazi."

"Yeah," Renee hedged. "That's the name that's been used for those people for the last hundred and fifty years. In a way it's sort of an insult to the modern Pueblo Indians, though. *Anasazi* is a Navajo word that translates to 'Ancient Enemy.' There's a movement to try and change the reference, but it's slow in coming. It's hard to break a long tradition, especially with so much in print about the subject.

"But we're getting away from what I was talking about.

"Around 900 C.E. some smart Pueblo came up with the idea of irrigation. They built dams to store water and cut channels in the bedrock to direct the runoff into their fields. With a steady supply of food available, they began to build permanent structures like Pueblo Bonito, Chetro Ketl, and the rest of them. This was a bustling place from about 900 to 1150 C.E."

"Yeah, yeah," Huey interrupted. "Then the weather changed and they all moved away. What does that have to do with skeletons?"

Renee was looking forward to getting back to Albuquerque. She was more than ready to start working on her evaluations. "It wasn't that simple. Even before the climate grew drier, there wasn't enough rainfall to support the agriculture of this canyon. At least that's what the currently accepted theory says.

"You have to remember, for whatever reason, Chaco Canyon was the religious and cultural center of a civilization that encompassed over sixty thousand square miles. People came here from as far away as Mesa Verde, Taos, and Cañon de Chelly to worship. And this went on for over two hundred and fifty years.

"They dragged logs over eighty miles from the nearest forest to construct their buildings. And when the buildings started falling into disrepair, they fixed them up. There have been at least twelve different styles of masonry construction identified."

"So how many people did live here?"

"Some archaeologists claim as many as five thousand people might have lived here at one time. But that was before the road systems were found. More than likely, the permanent population was closer to fifteen hundred people. It was probably their job to keep the buildings in good repair for the festivals or religious holidays."

"Well, if there wasn't enough rainfall to support

the people here," Dewey asked, "where did they get their water?"

"You guys took a hike up to Pueblo Alto, didn't you?"

Dewey nodded.

"Do you remember the huge trash heap of broken pottery?"

"Yeah."

"It's estimated over a million pottery vessels were dumped there. That's what Joel Conrad figured out. Pueblo Alto is essentially the hub of the road system. People came here from the outlying settlements to that one spot and threw away their pots."

"That's a long walk to a dump," Louie observed.

"They were coming to Chaco to conduct their sacred ceremonies. When they came they brought gifts. What's the most precious gift you can give to someone who lives in the middle of a desert?"

"Water?" Dewey guessed.

"It just so happens there's a series of canals cut into the bedrock that link Pueblo Alto to the canyon wall above Pueblo Bonito. At the base of the canyon wall is a catchment area where water was stored. It caught not only the runoff from rain and melting snow, it caught the water that was brought from the outlying areas by worshipers. Once the pots had been used for bringing the sacred gift of water, they were destroyed so they couldn't be defiled. At least that's what Joel Conrad contended in his master's thesis.

"For fifty years archaeologists who specialized in the Southwest didn't have an inkling what the trash heap represented. The first clue was the road system, but that wasn't discovered until the early seventies. Even then no one thought of combining climatology, hydrology, and archaeology to get a complete picture of the conditions in this canyon a thousand years ago.

"It was Joel who fitted the pieces of the puzzle together. So far no one's been able to disprove his theory."

"That's pretty cool," Dewey said. "But what does any of this have to do with skeletons?"

"That's one of the two great mysteries of Chaco Canyon. Why did the people leave here and, when they did live here, where did they bury their dead?"

"What about the pictures at the visitors' center? There are several photos of burial sites."

"In the hundred years that people have been digging in this canyon, only seven hundred skeletons have been unearthed. With a steady population of around a thousand people, there should have been close to forty deaths a year. Over a period of three hundred and fifty years, that adds up to over twelve thousand deaths. We're short by about eleven thousand burial sites. Maybe more."

"So what's the theory about that?"

"There isn't one," Renee admitted. "Even the most knowledgeable archaeologists figure the bodies were taken somewhere. It's just that no one knows where. Or why the site's never been found."

Renee looked up to see a cloud of dust being stirred up along the dirt road. "Looks like our truck's here, fellas. Time to go to work."

37

VENCEL PARKED HIS PICKUP NEXT TO RENEE'S FORD Escort, then got out to direct the paneled moving truck as it backed in. Renee and her three charges approached, awaiting instructions.

When Vencel was satisfied with the truck's position he signaled the driver to shut off the engine. He turned to his student crew. "Everyone cleared out their rooms this morning, right?"

All four nodded in affirmation.

"Good. I've closed out our accounts with the motel. We can head back to Albuquerque once everything's loaded."

"What about Joel Conrad's belongings?" Renee asked.

"I had the manager let me into his room so I could get his things. The three bags next to my tailgate are his. Would you see to it they get back to campus?"

There had been no word from Conrad in two days. Renee couldn't understand Vencel's nonchalant attitude toward the missing man. She knew the two had their differences, but she felt Vencel should display at least some degree of concern.

"What about the authorities?" she asked.

Vencel turned and stared at her. "What about
hem?"

"Shouldn't we try to find out what's happened to
oel? He could have been in a car accident, even a
:arjacking. He may be lying beside the road some-
vhere, hurt, dying. . . ."

"Mr. Conrad is free, white, and twenty-one. What-
:ver he does is his own business, unless it interferes
vith my concerns. All I care about is the fact that he
walked off this project without letting anyone know he
vas doing it. He didn't tell us where he was going or
vhy. In the military they call that desertion.

"Right now all I care about is wrapping things up
around here. I have a mountain of concerns waiting
or me back at campus. I don't have time to waste on
n impertinent, irresponsible slouch.

"To be perfectly honest, Miss Garland, this dig
vould have been a complete bust if you hadn't kept
hings in motion. I don't know why you keep defending
Conrad. If he's been anything at this dig, it's been a
urden."

"Do you mind if I try to get in touch with the
olice?"

"Miss Garland, as soon as that truck is loaded,
ou can do anything you want."

"I guess we should get busy, then."

"Indeed." Vencel turned to Huey, Dewey, Louie,
nd the truck driver and started barking orders.

While the men wrestled with the crates, Renee
vent to the storage trailer and began strapping all the
oose materials down. Another truck would come the
ollowing Monday to drag the trailer back to campus.

Once she was finished with packing away the
tools, she began a systematic search of the site. She
and the three undergrads had done a walk-around
that morning, but it didn't hurt to make one final
check. No more excavating would take place until the
following summer. She wanted to ensure no shards
were left exposed or tools left behind.

She was almost finished with her survey when
Vencel called to her. She walked over to where he
was directing traffic at the back of the paneled truck.

"Miss Garland, we're almost finished here. Have
you unloaded Mr. Conrad's gear?"

"No. I'll take care of that right now."

Renee walked to the back of Vencel's pickup
truck and began reaching for one of Conrad's bags.
That's when she noticed the three cardboard boxes
from the night before. Vencel had them strapped
down behind the cab.

She pulled Conrad's bags from the bed of the
truck and set them on the ground. She then checked
to make sure Vencel was still busy with the loading.
Using the bumper as a step, she climbed into the back
end of the pickup.

Constantly checking to make sure she wasn't
seen, she knelt next to the boxes. The top panels had
been overlapped to close the ends. She carefully pried
the panels of one box apart, just wide enough to reach
inside. Feeling around she recognized the spiral wiring
of a notebook. She grabbed the spiral end of the book
and pulled.

The opening she had made wasn't wide enough
for the notebook. As she pulled, the folded panels to
the box popped open.

"That's it!" Vencel announced from the back of the moving truck. "Close her down and let's get out of here."

Renee fumbled with the panels, trying to shut the box. Behind her she heard the rear door to the truck being closed. Crimping the corners, she bent the cardboard panels so that they would overlap and close.

The window to her car was open halfway. With no time to aim, she simply tossed the notebook at the window. The book hit the glass and fell. As it did, she jumped over the opposite side of the truck to the ground.

Vencel came around the side of the moving van as Renee picked up two of Conrad's bags and started for her car.

"You need some help there?" Vencel offered.

"No! That's all right. I've got them." She hurried to the side of her car and set the bags on top of the exposed notebook. She returned to the rear of Vencel's truck to get the last bag.

"All in all we did pretty good this morning," Vencel said, rendering a rare smile. "We might as well caravan back to campus. We can stop off in Crownpoint for lunch. My treat."

"I appreciate the offer," Renee said. "But I'm still worried about Joel. I thought I might get in touch with the local sheriff's office. See if they've heard anything."

Vencel nodded. The look on his face told Renee he disliked her decision not to join him for lunch. She could give a damn.

"By the way, the funeral for Dr. Giancarlo is set for

Sunday afternoon. I understand it will be for immediate family and close friends," Vencel said. "However, there will be a memorial service at the campus chapel at noon. It will be open to the public."

"Thank you for letting me know. I'd like to attend," Renee replied. In her worries over Conrad and trying to close down the dig she had all but pushed Giancarlo's death from her mind. The thought of the old archaeologist's funeral left an empty feeling in her stomach.

"Fine," Vencel said, walking around to the far side of his truck to get in. "I'll see you Sunday, then." He turned to the van driver. Raising his voice he said, "Just follow me out! We'll make a stop in Crownpoint for gas and lunch."

Huey, Dewey, and Louie piled into the junker they had been using for transportation all summer. Vencel pulled out first, followed by the trio. After arguing with the gears for a long moment, the truck driver was soon rumbling after the other two vehicles.

Renee waved the dust away as she opened the trunk to her car. She managed to stuff two of Conrad's bags inside. The third she had to toss into the backseat.

She then picked up the spiral notebook and opened it. Inside the cover, neatly printed in block letters, was JOEL CONRAD, followed by an Albuquerque address and a phone number. The writing on the first page was not so meticulous. Across the top Conrad had written, *Field Notes*. The page was dated three months earlier.

Her curiosity was piqued but she knew she didn't have time to read through the notes. Suddenly the need to find Joel Conrad was more important than ever.

She opened the door to her car and tossed the notebook onto the front seat. A minute later she was racing down the dirt road. She had no idea where she was going or who she was going to ask for help. At least, she reassured herself, she was making good time.

38

"YES," LANSING SAID INTO THE RECEIVER, "I'M TRYING to locate Querino Ortiz. I was told he works there at the casino."

"Could you hold?" the operator asked at the other end.

"Sure."

The line was silent for almost a minute and Lansing started to get impatient. It was a forty-minute drive from Las Palmas to the Pojoaque Pueblo. The casino itself was on Highway 84 as you headed into Santa Fe. He wondered if he would get better results if he just drove down.

"Hello?" the operator asked.

"Yes, I'm still here."

"Querino's shift starts at four. If you'd like I can have him return your call."

"Could you have him contact Sheriff Lansing in San Phillipe County?"

The operator hesitated before saying, "Could you please hold again?"

The Pueblos, like most Native Americans, had a deeply ingrained distrust of white men. Deservedly so, Lansing admitted. The distrust compounded when the white man was a law-enforcement officer. Lansing wasn't surprised with the operator's response when she got back on the line.

"Excuse me, but am I speaking to Sheriff Lansing?"

"Yes."

"I'm sorry, Sheriff. Our employees are strictly forbidden to make personal calls during their work hours."

"Does he have a home phone?"

"I'm not allowed to give out that information."

"Can I at least leave a message for him?"

"If you wish."

"All you have to say is 'Tyope needs to speak with him.' You can also tell him it's sort of an emergency."

There was silence at the other end. Lansing presumed the woman was writing down the information.

"Is there anything else, Sheriff?"

"No, that's it. Thank you."

Lansing hung up the phone, a little frustrated. But it was a frustration he had grown to live with. The Pueblos, the Apaches, the Navajos were all nations landlocked in a foreign country. Each fought to hold on to its culture, its heritage, its religion. Part of the strategy to prevent total assimilation into the American mainstream was to remain withdrawn.

Maybe because there was Tewa blood in his veins, Lansing felt an affinity for the Pueblo people. But he was considered an outsider and wasn't privy to the sacred rites.

Sure, visitors were allowed to watch the festivals, the dances, even the more public religious ceremonies. But each pueblo kept its secrets to itself. There were groups like the Bear Clan or the Corn Clan or the Water Clan. These were all based on blood relations.

Separate from the clans were the communal groups,

like the Kachina Society and the Koshare Society. These served not only a social function but a religious one as well. They were part of the tapestry that intertwined the family and clan groups with the community as a whole.

Beyond the clans and the social societies were the moieties. These were the most clandestine organizations in the culture. They protected the most sacred relics. They performed the most secretive rites. From what Lansing knew, their memberships were kept confidential. A man might belong to a moiety his entire life and his wife or best friend wouldn't know.

However, these were all things most white men refused to understand. In its infinite wisdom the federal government passed the Indian Reorganization Act in 1934. Disregarding centuries of Native American self-determination and traditions, Congress imposed an artificial and arbitrary government structure for every tribe in the United States. Each tribe was required to adopt a constitution, elect a president, vice-president, and tribal council, then govern themselves the same way the white men governed.

Lansing chuckled at the thought. The Pueblo people were building cities and governing themselves quite successfully when the majority of Europeans lived in thatched hovels and were essentially slaves to whatever king happened to be in power.

The Pueblos had an intricate and complex social system that had survived over a thousand years of invasion by Mayans, Aztecs, Navajos, Apaches, Spanish, and Americans. They had managed to survive by remaining united. Hundreds of years before the Spanish ever set foot in New Mexico, their ancestors had created a governing council comprised of representatives from every pueblo. Under Spanish rule it was officially called the All Indian Pueblo Council.

After six, seven, eight hundred years it still existed. And its purpose essentially remained the same: to protect their lands, their religion, and their culture from the invaders, whoever they might be.

Yeah, Lansing admitted to himself. He was frustrated. But there was nothing he could do. He could only hope that Querino Ortiz got his message and understood. Without Ortiz, Jonathan Akee wasn't going to say anything in his defense.

The door to his office swung open. An angry Margarite Carerra stood with the knob in her hand, glaring.

"Since the door's open, you might as well come in," Lansing quipped.

"What's this noise about you arresting Jonathan Akee?"

"Guilty as charged." Lansing raised his hands in surrender.

"How much is the bail?"

"It hasn't been set."

"So what am I supposed to do to get him out of here?"

"There's nothing you can do. Why don't you close the door and sit down?"

"This isn't a social visit," Margarite snapped. "Susan came to me in tears this morning. She said you arrested Jonathan for no reason at all."

"I got him for wife beating."

"Susan said she's not pressing charges. After what those two just went through, why are you doing this?"

"If you close the door, sit down, and calm down,"

Lansing said sternly, raising his voice just enough to show he meant business, "I'll explain."

Margarite tapped her foot on the floor and stared at the ceiling for a moment, looking as if she was trying to make up her mind. "All right," she said, closing the door, though not very gently.

Lansing noticed the doctor appeared tired. There were dark rings under her eyes and a huskiness to her voice. "You look like you didn't get much sleep last night."

"I didn't get any sleep last night," she snapped, taking a seat in front of Lansing's desk. "I didn't get back to Burnt Mesa until nine this morning."

"What happened?"

"Police Chief Vicinti took his posse into the mountains yesterday, slaughtered a handful of mountain lions and bears, and got two of his men killed."

"Hunting accidents?"

Margarite shook her head. "There is something loose out there on the west slopes. I don't have the slightest idea what it is, but it's not afraid of men. Doctor Velarde and I spend all night working with dead dogs and dead humans, trying to recover hair samples, saliva samples, blood samples, anything that can be analyzed. We sent samples to the University of New Mexico biology department and the State Police Crime Lab. We're hoping someone can tell us what we're supposed to be looking for."

"Do you think it could be the same animal that's been attacking livestock in the western part of the county?"

"Lansing, I have no idea. All I know is that I'm dead on my feet. As soon as I get Jonathan out of here, I'm going to bed."

"I'm afraid Jonathan's not going anywhere."

"Just because you saw him slap Susan?"

"No. That was my fault anyway. I kind of badgered him into it."

"Then why are you holding him?"

"The Albuquerque police want to arrest him for Dr. Giancarlo's murder."

"What?"

"They found his fingerprints at the scene of the crime. Bloody fingerprints."

"I can't believe Jonathan killed anyone."

"Neither can I. That's why I arrested him."

"That doesn't make a lot of sense, Lansing."

"As long as I have Jonathan in custody, it will be easier for me to help him. Once they drag him down to Albuquerque, he'll be out of my control. I don't know if I can do anything for him then."

"What does Jonathan have to say about all this?"

"Not a damned thing, which makes helping him awfully hard."

"He won't talk."

"Not to me. At least not yet. He said he can't say anything until he talks to a man from Pojoaque Pueblo. After that, who knows?"

"Susan didn't say anything about murder charges."

"She doesn't know yet. I didn't want her to hang around and cause a big scene with them. To keep Jonathan here, I had to play dumb to the police lieutenant who came to pick him up. I've got him pretty much convinced I'm a stupid, hick sheriff."

"Well, if the shoe fits . . ." Margarite said, half joking.

"I can see I'm going to get a lot of support from you."

"You'll get all the support you need," she promised. "But first let me go take a nap for a couple of hours. A little sleep and a shower, and I'll be as good as new."

"I'm sorry you wasted your trip down here," Lansing said, walking around his desk and helping her up from the chair.

Margarite put her arms around his neck and pulled him close. She forced him into a long, lingering kiss, though he didn't fight very much to get away. "As long as you can still pucker like that," she whispered, "it wasn't a wasted trip."

"Can you make it back to the pueblo?"

"I'll be fine. What should I tell Susan if I see her?"

"You can tell her the truth. You can also tell her the police won't be here to pick him up until Monday. She can come by and visit him anytime."

"Will do."

Margarite released her hold on his neck and stepped to the door. "Would you mind if I looked in on him before I left? He still is a patient of mine."

"Go ahead. Just remember. You need to get some rest."

"That's something you don't have to remind me about."

39

RENEE WASN'T WORRIED ABOUT RUNNING INTO VENCEL. His caravan was heading south. They would catch Highway 371 just north of Crownpoint and continue south to I-40. It would be a straight shot to Albuquerque from there.

She was going north. Conrad had talked about the ceremonial roads leading to Chaco Canyon. All the roads that had been discovered came from the north or the east. If he was developing a theory connected to the road system, north or northeast of Chaco was where he was conducting his surveys. And with no other facts to go on, she surmised he must have disappeared while doing his research.

Renee took the back exit from the canyon. The dirt road she was on forked five miles from the canyon rim. The right fork led to Nageezi and the road to Counselor. She had been on that fifteen-mile stretch three times in the past two days and there had been no sign of Conrad.

She took the left fork.

Pulling out her highway map as she sped down the dirt road, she quickly located her position. In another twenty miles she would reach Carson Trading Post.

There was a chance someone might have seen Conrad recently. She could only hope.

She kept glancing from the road to the notebook on the seat next to her. She couldn't figure out why Vencel had a copy of Joel Conrad's field notes. From the way Vencel had acted the night before, he obviously didn't want anyone to know he had the boxes. Were all three full of Conrad's work? Did Vencel know what had happened to him? Had Vencel done something to Conrad?

Nothing was making any sense. Vencel had been out of town when Conrad disappeared. He couldn't have had anything to do with that.

Conrad's field notes could be for the Chaco dig. As senior archaeologist at the site Vencel was entitled to review his subordinates' notes for the final report. But that didn't explain why he was being so secretive about it.

Renee chided herself for being suspicious. All that mattered for the moment was that she find Joel Conrad. She was sure all the pieces would fall into place once he turned up.

Three vehicles were parked in front of the trading post when Renee pulled in. Two were late-model pickup trucks, much newer than what Conrad drove. The third was a pink 1962 Cadillac convertible with its top down. The Cadillac had seen better days.

Renee went into the store. A dozen Navajos stood in line to pay for the goods they were holding. There was a assortment of men, women, and children talking amiably among themselves until they saw the white woman. They immediately grew silent, obviously uncomfortable with the new addition.

The proprietor, an older white man with a full head of silver hair, was ringing up prices and making change. He casually glanced in Renee's direction but seemed more interested in tending to his immediate business.

Renee decided she could wait until the customers cleared out. She found herself just as uncomfortable as they appeared.

She strolled to the side of the store that contained Native American handicrafts and works of art. She was enthralled with several of the pieces she looked at. However, her enthusiasm was shattered when she saw the prices. She carefully replaced the ceramic piece she was holding. It would take her six months to earn enough money to pay for the bowl if she broke it.

She contented herself with simply browsing at the items.

It took nearly ten minutes for the customers to clear out.

"Is there anything I can help you with, miss?" the man behind the register asked.

"I hope so," Renee said, approaching the counter. "My name's Renee Garland. I'm a grad student with an archaeological dig near here."

The proprietor extended his hand. "Harvey Sparks, desert rat and sometime store operator."

Renee took the proffered hand. She found Sparks's smile disarming. "I'm looking for a friend of mine," she explained. "He mentioned coming in here before."

"Got a name?"

"Yes. Conrad. Joel Conrad. We've been working together at the dig."

Sparks wrinkled his brow in deep thought, then shook his head slowly. "No. The name doesn't ring a bell. What's he look like?"

"He's Caucasian, about five nine. Dark brown hair. Slim. He's around twenty-seven, twenty-eight. No mustache or anything like that."

This time Sparks nodded. "Yeah. Sounds familiar. He was in here once or twice. I think all he ever bought was beer."

Renee beamed. "That's Joel, all right. Have you seen him recently?"

"Earlier this week. Like I said, all he ever bought was beer."

"Earlier this week? He wasn't in here yesterday, was he?"

Sparks shrugged. "Might have been. I wasn't here yesterday. I have a Navajo woman comes in here and helps on occasion. That gives me a little time to go ratting around in the desert. Kind of a passion of mine."

"Is there any way you can contact her? See if he was here?"

"No problem."

Sparks reached under his counter and pulled out an old black dial phone. A moment later he was talking to someone. "Blanche? Harvey Sparks. Listen, I have a young lady here looking for a friend of hers. He's been in the store once or twice before. A white boy, late twenties, brown hair. She was wondering if he stopped by yesterday. . . . No one like that, huh? Okay. Just thought I'd check. Thanks a lot."

Sparks hung up the phone. "Sorry, miss. No luck."

"I know he was doing some survey work somewhere around here. I don't know exactly where. I don't suppose he mentioned anything about what he was doing."

"We never talked about anything except the weather and the price of beer," Sparks said, smiling. "Would you like to leave him a note or something, just in case he stops by?"

"Uh," Renee uttered indecisively, "yeah, I guess so. Do you have a pen and paper?"

"Sure." Sparks produced a small notepad and a pencil. "Here you go."

Renee was brief with her message. It simply said: *Joel, The dig's over. See you around on campus. Renee.* Putting any more information down was a waste of time. She knew she couldn't spend more than a day looking for him in the hills. If she didn't find him by Saturday night, she'd have to head back to Albuquerque.

She handed Sparks the pad. "Would you mind if I called the Sheriff's Department? He might have been in a traffic accident or something."

"Not at all. I'll even dial the number for you." Sparks pushed the phone across the counter and handed Renee the receiver as soon as the phone at the other end began ringing.

"San Juan County Sheriff's Department," the operator said. "Can I help you?"

Renee explained the situation and the operator switched her over to the dispatch desk. They would have a record of any accident reports. After a few minutes Renee hung up the phone.

"No luck?" Sparks asked.

Renee shook her head. On the wall behind Sparks

she noticed an advertising calendar. The picture on the top half promoted Kodak film. Renee remembered her conversation with Conrad two days earlier. He had mentioned that he was waiting for some film to be developed.

"When Joel was in here a couple of days ago, did he happen to drop off some film?"

Sparks shook his head. "I'm not equipped to handle things like that. He'd have to go into Counselor or Bloomfield to get anything developed."

"Oh." Renee sighed. "Well, thank you for all the help."

"I'm sorry I couldn't have helped more. What are you going to do?"

"I don't know. Drive around, see if I can spot his truck somewhere. Maybe ask some of the ranchers around here if they've seen him."

"Do you know what your friend was looking for?"

"Not exactly. I know it had to do with the Chaco Canyon road system."

"Then I'd suggest you head west. Pierre's Ruin isn't more than fifteen miles from here. That's on the main Anasazi route from Aztec. If he's studying the roads, I'd start there and work my way north."

Renee nodded. "Thanks. Maybe I'll do that." She walked over to one of the coolers and pulled out a Coke. Before she could dig in her pocket for change, Sparks stopped her.

"That's on the house, miss."

"Thanks." Renee returned Sparks's infectious smile. "And thanks for all the help."

"Anytime." Sparks waved. "Anytime."

As the graduate student walked out the door, Sparks reached under his counter and pulled out a

processed film package. It had arrived via the postman
that morning and he hadn't had a chance to look
through it yet.

He removed the photos and negatives, then tore
up the outer envelope. Tossing the envelope into the
trash, he began thumbing through the pictures.

The first three photos showed stone lions with
menacing snarls. The others showed long shots of a
broad canyon. Above the canyon were several peaks
that Sparks recognized.

He smiled to himself. He hadn't found the final
resting place of the Lost Patrol yet. But he would now.

40

IT TOOK FORTY MINUTES TO REACH THE HIGH MEADOW
where Roberto Sanchez kept his flock. He had
told Gabe that it was a small flock, no more than
a hundred sheep. But it was large enough to keep
him in food and pay his taxes. That's all he really
needed.

The flock was crowded near the metal gate to the
high pasture but there was no sign of Antonio,
Sanchez's nephew.

"It is lunchtime. Maybe he is in his trailer,"
Sanchez suggested.

The trailer, a tiny one-room outfit with no in-
door facilities, sat along the fence line not far from
the gate.

Gabe parked next to the gate and the two men
walked over to the trailer. Sanchez knocked once.
When there was no immediate response he opened
the door. The trailer was empty.

"He is not here," Sanchez said, shaking his head.

"Maybe he's in another pasture," Gabe suggested.

"He shouldn't leave the flock like this." The old
man scowled. He walked over to the gate and cupped

his hands in front of his mouth. "Antonio!" he bellowed. He listened for a response. When none came, he yelled again. "Antonio!"

Again there was no answer.

The back part of the pasture disappeared behind a small hill. "Why don't we drive on in? It will take us just a minute to check out the rest of the pasture."

Sanchez nodded. "I will get the gate."

The gate was built of welded metal pipes and was hinged so that it could swing in either direction. Sanchez unhooked the chain holding it in place, then pushed it inward, shooing the sheep back so they wouldn't escape. The animals, used to taking directions, meekly got out of his way.

When the gate was open wide enough, Gabe edged his Jeep into the pasture. Sanchez secured the gate behind him, then climbed into the Jeep.

Once on top of the hill that the divided the field they had a clear view of the surrounding land all the way up to the tree line. The pasture fence stopped a few yards short of the trees.

There was no sign of Antonio.

Gabe glanced at his passenger. Sanchez's face was a mask of worry.

"I don't see Pepe anywhere either," the old man said.

"Who's Pepe?"

"My dog. He always stays with the sheep."

"Maybe they went into the woods." Gabe said. "Maybe one of your sheep got out and they went after it."

"That is probably what happened," Sanchez agreed,

nodding. He sounded unconvinced. "Maybe if we drive to the end of the pasture."

Gabe continued over the hill, parking just short of the barbed-wire fence that marked the boundary of Sanchez's property. Sanchez got out of the Jeep. Walking up to the fence, he put his fingers to his mouth and let out a shrill whistle.

From deep within the woods came a barking sound. Sanchez turned to Gabe and smiled. "Maybe you are right!" He put his fingers to his mouth and repeated the whistle.

The barking came again, this time a little closer. The two men could hear the rustle of dried leaves down the side of the mountain. A moment later Pepe popped out of the woods. However, instead of running to his master he stopped. Barking wildly, he turned as if he were heading back into the woods. At the tree line he stopped again, turned, and continued his barking.

The two men looked at each other. Nothing needed to be said. They were supposed to follow the dog.

Sanchez carefully squeezed between two strands of wire. Gabe followed his example. By the time they were through the fence, Pepe had already run back into the woods.

There was no distinct trail. All they had was the sound of the animal ahead of them, and it took a few minutes to catch up to him.

They found Pepe standing over the motionless body of a young man lying facedown. Sanchez ran to the spot and fell on his knees.

"Antonio?" he said softly. He touched the boy's

shoulder but there was no response. He began to turn the body over. Before he was halfway through the action, he let out a horrified "O-oh!" and jumped back.

Gabe hurried to the body. He knelt and gently turned the body over. The eyes were open, staring wildly into oblivion. There was only a gaping wound where the neck should have been. Next to the body was a shotgun. Gabe guessed the young man never had a chance to use it.

The deputy got up and turned to Sanchez. The old man stood a few feet away, his face buried in his hands.

"Is this Antonio?"

Sanchez nodded. "It is my fault," he whimpered. "I should have come yesterday when you first told me."

"He could have been here a couple of days, Mr. Sanchez. You probably couldn't have done anything."

Gabe hesitated. He didn't know if he should leave the body there or wrap it up and take it to town. He had heard about the animal attack on Chief Vicinti's son. This looked like a repeat of that tragedy.

He looked around on the ground for any trace of what kind of animal had done this. It took him only a minute to realize he was no sort of tracker. He knew he couldn't tell the difference between a bear track and the paw print of a large dog.

"Do you want to wait here, Mr. Sanchez? I need to get a body bag from the back of my Jeep."

The old man nodded, his face still covered. "I will stay."

Gabe started down the mountain to the pasture.

After going a dozen yards he looked back toward Sanchez. The old man was on his knees next to the body, praying.

Gabe shook his head. He realized at that point that was all anyone could do.

41

LEAVING THE TRADING-POST PARKING LOT, RENEE found herself turning toward the southeast on Highway 44. The map indicated several dirt roads that would take her to the east and northeast, toward the mountains.

It wasn't that she didn't believe Harvey Sparks. It made perfect sense to use Pierre's Ruin as a starting position if she was going to look for Conrad. The ancient road that led from Aztec to Chaco Canyon was certainly the longest in the Chaco road system. Because of its length and the fact that it traversed barren desert, the Aztec road was probably the least explored of any. Pierre's Ruin, only twelve miles north of the canyon and one of the way stations along the road, wasn't even discovered until the early 1970s.

But the way Conrad had talked about the road system told her she should be looking somewhere else. He said the roads had been built to guide people to the sacred canyon. He also suggested the possibility that some of the roads had been built to lead people away from Chaco to an even more sacred place.

As far as she was concerned, the Aztec road was not where she should be looking.

Just before reaching Nageezi she spotted a dirt road heading off the highway toward the east. Giving herself a mental shrug, she slowed, then turned onto the gravel track. Two miles down the road she went over the top of a small rise. At the bottom of the hill the road ended, terminating at a decrepit-looking ranch a mile away.

She stopped her car immediately. It didn't make sense to go any farther in that direction. She pulled out her map for a quick reconnoiter. She found Nageezi and estimated her approximate position.

There were three dirt roads that headed to the northeast between Nageezi and Counselor. The three appeared to join up with a major gravel road that led north out of Counselor.

She sipped on her Coke for a moment, thinking. Her eyes wandered from the map to the notebook.

"Well, stupid," she said out loud. "Why don't we see what Joel has to say about all this?"

She picked up the book and opened to the first page:

I've been toying with the question of why no more branches have been found to the Chaco Road Complex. I think part of the problem is erosion. Less than half of the Aztec road showed up on aerial photography, although at ground level the path is quite distinct.

Out of sheer curiosity I walked a ten-mile stretch of Nageezi road, that glorious monument to road graders that leads from Highway 44 to the Chaco back door. I honestly believe I found a portion of one of the ceremonial roads. Most of the road has been obliterated by modern road construction, but I did find a "curb" of stones through one of the adjacent cow pastures. (Reference Photos 1–12)

When the highway engineers laid out Nageezi road, they simply ran the graders and plows around the hills, rather than over them. It's still a relatively direct route, but not nearly as direct as what the pre-Pueblo people used. As we've seen on the Aztec road, their highways are straight lines. If they came to a butte or a cliff, they didn't go around. They cut steps into the nearly vertical walls so that they could continue in a straight line. (Religion can be a hard taskmaster.)

The straight-line principle is in use around the Nageezi road. Also, unlike so many of the ceremonial roads that radiate out only a few miles from the canyon and terminate, the Nageezi-Chaco road extends well past Highway 44. I found traces of an ancient track three miles past the town.

Unfortunately, I haven't found anything that extends all the way to the foothills. At least not in a straight line. Like other Chaco tracks this one may also have a dogleg in it. Simply extending a straight line from the Nageezi road to the foothills may not point out the exact location of the site.

I'm afraid I may have to use the very unscientific method of tromping up and down hills until I find it. At least the discovery of the Nageezi road confirms my belief that the roads lead to and away from Chaco Canyon.

" 'Exact location of the site'? Find 'it'?" Renee muttered. "What are you looking for, Joel?" Then she thought about the jade skull he had shown her two days earlier. "Maybe the better question is, 'What have you found?' "

She looked at her map again. Using the edge of the notebook, she tried to create a straight line using the Nageezi road as a pointer. Fifteen miles past Nageezi was Canyon Largo. Beyond that wash were the foothills, canyons, and valleys leading into the mountains. The high desert stretched for sixty miles, north to south, thirty miles to either side of where her imaginary line intersected the hills.

Joel could be anywhere up there, she thought. And sitting there sipping a Coke wasn't going to help find him. For the moment she was reassured that she was heading the right way. Pierre's Ruin was due west of her and in the exact opposite direction from where she needed to go. Of course, there was no way Harvey Sparks could have known that. He had done his best to help her.

She glanced through the next few pages of the notebook. Conrad had page after page of narrative. Sometimes the field notes were interspersed with Conrad's own particular interpretation of history as it related to the hard evidence he had at hand. Sometimes his ideas were just a series of wandering notions that didn't culminate in a cogent point.

When he was dealing with hard evidence from his field surveys he made references to photos he had taken or maps he had drawn. Unfortunately Renee had none of those items to work with. She decided her best bet was to head in the general direction of the mountains northeast of Nageezi. Maybe she'd get lucky and find something.

She made a U-turn on the dirt road and headed for the highway. Heading south again on Highway 44, she turned again toward the east on the first dirt road after Nageezi. Having finally referred to the map, she was fairly certain she wouldn't run into another dead end, at least not for a while.

Twenty minutes after departing Highway 44 she reached the gravel road that led north from Counselor. She looked up and down the road in both directions, trying to decide which way would be better.

Using a backward logic she didn't understand herself, she decided to turn right and head south. There was less territory to cover in that direction. If she didn't find anything, she could turn around and tackle the vast expanse of the northern part of the range.

Renee headed south on the road, driving slowly. Most of the land had been partitioned with barbedwire fences. Numerous dirt roads, some no more than two-rut tracks, entered the fields beyond the fences. Some of the fences had gates. Some simply had openings with cattle guards, pipe bridges that hoofed animals refused to cross.

There was a chance Conrad had gone up any one of those roads. For Renee to check each and every one would take a week. She had a day. She decided to simply continue south and hope she could spot his truck along the way.

She had been on the road for ten minutes when she spotted a Jeep pulling onto the highway in front of her. She just caught a glimpse of the side of the vehicle, but it appeared to have some sort of decal. The top of the Jeep had blue and red lights and the lights were flashing.

She accelerated to catch up. It took her a moment to realize the other driver was accelerating as well.

What was worse, the Jeep was kicking up a cloud of dust and there was no way she could be seen.

She started beeping the pitiful horn on her car, hoping she could catch the patrolman's attention. The Jeep continued to pull away, stirring even more dust in its wake.

Renee veered into the opposite lane, trying to get clear of the dust cloud and catch the patrolman's attention. The fine powder in the air dissipated just enough for her to see past the patrol Jeep. A quarter mile in front of her another car was approaching, head on.

Renee slammed her foot on the brake. The tires locked and she began to skid on the gravel surface. She immediately let up on the pedal and hit the accelerator again. Her car skidded and lurched but she managed to swerve onto her own side of the road. She hit her brakes again and slid to a stop, her engine suddenly dying on her.

The oncoming car had performed a similar maneuver, swerving onto the soft shoulder with enough momentum to end up on the road again. The driver leaned out his window and yelled several expletives in Spanish while he shook his fist at her. He continued down the road without stopping.

Ahead of her, the Jeep proceeded on its way, the driver oblivious to the accident that she nearly caused.

Renee closed her eyes and took a deep breath. She held on to her steering wheel tightly to keep from shaking. It took a few seconds before she calmed down enough to open her eyes.

By then the dust had settled and she had a clear view of her surroundings. She was on a hill and could see almost twenty miles in any direction. The road stretched in front of her, toward the southeast. Five, maybe six miles ahead, by her estimate, and parked to the side of the road, was a truck with a tan-colored camper shell.

From that distance it looked tiny, but Renee had no doubt whose truck it was. She had found Conrad.

Mentally crossing her fingers, Renee turned the ignition key. The engine started up immediately. Checking for traffic first, she slipped the gear into drive and headed down the road again.

As she got closer she could see that Conrad was walking along a side road, surveying the ground around him, as if he was looking for something. She pulled off the main road and parked behind the truck.

Renee had already jumped out of her car and was running toward Conrad when he finally noticed her. She nearly leapt into his arms. "Joel, I was so worried."

Conrad was surprised at both her arrival and the sudden show of affection. "What are you talking about?"

She stepped back to get a look at him. He was still a mess, despite the fact that Mrs. Rodriguez had cleaned him up earlier that day. "My God, what happened to you?" She was almost in tears.

He touched the bandage on his scalp. "You mean besides being shot?"

"Someone shot you?" Renee cried. "Who? When? What in hell is going on around here?"

Conrad couldn't understand her overflowing emotions. "Why are you so upset?"

"I was afraid something had happened to you." She sobbed. "And I was right!"

He hesitated a moment before putting his arms

around her to comfort her. "You were worried about me?"

"Yes, you big dummy! I was worried about you."

Conrad found himself completely confused. He had always thought Renee was a career woman with tunnel vision. Despite her attractiveness he had never seen her flirt, especially with him. "I—I didn't think you even knew I existed."

She pulled back slightly so she could look him in the eyes. "You are some thick, Joel Conrad."

"What do you mean?"

"I've been trying to get you to look at me for three years. The main reason I volunteered for this dig was so we could work together. I thought I'd be able to get your attention. But hell, no. You've got your own agenda, and there's no room for anyone else. I shouldn't have wasted my time looking for you!"

"You came looking for me? Won't Vencel have your hide for leaving the dig?"

"The dig's finished for the season."

"Huh?"

"And Dr. Giancarlo's dead!"

"What?" He couldn't believe the news.

"And on top of everything else I nearly wrecked my car looking for you!" She began sobbing once more.

Conrad put his arms around her again. This time, though, it was to steady himself as much as it was to comfort her. "I think I've just been overwhelmed," he admitted. "We need to sit down and talk somewhere. All this is a little much."

"How far are we from Counselor?"

"Twenty, twenty-five minutes. I guess we can stop at our motel."

"It's not our motel anymore. We checked out this morning."

Conrad shook his head. Things were moving way too fast for him. "We can go to the grill a half mile past the motel. I'm dying of thirst and I need to eat something."

Renee frowned. "Are you all right to drive?"

"Yeah. Just lead the way. I'll be okay."

42

LANSING WAS FINISHING A PILE OF PAPERWORK ON HIS desk when the phone rang. He picked up the receiver. "Yeah?"

"Sheriff, I have a Mr. Querino Ortiz out here. He said you'd be expecting him."

Lansing really wasn't expecting him. In fact, he had doubted Ortiz would even bother to return his call. He glanced at his watch. It was two-thirty. Evidently news traveled fast around Pojoaque. "Send him in."

Lansing went to his door and opened it. A short, thin man in his late fifties approached. He wore a long-sleeved white shirt that was neatly tucked into blue jeans. His long gray hair was gathered at the back. He carried a flat-brimmed hat in his hands. His weathered face and hands attested to a lifetime of hard labor. He didn't look anything like a blackjack dealer.

"Mr. Ortiz?" Lansing asked.

The older man nodded. "You said Tyope needed to speak to me. You said it was an emergency."

"Jonathan—Tyope, I guess—is in one of my jail cells. The Albuquerque police want him for the murder of a man from the University of New Mexico. He said he didn't do it and I believe him. Unfortunately, taking his word for it isn't going to get him turned loose. The police have proof he was at the scene of the crime.

"I want to help him, but he won't tell me a thing. He said he can't tell me anything until he speaks to you."

Ortiz nodded. "May I speak with him?"

"Sure."

Outside the cell area Lansing patted Ortiz down, checking him for any weapons. He searched the hat as well. Satisfied this wouldn't result in an attempted jailbreak, he let Ortiz into the lockup.

The old Pueblo turned to Lansing. "May we speak in private?"

"I'll be right outside."

As Lansing closed the door to the lockup he thought about his antiquated facilities. There were many times when he wished his jail were outfitted with twentieth-century technology. There were no surveillance cameras, no hidden microphones to pick up jailhouse chat, no electronic alarms to announce break-ins or breakouts.

Deep inside he was looking forward to the construction of a new jail. San Phillipe needed one. Had needed one for twenty years. His major resentment was the way Peter Alvarez, Roger Kellim, and the other commissioners were ramming it down his throat with one hand and stripping him of his budget with the other. It was too bad politicians had decided crime was a good way to generate income. Then again, politics and money always seemed to go hand in hand.

He went into his office and retrieved his coffee cup. He didn't feel too guilty about filling his cup again. This was only his third round of coffee for the day. Nothing like the dozen cups he'd had the day before.

He strolled over to the reception counter. Marilyn was just picking up a transmission from Deputy Hanna.

"I just passed Angelina Peak. How do you read me now?" Gabe asked.

Lansing glanced at the map. Gabe was crossing the mountains at the southern end of the county, rather than going north through Dulce. In the summer months, when snow wasn't a problem, it was usually the quicker way across the Continental Divide.

"You're loud and clear," Marilyn responded. "We were expecting to hear from you sooner."

"Had some unseen complications."

Lansing signaled for her to hand him the microphone. "This is Sheriff Lansing. Do you have Mr. Conrad with you?"

"He refused treatment. Didn't want to come in."

"What were your complications, then?"

"I went with Mr. Sanchez to check on his nephew up in the meadows. We found him dead. Something had attacked him."

"Any clue as to what?"

"No, sir," Gabe responded. "I have the body with me. I'll take it directly to the funeral home. I thought Dr. Carerra might want to take a look, since she saw the Vicinti boy."

"Roger. I'll get in touch with her. Anything else?"

"No, sir. My ETA is about thirty minutes."

"Ten-four." Lansing handed the microphone across

the counter. "I don't know what the hell's going on around here, Marilyn. So far this week that's four people killed by some wild animal, and two of them were experienced hunters. I have no idea how much livestock's been attacked."

"Sounds to me like you need to get in touch with the forestry service. They should have some animal experts around."

"I don't think I have much choice."

Ortiz emerged from the lockup. Whatever the conversation had been was short and to the point. "Sheriff, may we speak together?"

"Yes, let's go in my office."

Lansing invited Ortiz to sit in one of the chairs in front of the desk. The sheriff knew that sitting behind his desk put him in a position of power over any of his visitors. He admitted to himself he used the desk as a mind game on many occasions. He wanted to avoid that situation now. Instead of taking his usual seat, he sat in the chair next to Ortiz, turning it slightly so he could face him better.

"Dr. Giancarlo was a great friend to the Pueblo people," Ortiz began. "He studied our languages, our customs, our religions, with great respect. Our hearts break because of his death. None of us would ever have wished him harm.

"Jonathan went to Dr. Giancarlo to discuss a sacred matter. It took several days to make the arrangement, and Jonathan had to wait.

"When the appointment was made, Jonathan went to the doctor's office. Dr. Giancarlo was already dying. Jonathan attempted to save his life, but he was too late.

"Instead of calling the police, he panicked and ran.

Most Indian men would in that situation, because we are always blamed for the misdeeds of others."

Lansing thought about the story. It was conveniently short and to the point. It just seemed too convenient. "What happened to the emerald that Giancarlo had with him?"

"Jonathan does not know. It wasn't there when he arrived."

"What about this religious matter they were supposed to discuss? What was that all about?"

"It is something I cannot discuss with you."

"Okay," Lansing said doubtfully. "Why did this appointment have to be at night? I realize Giancarlo was a busy man, but surely he could have made arrangements for an office visit during regular office hours."

"The time and place for the meeting was his choice."

Lansing considered the statements for a long moment before shaking his head. "Are these the answers you told Jonathan to give me?"

"These are the answers he gave me."

"Why couldn't he have told me all this?"

"He will tell you now."

"I'm afraid this isn't going to get him off the hook. Unless he can prove someone else was there, the Albuquerque police will be convinced he did it, and there won't be a thing I can do for him."

"The one who took the stone. He is the one who killed Giancarlo."

"There is no way I can prove Jonathan didn't take the stone. He had plenty of time to hide it after the murder."

"Find the stone. You will find the murderer.

That's all I can tell you." Ortiz stood and started for the door.

"Ortiz"—Lansing stood and spoke in the most apologetic tone he could find—"may I ask you one more question? It has nothing to do with Jonathan."

The older man stopped at the door and turned. "I will answer if I can."

"The Pueblo people have been here since before time began. I know some of your stories. I know how they have been handed down from mother to daughter and from uncle to nephew, preserved, protected. I know some of your stories carry great power and they can speak hidden truths."

"This is all true," Ortiz admitted.

"Something is happening in the mountains. Something I don't understand."

"What is that?"

"Several ranchers over on the west slope have lost sheep to some predator. Recently two shepherds, one just a boy, have been killed. From what I've heard their throats were ripped out by some wild animal.

"Several men, hunters and trackers from the Jicarilla tribe, went out yesterday to destroy the animal. They managed to kill two bears and two mountain lions. But they didn't kill what they were after. In fact, it came after them. Two hunters and half a dozen hunting dogs were torn apart.

"In the stories of your people, did you ever have an animal that came out at night, that had no fear of man, that killed anything that came across its path?"

Ortiz's face clouded with concern. "There are many stories about monsters. There are great tales about Monster Slayer, Son of Corn Maiden. He destroyed the monsters that roamed the earth and made it safe for the human beings to emerge from the Sipapu."

"I'm not talking about monsters. I'm talking about something real."

"Who's to say the monsters in our stories were not real?"

"I know about the before time, when all thing were possible. But I'm talking about here and now today, and what's logically possible."

"You want an explanation I cannot give you."

"An explanation you cannot or will not give me?"

"Either way, you would not believe me. You have to find the answer within yourself."

"What do I have to do with some wild anima rampaging through the mountains?"

"It is on your shoulders, Sheriff Lansing. It is you who found the stone, the emerald fetish."

"The emerald was stolen."

"We are in a circle with no beginning and no end. Find the man who killed Giancarlo and you wil find the stone. Then I can help you."

"You're saying I have to get Jonathan off the hook, then you'll help me?"

"No," Ortiz said, shaking his head. "I cannot help you until you find the stone." With that the Pueblo opened the office door and left.

43

ANSING WATCHED AS ORTIZ EXITED THE OUTER OFFICE.
Ie was confused about how he was supposed interpret
he Pueblo's words. Somehow or other Lansing was
upposed to blame himself for Akee's situation. Ortiz
aid it was on his shoulders. He was the one who had
ound the stone.

Lansing couldn't figure out how any of this was
is fault. Yes, he had found the stone. Then he'd
urned it over to people who knew about such things.
Iis actions, all the way through, had been innocent.

Lansing realized he was becoming angry. Ortiz
new more than what he let on about. All Lansing
as trying to do was keep Jonathan Akee from going
o prison for something he hadn't done. Akee would
nly talk to Ortiz. He had, and now both he and
ansing were left twisting in the wind.

Marilyn opened the door leading to her reception
rea. She was holding a handful of fax paper. "Oh,
Cliff. This just came for you."

"What is it?" He wasn't particularly interested.

"It's from the university. More of the journal."
he walked across the waiting area and handed it to

him. "I read a little of it. I think it's still talking about the Mexican War."

Lansing took the pages. "Thanks. I'll be in my office. I need to make a couple of phone calls."

Once he was at his desk, he picked up the phone and dialed. The phone at the other end rang four times before it was answered.

"Hello?" a very groggy Margarite said.

"Sounds like I woke you."

"What time is it?" she asked, yawning at the same time.

"Three o'clock."

"In the afternoon?"

"Yes. Should I let you go?"

"No. I need to get up or I'll never go to sleep tonight. What's going on?"

"We've had another animal attack."

"Oh, no!" That news woke Margarite up. "Who? When?"

"Deputy Hanna's bringing the body into the funeral home right now. It was a shepherd over on the west range. Sounds like the Vicinti boy all over again."

"My God . . . I'd like to see it if I can."

"I figured you would. That's why I called."

"Give me time to clean up. Could you call Mr. Sellers and tell him I'll be there in about an hour?"

"Yeah. And I'll meet you there. I'd like to get a firsthand view about what's going on."

"See you then."

Lansing made a quick call to the Las Palmas Funeral Home. Ed Sellers, the mortician there, hadn't been informed about the new body arriving. At the moment he had two slabs that weren't occupied, so there wasn't any problem with storage. He was currently preparing two bodies for burial. If no one was upstairs when Lansing and Margarite arrived, they could come on down to the basement. That's where he'd be.

Hanging up the phone, Lansing glanced down at the pages Marilyn had handed him. The journal had been interesting on a personal level, but so far it had yielded nothing that he had found useful. He was tempted to simply stuff the papers into a folder he had started and read them later.

He glanced at his watch. Margarite would be in town in less than an hour. He was caught up with his office paperwork and an hour wasn't long enough to start any new projects. He decided he needed to kill the time somehow. He picked up the first page and began to read.

44

JOURNAL OF VIRGIL LANSING (CONT.)

Having faced no hostilities with marauding Navajos after traveling north from Zuni, I delivered my detachment to the base of West Mesa along the Chaco River. It had been agreed this would be the rendezvous point with Major Phillips and his contingent.

Our horses had been without water for two days and the alkali pools that still remained in the Chaco Wash were unfit for consumption. There was no way we could make an extended encampment while we awaited Major Phillips's arrival. We needed to begin the march back to Santa Fe as soon as possible or we would start losing animals.

Early the next morning I sent a rider east through Chaco Canyon to see if there was any sign of the other detachment. He reported back by noon. There had been an encampment at the large ruins in the middle of the canyon. He reported that several pits had been dug within the ruins, but for what purpose he wasn't sure.

He had retrieved several carbine shells from around the encampment, so we were sure Major Phillips had been there ahead of us. My scout had continued down the canyon. He found where Phillips and his troops had entered the canyon from the south, just west of Chacra Mesa. He also discovered their departure route. Phillips was now heading due east.

Aside from Kit Carson, General Carleton's chief scout, I knew more about the terrain in the high desert than anyone else under Carleton's command. I directed Lieutenant Grimes to lead our troops directly back to Santa Fe. He was to report that I would attempt to overtake Major Phillips and guide his unit back to the fort.

There was no logical explanation for Major Phillips's departure from explicit orders. Our units had been dispatched on routine patrols. We were to make rendezvous and return to barracks. The only thing I could surmise was that Phillips had encountered hostiles and was now in close pursuit. I would have followed with my entire regiment if the water situation had not been so tenuous.

Immediately after issuing my orders I set out to pick up the trail, unsure of how far ahead Major Phillips might be.

At the easternmost end of the canyon the trail turned toward the northeast. Judging from the impressions of the hooves the horses were kept at a leisurely pace. This gave me cause to doubt the theory of close pursuit.

I continued following the trail, keeping a watchful eye for any convenient source of water. But it was not until dusk that . . .

[NEXT SEVERAL PARAGRAPHS UNREADABLE]

—though it was not surprising that I should overtake them by the evening of the second day. Unfamiliar with the high desert, Phillips and his scout had missed two opportunities to water their horses and fill their canteens.

Their encampment was located at the broad end of a valley. Hidden by stunted willows and close to the entrance were two extraordinary stones, carved in the likeness of crouching mountain lions. Facing away from the valley they seemed like sentinels, warning anyone who dared pass beyond them.

Major Phillips was very agitated at my arrival. He very nearly became belligerent when I questioned him as to why he hadn't joined up with my force. I reminded him we were operating under explicit orders. Further, I was his superior officer and his actions were answerable to me the moment we left Santa Fe.

He none too delicately reminded me that he was General Carleton's personal executive officer. As such he was operating under the general's orders and would only answer to him.

The strain of three weeks in the field was telling on us both. I deferred any further conversation until the next morning, after we both had had a good night's rest.

My intentions were going to be clear. I would lead his men to the nearest water source first thing in the morning. After that we could proceed directly to Santa Fe via the Jémez Pueblo.

Instead of greeting the morning with a clearheaded Phillips to talk with, I found myself being guarded by two of his men. I was informed that I was under arrest for deserting my own regiment.

Major Phillips could not be reasoned with. Direct orders and threats of court-martial were ignored. His claim was that he was operating under General Carleton's personal orders. Any attempt on my part to subvert those *orders* could result in my immediate execution. We were, *he* reminded me, in a state of war with the Confederacy. And with me being a Virginian by birth, General Carleton *had* already questioned my allegiances.

I was dismayed over the circumstances. But I was *more* mystified at Major Phillips's actions. I couldn't *understand* why he had come to this remote, strategically *unimportant* location.

It was at this juncture that I was placed with the Navajo shepherd boy they had captured some days earlier. The child had been beaten repeatedly and was suffering *from* dehydration. I let him have all the water he could *stand* from my canteen. Fortunately, we were able to *communicate* through Spanish. He had been taken near Chaco Canyon, his flock dispersed.

He was told he would not be allowed to return home *unless* he led Phillips to Montezuma's gold. The boy *thought* they meant the fallen cities in Chaco Canyon, so *that* is where he took them. Dissatisfied after two days of *digging,* Phillips beat the boy, demanding to know the *truth.*

The poor child knew only the legends of his people. He told Phillips there was a valley of graves. It was the Tombs of the Anasazi. It was a forbidden place guarded *by* two stone lions. The lions were demons put there by the Anasazi gods to protect the dead.

I don't know what providence guided him to that spot. The shepherd insisted he had never been there before. I do *know* he was frightened out of his wits. The Navajo have *no* great love of the darkness and they harbor a mortal fear *of* the dead.

But armed with the boy's explanation, I now under*stood* the nature of Phillips's mission. He was acting on

sheer greed. I do not know if he was truly acting directl
on General Carleton's orders.

(My personal belief came to be that Carleton was ɑ
man of guile and deceit. He broke promises with the native
of the land and stole from the Navajo at every opportunity
He eventually herded them like cattle onto Bosqu
Redondo, where they were nearly starved out of existence.)

I requested permission of the two guards to speak witl
Major Phillips. They escorted me past the crouching lion
to the valley beyond. The basin was long and low, witl
steep sides. For perhaps a hundred yards, set at regula
intervals and in pairs, were mounds of earth. The mound
were ten feet high and oblong in shape. There were dozen
upon dozens of these mounds, all uniform in their desig
except one. The farthest mound from the lion guards wa
perhaps twenty feet high and looked like a pyramid tha
had been flattened at the top. The resemblance to templ
ruins I had seen in Mexico was striking.

It was at the large mound that I found Major Phillip
and his troops. Apart from the two soldiers watching m
and the boy, Phillips had twenty-three men to do his bid
ding. Every one of them had been put to the task of tearing
down the mound. A few had shovels. The rest wer
reduced to ripping at the earth with their bayonets anc
hands.

Approaching the major, I demanded he release th
Navajo. The boy had done his bidding. . . .

[NEXT TWO PAGES UNREADABLE]

Phillips talked in low tones with his sergeant, I am confi
dent, about the water situation. I do not know how th

treasures they had found were to be divided amongst the men. But all the gold in the Americas is worth little to a man dying of thirst. That would soon be our situation if we did not depart soon.

I had seen little of what they had recovered. But the men talked of gold chains and rings, beautifully carved beads, and a green stone the size of a man's fist. From their description there was nothing left of the great mound. But they still had a hundred of the smaller ones to plunder.

By making his men confederates to his greed, Phillips abandoned his right to authority. Rations were short, the soldiers were tired, and fights broke out, if not over food, then over some ancient trinket they had found.

I was tied to a willow tree, apart from the rest. My guard did allow me my wool tunic before my hands were bound to prevent my escape, and it did provide some warmth. But the chilling desert air descended upon us as completely as the darkness and I found myself shivering uncontrollably. I couldn't help thinking of the Navajo boy, alone, somewhere out in the darkness. I know Phillips believed the boy would die on his own. That was the only reason he had allowed the boy to be released. I prayed that night that he was safe.

Two guards were posted to prevent intruders, but discipline was nowhere to be found. They both huddled over a fire, ignoring their watch on the perimeter.

Despite the chill I must have been overcome by my own exhaustion. The first scream, though, shocked me into consciousness. At the far end of the camp a man asleep in his bedroll had been attacked. His screams continued for several seconds as he was dragged into the darkness beyond the light of the campfires.

Men jumped to their feet, rifles at the ready. The two

guards, dozing near a fire, began firing. Phillips rushed from his tent, demanding to know what was going on.

During the confusion the screaming man had been silenced. Phillips ordered the two guards beyond the perimeter to see what had happened. Their reluctance was understandable. Phillips drew his pistol and repeated the order with his gun cocked and ready.

Seated on the ground and a hundred feet away, I could see little of the activity. The soldiers in the encampment were all up and armed by this point, their attention directed at the spot where the two sentinels had been dispatched. Several minutes passed. One of the guards yelled back. He had found the body of their companion.

Then one of the guards began to scream. The other began firing his weapon. Terror had gripped the entire camp. Men started firing their rifles in the direction of the scream, disregarding the fact that their comrades would be at the receiving end.

It took Phillips a full minute to get the shooting to stop. He turned to the darkness and called out the names of the two guards. Silence answered.

The horses were tethered not far from where I sat. They had already become skittish from the rifle fire. Now they were in a complete panic. I turned my head to see a great black shape leap from the darkness onto the back of one of the animals. The horse reared. Restrained by its rope it fell sideways onto the ground.

The dozen horses tethered to that line pulled the rope free from its anchoring. Still joined together by the main hitch, they escaped into the darkness.

A half-dozen men began to run after them until they realized they would be abandoning the artificial safety of the campfires. Even the threat of Major Phillips's pistol could not get them to budge from the camp. I believe he saw the real possibility of a mutiny if he pressed his orders any further.

Phillips ordered the fires to be rebuilt.

[NEXT PAGE UNREADABLE]

Counting Phillips and myself, only a dozen of us remained. In the morning light the carnage could be seen everywhere. In some instance the bodies had been dragged fifty yards from the camp, though most of the dead lay where they had been attacked, well within the supposed safety of the fires.

I had no explanation for why I had been spared. I was the farthest from the fires and certainly the most vulnerable.

Phillips came to me, knife drawn. He was haggard and wild eyed and I expected the worse. Instead he cut the ropes that bound me and handed me a pistol. I could join in the defense. He was convinced that the shepherd boy had encountered a Navajo raiding party and that Indians were responsible for this massacre. As I walked around and surveyed the scene I knew otherwise. Navajo warriors would not attack at night. And if they had, it would have been with rifles, and bows and arrows.

Phillips demanded to know, if not Indians, then what? I had spent most of the last fifteen years in New Mexico. I most certainly should have known what had attacked them.

I honestly didn't know, though the shredded bodies and uniforms argued that a wild animal had attacked. I told him I had never seen that kind of carnage around there, except for what men perpetrated against other men.

Phillips ordered immediate withdrawal. We still had fourteen horses on tether. Two of the horses could be used for packing the small fortune they had amassed. I suggested they leave their trove behind, if for no other reason than it would slow us down.

The major would hear none of that. He reached into his personal saddlebag and produced a large green, almost translucent stone. He would see more money from that one stone than a lifetime in the army.

I asked if I could look at that one treasure. Reluctantly, he agreed.

When he flashed it in front of me it seemed vaguely familiar. As I held it in my hand the memories of the Yucatán campaign flooded over me. It was an emerald, painstakingly and delicately carved to resemble a jaguar. Why and how it was there I do not know. But it was identical to the stone I had seen at the Temple of the Jaguar so many years before, the one the Mayan priest held above his head and prayed to.

I reached beneath my tunic and felt. I still carried with me the jade skull the priest had given me. We each create our own superstitions, and that had become mine. The charm had protected me that night on the temple. As I have written previously, the cube was drilled with a hole completely through it. I had suspended the skull from a leather strap and worn it around my neck throughout the rest of the Mexican campaign. That I had survived when so many of my comrades fell was testament to me that the charm might have powers.

As a rational man and a Christian I kept that absurd belief to myself, though I privately accepted the notion that my survival might be attributed to that pagan stone. I mention this now because of the massacre of the previous night. Despite my vulnerability I would not be harmed.

Whatever demons the Mayan priest had conjured up that night on the Temple of the Jaguar now existed in this place. The long dead had been sacrileged and the punishment was death.

Since it was now beyond Major Phillips's capability to follow orders, I pleaded with him to return his stolen artifacts. I explained my belief that he had violated sacred ground. Only by reburying his treasure could we escape the consequences.

This was beyond his comprehension. He directed his men to saddle up as quickly as possible and ordered me to guide them to the nearest source of water.

[NEXT SEVERAL PAGES UNREADABLE]

45

"I STILL CAN'T BELIEVE HE'S DEAD," CONRAD SAID, shaking his head. "I've studied under him for the last ten years. He was like a second father to me."

Renee had liked Giancarlo, too, but she'd had no idea how hard Conrad would take the news. She stared into her cup of coffee, trying to avoid his eyes. Every time she looked up she could see him fighting back the tears.

"I'm sorry," he finally said, clearing his voice. "I need to get hold of myself."

Whatever feelings Renee thought she'd had for Conrad before that moment had been increased tenfold. Joel Conrad was intelligent, handsome, enthusiastic, flip, and candid. She now saw he had emotions that ran deep and when he hurt he wasn't afraid to show it. He had a vulnerability she had never seen before and that made him all the more desirable.

She had avoided eye contact, not because she was embarrassed, but because she didn't want to get caught up in his pain. A very genuine pain. At that moment he could have asked her to do anything in the world and she would have done it.

Their conversation in the restaurant hadn't gone

far. Conrad had brooded over the death of his mentor the entire drive there. For the first twenty minutes in the booth all he could talk about was Giancarlo and how he couldn't believe the man was dead.

When enough silence had passed that Renee felt it was safe to change the subject, she asked what had happened to him over the past two days. Conrad told her what he could.

He had been attacked while he was in his truck and knocked unconscious. He eventually woke up and wandered for hours. When he reached the closest ranch, the Sanchez place, the old man thought he was breaking in and shot him. A neighbor patched him up. Then when he got back to his truck he discovered all of his research material had been stolen. When Renee found him, he was looking to see if any of his notes or artifacts had fallen out.

"That road where you were pulled off, does that go up to the site you found?"

"What do you know about that?" he snapped.

"First off, you showed me the jade skull the other afternoon." From the seat next to her she produced his notebook. "And then I read part of this."

"Those are my field notes!" He almost grabbed the notebook from her hand. "Where did you get this?"

"From the back of Dr. Vencel's truck." She said that the night before, Vencel had arrived at the motel late. She described how he sneaked three boxes into his room, checking to make sure no one saw him. The same boxes were in his truck that morning. She admitted she hadn't been able to help herself. She'd had to know what was inside. That's where she'd found the notebook. She hadn't had time to see what else Vencel might be hiding before he came back to his truck.

"That son of a bitch must be the one who hit me!" Conrad steamed.

"The night before was when he went to Santa Fe. As far as I know, he didn't get back to the motel that night. He said he spent the night out of town. The first time I saw him again was at the Chaco dig. That was yesterday morning."

"What time?"

"It must have been around eight-thirty."

"I got clobbered about five-thirty. He could have followed me out there. After knocking me out he had plenty of time to clean out my truck and get back to the canyon."

"Why would he have done that?"

"He's after my research. He plans on putting his name on my work and calling it his own."

"That sounds a little paranoid, Joel."

"You don't know Vencel like I do. He was a big deal in archaeology twenty-five years ago. He was one of the first scientists to describe the Chaco road system. There was even some debate about whether Baron Vencel or Pierre Morenon was the first to describe the tower they now call Pierre's Ruin. Vencel's still pissed about that one.

"The trouble with Vencel is that he hasn't had an original idea in the last two decades. He's written six books. He got a lot of praise for *The Road to Chaco Canyon*. Since then everything he's written has been a flop. He's been accused of stealing ideas, repackaging old theories with new terminology and calling them original proposals. He even got caught plagiarizing someone else's work in an article he did for the Smithsonian four years ago.

"You've heard the rule before: Publish or perish. Vencel's desperate. He runs these archaeological digs every year so that he can have something in print. But none of it's his own work. He takes the field notes from his students, rewrites the material, and takes credit for their efforts. Have you ever read any of his work?"

"A few things, sure."

"His articles read like an inventory." Conrad did his best to imitate Vencel's speech pattern. " 'The first stratum we encountered represented classical Pueblo Two. The mixture of Chaco and Mesa Verde ceramics indicates an extensive trade between these two sites. This proves conclusively that Mesa Verde was being occupied by 1035 C.E.' "

Renee giggled at the recitation.

"Where is the originality in that statement? Thirty years ago archaeologists proved Mesa Verde was occupied by 1000 C.E. But Vencel will make it sound like it was an original discovery and he that had just come up with it."

"You really don't like the man, do you?"

"He's a liar and a fraud, and those are his good points."

"What happened between you two?"

"Over the last twelve years I've spent every free moment I could scrambling around the cliffs in Chaco Canyon. During the summers I worked on the litter patrol and cleaned the septic tanks. It was crap work and crap wages, but I did it just so I could spend time at the canyon.

"By the time I reached my junior year in college I

had already decided I wanted to solve the mystery of the pottery dump near Pueblo Alto. I began the preliminary work as an undergrad, but I knew that would be my master's thesis. That's when I got into computer modeling, trying to reconstruct the weather patterns around here a thousand years ago. I estimated population density based on crop potential. I found there were more people and more crops than what the weather allowed. The water had to come from somewhere. After nearly two years of work all the pieces fell into place.

"Other scientists had guessed that the pottery dump was the result of a religious rite. I filled in the blank space. The people from the outliers brought their most precious resource to the canyon. They brought water."

"Vencel didn't like your idea?"

"Oh, Vencel loved my idea. He knew what I had been doing. I spent my summers working on digs he supervised. Sometimes in the evenings I'd bounce my ideas off him. That bastard would go back to his room and write everything down.

"Dr. Giancarlo was head of my thesis committee. Halfway through my second year in graduate school I submitted my thesis topic. He almost turned it down."

"Why?"

"Because he had just read a paper Vencel was submitting for publication. It had to get department-head approval before it could leave campus. Vencel's paper was the core of my thesis and if he published before I had finished my work, I would be the one being accused of plagiarism."

"What happened?"

"I asked Dr. Giancarlo if I could challenge Vencel's

right to publish in front of a faculty review committee. I knew I'd get put through the wringer. I was some punk grad student disputing the work of a tenured professor. I know Vencel didn't think I could prove anything.

"Boy, was he wrong. I had all of the research material I had been assembling for almost two years. I had computer models of the weather patterns, broken down by years and months. I had hydrology reports on the percolation rate of rainwater and snow runoff for the Chaco Plateau. I had ceramic vessels that I had reconstructed from the Pueblo Alto dump, nearly fifty of them. I could tell you how much water they held. I could provide a scientific estimate on the total number of pots in the dump and the amount of water that had been delivered."

"What did Dr. Vencel have?"

Conrad smiled. "All he had were the notes he made after he had talked to me. What was worse, Vencel compounded his guilt by claiming he had directed me to make those studies. To get access to computer time for my research, I had to have faculty approval. To get hydrologists into the field for their studies, I had to tap into department funds, which also needed faculty approval.

"I asked Vencel, since all these studies were done under his direction, could he tell the committee when he'd first authorized my access to the university mainframe? Had he kept a record of the authorization for auditing purposes? Did he remember how much money had been authorized from the department budget for the hydrology reports?"

"And?"

"And he turned as red as a tomato. I thought his head was going to explode. He sputtered and stammered for a moment, then muttered something about the fact that I had done all that work without proper authorization."

"Had you?"

"Hell, no! Dr. Giancarlo authorized everything and I had his signature to prove it. He knew what was going on the entire time. He knew Vencel was trying to steal my work. He just wanted to see if I was willing to stand up for myself. He also wanted a public forum to prove that Vencel was the fraud that he was."

"Was Dr. Giancarlo trying to get rid of Vencel?"

"I think so. He probably could have if Vencel had published that paper. He'd been caught plagiarizing before. But if Vencel published, all of my work would have gone out the window. Giancarlo wanted to make sure that didn't happen."

"I can see why you two don't get along. What did they do to Vencel?"

"He was publicly censured and told he couldn't publish for a year. They removed him from the chairmanship of all his committees and told him he could kiss off any thoughts of advancement."

"But he is the chairman on two or three committees."

"Now. He played the recalcitrant for a year, waiting for everything to blow over. He spent that time grooming some political allies in the upper administration. With an influential word here and a forceful suggestion there, he eventually clawed his way back into power."

"I guess you don't know he's been appointed acting head of the department."

"You're kidding!"

"I wish I was."

Conrad shook his head. "I don't know if it's possible, but I think Dr. Giancarlo hated Vencel worse than I do. I know Giancarlo planned to stay on for only a couple more years. I also know he was going to pick his own successor and I can guarantee you, it wasn't going to be Vencel."

"Was Vencel aware of all this?"

"Oh, he knew. There was no love lost between them. They barely spoke to each other anymore."

Renee hesitated for a second, not sure how to couch the next bit of news. "I'm afraid I have one more bulletin for you. He told me to tell you that you were fired from the dig and that you were finished at the university."

"That son of a bitch!" Conrad swore, clenching his teeth as he did. "That fits in with everything. Steal my work, then kick me out of the department so I can't do anything."

Renee reached across the table and took his hand. "What happens now?"

"Now?" Conrad squeezed her hand and gave her a reassuring smile. "Right now, I'm going to get something to eat. Then I'm heading back to Albuquerque and get all of my research material back from Vencel."

"Do you think he'll just hand if over?"

"I know he won't. But I'll get it back, one way or the other. And now I don't have a damned thing to lose. He may be able to kick me out of the school, but I'll be damned if he's going to take credit for my work. I can get a sheepskin anywhere."

"Do you know what you're going to do?"

"Albuquerque's a four-hour drive from here. I'll have plenty of time to figure it out."

"Do you mind if I tag along?"

"I think I'd like that. But are you sure you want to?"

Renee shrugged and gave him a slight smile. "I think you already know that I enjoy the company."

"I don't want you to get in any trouble."

"To use Vencel's words: I'm free, white, and twenty-one. I can make my own choices."

Conrad handed her a menu. "Then let's get something to eat. It's a long drive back."

"Yes, sir." It wasn't exactly a first date, but after three years of trying it was finally something. She emitted a slight giggle.

"What's so funny?"

"Nothing," she said, smiling. "Nothing at all."

46

For a Friday evening the crowd in Paco's Cantina was very light. Christina was able to seat Lansing and Margarite immediately. Neither was in a big rush, so they ordered two beers while they looked over the menu.

"You didn't say much back at the funeral home," Lansing observed.

"Not much to say. It looked exactly like the same wounds I saw last night. For the life of me, though, I can't tell you what I was looking at. Yes, it was an animal attack. Obviously the same kind of animal. But what kind of animal?" She shrugged in frustration.

Lansing nodded. He was facing his own frustrations at the moment. "Jonathan's associate from Pojoaque came in this afternoon."

"Are things getting straightened out with Jonathan?"

"Not in any legal sense." He described Ortiz's visit and the story he and Akee were sticking to.

"Just before Ortiz left, I mentioned the trouble with the animal attacks in the mountains. I asked if he could help me. You know, did he remember anything like that happening before. Maybe there were some stories they told around the Pueblo. He said something about monsters and monster slayers. Then, he said I was to blame because I found that carved totem under my house. He said he couldn't help until I recovered the emerald."

"Do you know what he meant by that?"

"No. He provided me with a brilliant revelation, though. If I find the emerald, I'll find the real killer."

"Well?" Margarite said with a twisted smile. "It does make sense."

"Believe it or not, I had actually developed a very similar theory myself."

She patted him on the forearm. "You must be proud."

Lansing never feared that his sarcasm would be wasted when Margarite was around. His only problem was getting a snide remark out without being "one-upped."

Margarite noticed the hurt look on his face. "You really don't think this is all your fault, do you?"

"Let me reserve comment for the moment." He had brought a manila folder with him. He picked it up from the table and handed it to her. "I'd like you to read something. I won't interrupt you. Just read it straight through."

Margarite spent the next ten minutes reading through the fax pages. Periodically she would adjust the angle of the page to pick up more light in the dim interior.

Lansing had been bothered by the most recent pages of the journal. He needed someone intelligent to discuss it with, and Margarite was the most intelligent person he knew. The journal was, as far as he was concerned, a preposterous tale.

He accepted Virgil's story about the Yucatán. Virgil saw the Mexican soldiers attacked. They had obviously been attacked by Mayan warriors in some type of ceremonial fighting costumes. The fact that he saw no native bodies the next morning was no surprise. He had said that when he and Captain Christmas returned to the village, after the Mexican soldiers began chasing them, the bodies of the dead had already been removed. The same thing had happened that night.

There was no need to believe that a priest conjured up wild animals in the middle of the night to attack the soldiers. Things like that didn't happen.

The tale about Major Phillips stepped beyond the bounds of credibility.

Margarite let out a soft whistle when she was finished.

"What do you think of it?"

"Either your great-great-grandfather had some extraordinary experiences in his lifetime or he was hitting the tequila pretty good when he was writing this."

"So you don't believe it either?"

Margarite shook her head. "I didn't say I didn't believe it. I just said it was extraordinary."

"Well, I'm having a hard time believing it. I can rationalize and explain away almost everything Virgil describes. I cannot believe that a Mayan priest conjured up demons way back when on the Yucatán. I will not believe that this Major Phillips dug up some grave, uncovered a gem, and caused a raft of hobgoblins to attack his men. And I—" He cut himself off in midsentence.

"And you, what?" Margarite asked.

He closed his eyes and thought through the words he wanted to say. "The carved emerald jaguar Old Virg describes in his journal has to be the same one he placed under his house."

"Yes. And?"

"And I refuse to believe that there's any connection between the fairy tale he told and what's going on up in those mountains now."

"A part of you wants to believe, or you wouldn't have brought it up."

"I'm a little old to start believing in ghosts and goblins and things that go bump in the night."

"Just what do you believe in, Lansing?" Margarite was being very sincere with her question.

"On a good day I almost believe what the preacher says on Sunday. But good days don't come very often. I think most people are satisfied with just getting along in life. I try to live by the Golden Rule. And most of the time I think God's too busy to really fix the mess he created down here."

"I didn't think you were that much of a pessimist."

"You're the one who asked."

"What are you really angry about?"

Lansing waited until the new beers were in front of them before answering. "What makes you think I'm angry about something?"

"Because I'm getting to know you, Lansing, as much as you may hate that. You're like a deep, dark lake. You can be smooth as glass on the surface, but underneath there are all sorts of things going on."

"You're right, I do hate it."

Margarite waited calmly for his real response.

Lansing took a sip of his beer and stared at nothing in particular. Finally the silence was too much even for him. "All right. Where the hell does Ortiz get off blaming me for everything that's going on? That doesn't make any sense."

"Maybe he's not saying you're the one to blame. Maybe he's just trying to say, you're the only one who knows enough to correct what's gone wrong."

"What do I know, Margarite?"

"You know something strange is going on up in these mountains. Tonight, you found out Virgil Lansing saw something just as strange a hundred and fifty years ago.

"Don't turn your back on the possibilities, Lansing. Virgil had a strange event happen to him. The experience was important enough that he had to write about it.

"You discovered the emerald under your house. Virgil left instructions about what had to be done if anyone ever found it. That's what the journal's all about."

"Do you really believe that?"

"Why was it hidden there, instead of handed down through your family? Have you ever thought about that?"

"I didn't give it any serious thought."

"Maybe you should."

"All right. I will."

She studied Lansing's face for a moment. She never remembered having seen so much confusion. "Do you have any idea where you're going to start?"

"I'm going to start by asking the lab folks to hurry

up with the journal. Then I'll see if I can find the stone. I'll ask my old buddy Chet Gonzalez to let me look over the police evidence. Maybe take a look at the crime scene. Talk to any of their witnesses."

"You're going down to Albuquerque?"

"I have an excuse. There will be a memorial service for Giancarlo on Sunday. I'll explain that since I'm in town, I'd like to look at what they have, purely out of professional curiosity."

"Do you think they'll cooperate?"

"They think I'm stupid. What possible harm could I cause?"

"You have a very good point there."

"Which point is that?"

Margarite picked up her menu, trying to avoid answering.

"I see." Lansing said. "And I was just about to ask you if you'd like to come along."

"What? Albuquerque for a couple of days? Aren't you going to spend some time with C.J.?"

"Frank and his mother took him to California for a couple weeks. One last trip before summer vacation's over."

"You really want me to come?"

"You blew it."

"Aw, come on, Lansing. I have two months of comp time saved up. I'll bet I could get John Tanner to cover any emergencies. I know a great Mexican restaurant. It'll even be my treat."

"All right, all right. I hate it when you whine. Could you be ready to go early tomorrow?"

"Tell me what time you want me at your ranch. We can just take off from there."

"Why couldn't you spend tonight down there? Then the morning won't be so rushed."

"I'll have to think about that. You're in one of your moods. I'm not sure I can take a whole night of one of your moods."

"Not even if you try real hard?"

She signaled Christina they were ready to order. "I'll let you know after I eat."

47

"Dr. Gill, I'm Sheriff Cliff Lansing. This is my friend Dr. Margarite Carerra."

Mary Ann Gill shook hands with her two visitors. "Welcome to my inner sanctum," she said, gesturing to the low-ceilinged but brightly lit lab behind her. There were half a dozen students busy working at microscopes and assembly tables. They seemed totally engrossed in their projects. "Did you have any trouble finding your way down here?"

"No. Your directions were perfect. I know this was short notice. I appreciate you giving up part of your weekend to see us."

"Usually the only way I know it's a weekend is that I don't have a class to teach. Otherwise, I'm down here."

Lansing was surprised how closely Dr. Gill looked the way she sounded. Her voice was low, hoarse, and gravelly, reflecting a lifetime of cigarette smoking. In appearance she was short and heavyset with muscular calves. He guessed she spent a lot of time on her feet, though there was a slight waddle in her walk. Her age was a vague fifty-something. Her eyes were a deep

lue that sparkled with enthusiasm whenever she
alked about her work. Lansing liked her immediately.

"Of course, none of the faculty is getting this
reekend off," she continued. "We have the memorial
ervice tomorrow. But as if that wasn't enough, the
cting chairman of our department called a meeting this
aorning. He said he wanted to clarify his position."

"I'm sure he just wanted to allay everyone's fears,"
ansing guessed. "Let everyone to know there would
e no drastic changes just because Dr. Giancarlo
assed on."

Dr. Gill shook her head. "That's so far off the
aark, it's almost laughable.

"No, he wanted everyone to know there were going
> be changes. Big ones. We're supposed to supply him
ith a summary of every project in the department
>proved by Giancarlo. First thing Monday morning.
Ie'll personally decide if any of these studies are worth
ursuing."

Lansing looked from Margarite back to Gill.
Who is this guy? He sounds like a real jerk."

"Dr. Baron Vencel. He's been in the department
.most twenty years. And calling him a jerk would be
compliment."

"How'd he get selected to replace Dr. Giancarlo?"

"Campus politics. He's big into tennis and racquet-
all. Whenever the university president needs a play-
ig partner, he seems to be available. He conveniently
•ses too."

"Yeah, I know the type. From what I remember,
r. Giancarlo didn't suffer fools too readily."

"You remember correctly, but that's a whole other
sue we don't need to get into. Anyway, enough about

my problems. I suppose you came here to talk about Virgil Lansing's journal."

"That's only part of my reason for being here. But we can start there."

"Let me show you the problem we're having with the pages."

As she led them to a table at the back of the lab they passed several of the other projects being worked on. There were trays of ceramics in various stages of reconstruction. There were terrariums where different types of native grasses and grains were being raised under hot lamps. One section was reserved for assembling human skeletons. The industrious students hardly noticed them going by.

At the back of the lab were two young women working at a table alone. One was looking through the magnifying glass of a jeweler's lamp, trying to separate moldy, crumbling pieces of paper with a razor. The other had her face planted on a light-protective viewer. She was looking through a glass filter into a machine that emitted a pale blue light. She would study the contents of the machine for a few moments, then make notations on a pad next to her.

"Sharon, Patricia," Gill said, "I'd like you to meet Virgil's great-great-grandson."

The two students looked up from their work and smiled.

Sharon, the one with the razor, extended her hand. "You must be Sheriff Lansing. I wish we could have saved more of this journal. Virgil Lansing was cool."

"All three of us have become real fans of his," Gill said. "I hope you don't mind us talking about him the familiar. We feel like we've discovered a new American hero and he belongs to just us."

"It doesn't bother me in the least. If it wasn't for our work, I wouldn't know anything about him."

"His life was fantastic," Sharon continued. "I mean, he was in the middle of the Mexican-American War. He met actual Mayans. He knew Kit Carson and John Frémont."

"I haven't read anything about that yet," Lansing said, a little disappointed.

"Unfortunately, there's not much to read," Patricia said. "The parts referring to Kit Carson and California are mostly fragments. We've been able to piece together a sentence here and there. But mostly we're getting single words or half a date. Then we lost thirty pages during our accident. That doesn't yield a very complete history."

"No," Lansing said, "I suppose not."

"As I told you before," Gill explained, "the pages are glued together. Separating them is like trying to separate sheets of plywood."

"Have you tried immersing them in a solvent?" Margarite asked.

"We experimented with a couple of mixtures," Patricia said. "Acid-based formulas were a big mistake. We tried acetone and some petroleum-based products. The problem we had was, anything strong enough to separate the pages dissolved the ink."

"We tried an X-ray device in an attempt to see through the paper," Gill said. "The writting came out a smudge on the film."

Margarite had wandered over to the manuscript Sharon was working on and peered over the student's shoulder. The leather binding had been removed and what remained of the journal looked like a solid bloc of wood. "How are you separating the pages?"

Sharon shifted on her stool so Margarite coul get a better look. "I take the razor at the corner an try to shave the top page from the one below it. If I' lucky it will begin to peel apart. Usually, I end u shaving the paper as if I were using a plane on a piec of wood."

"Have you tried moistening the paper befor trying to separate it?"

"Everything from water to mineral oil. Too muc moisture and the paper just dissolves."

"Have you tried using saliva?"

"What?" Sharon asked, sounding a little disguste

"When we eat, the digestive process begins in th mouth. And I'm not just talking about the chewin The saliva has enzymes in it that starts breaking dow the carbon chains in the food.

"The gluing process you've encountered is probab a carbon bonding of some type. It's possible the saliv enzymes might be strong enough to weaken thos bonds. Maybe dissolve them completely."

Gill was fascinated at the prospect. "Let me t that."

She scooted Sharon out of the way and sat dow on the stool. She put the tip of her index finger to h mouth and moistened it. She took the saliva and p it at the corner of the top page. Waiting a moment f the moisture to soak in, she looked through the lamp Taking the razor blade, she carefully attempted separate the pages.

The top page began to peel away. A little to anxious at the success, Gill tried to wedge the blac farther into the document. The brittle paper immed ately broke away when she extended the razor past the moistened corner.

"Damn," she swore. "I got greedy." She looked up from the lamp, smiling. "At least we know it works! Thank you, Dr. Carerra. I would have never thought of something like that."

"You're welcome. And call me Margarite."

"Am I going to have to lick every page that's left?" Sharon made a sour face at the thought.

"Either that or we can walk around campus and get everyone to spit in a bucket for us," Patricia said, laughing.

"Try the med school or the chemistry department," Margarite suggested. "They may be able to replicate saliva enzymes in large batches."

"That's exactly what we'll do," Gill said. "This is fantastic. Have you ever considered a career in research science?"

"I think my medical patients would like me to stay right where I am."

"Well, if you ever want change, let me know."

"Doctor Gill," Lansing interrupted, "would it be all right if we talked in private for a while?"

"Not at all. We can go in my office."

48

LANSING AND MARGARITE FOLLOWED GILL TO THE front part of the lab and into the hall. A few doors down she ushered them into her office.

The room was nearly as sterile as the laboratory. Except for a display of diplomas behind her desk, the walls were completely bare. A bookcase neatly filled with dozens of textbooks stood along the wall across the small room. The desk itself held only an ink blotter, an appointment book, and a phone.

Lansing could only wonder if this peculiarly dedicated woman allowed herself any extravagances. He soon found out.

"Margarite, would you mind locking the door?"

"Certainly."

"Please, sit down." She indicated two chrome-and-Naugahyde chairs along one wall. "You can pull them up if you want."

As Lansing brought the chairs closer to the desk, Gill opened a desk drawer. She pulled out a aerosol can of air freshener, a pack of cigarettes, an ashtray, and a battery-operated air cleaner. "Needless to say, there's no smoking in any campus buildings. I have to be careful." She held up the pack of cigarettes. "Hope you don't mind."

"It's your office," Margarite said. Lansing nodded in agreement.

"Believe me, except for overeating and too much beer during a football game, this is my only vice." She tapped out a cigarette and lit it. "So, Sheriff, what did you want to talk about?"

"Do you remember the pages you faxed yesterday?"

"Chaco Canyon and the Phillips regiment? That's one of the most remarkable things I've ever read in my life."

"The whole journal was written by a man in his fifties, trying to remember things that had happened to him ten and twenty years earlier."

"So?"

"Don't you think his memory might be a little warped? A Mayan priest conjuring up creatures of the night? Opening Anasazi graves and being attacked by demons?"

"Let's back up a little. It had been a long time since I had read about the Mexican-American War," Gill admitted. "Not since my undergraduate days. I was really curious when Virgil wrote about the Battle of Monterrey. I was wondering how accurate his memory was. So I went to the library and checked out a couple of books on the subject.

"Virgil's memory was right on target. He didn't do a great job of describing the layout of the town so that the reader understood the location of La Tenería in relation to the fort. But he described the attack he was involved with and the eventual outcome of the campaign the same way as historians have.

"As far as his story about the Mayan village, there's

no way to corroborate what he said. But I did pull out a map and tried to trace his route. The conical hills that he and Captain Christmas spent the night on, the hills that turned out to be ruins, really do exist. It's a place called La Venta. It was built by the Olmecs and later occupied by the Mayans. One of the ruins there is known as the Temple of the Jaguar. I don't believe he made any of that up."

"And what about the things he described as happening?"

"Why couldn't it have happened?"

"Because it flies in the face of logic."

"Are you a Christian, Sheriff?"

"I was raised Christian."

"Two thousand years ago the son of a Jewish carpenter, it turns out, really wasn't the carpenter's son. He was actually the son of the one God and his mother was still a virgin after he was born. When he became a man, he taught other men to love their brothers and believe in the one true God, his father. He was crucified for his teachings and he died. But three days later he rose from the grave, resurrected, reborn. After walking among his followers he was carried to the sky by angels to be with his heavenly father.

"Do you believe that story, Sheriff?"

"I was taught to believe it."

"On the surface, though, if you think about it, it flies in the face of logic."

"I suppose that's where faith comes in."

"Most certainly. Faith is the glue that holds any religion together, whether it's Christian, Muslim, Hebrew, Mayan. One of the remarkable features of every Native American religion is that there is only one Creator. There may be a pantheon of lesser gods that were created to help explain how nature worked. But there was only one Creator, who made everything.

"In Islam and Christianity there is the one Creator. But there are also hosts of angels, powerful beings who assist God with the mundane business of helping mankind. They operate in much the same way as the lesser gods of the Native Americans. Does that make sense to you?"

"If I set aside the issue of faith, I guess so."

"Okay, then, we'll start with the foundation of most major faiths. There is one God, one Creator. In His infinite wisdom for us to achieve Paradise, Nirvana, Heaven, whatever you choose to call it, He has provided us with numerous paths. Some follow Christ, some follow Muhammad, some follow Buddha. But the path always leads to the one God."

"This is getting away from what I wanted to talk about," Lansing said uncomfortably.

"No, Sheriff. This is exactly what you were talking about. Virgil Lansing saw a Mayan priest call upon his Jaguar God to destroy his enemies. That priest called upon the same type of faith that Moses used when he parted the Red Sea, then destroyed Pharaoh's army."

"There was no Mayan priest around when Major Phillips started digging up those graves."

"No. But some places have great mystical significance in different religions. Lourdes in France is a place of healing. Non-Catholics have gone there and have been relieved of lifelong ailments. Doctors can't explain it. But it happens."

"In the journal Virgil thinks that if they rebury the emerald jaguar and all the other stuff they'll be safe, that whatever is attacking them will go away. He wants us to believe some inanimate object, like the emerald, has the power to evoke the supernatural. To believe that you're asking me to disregard everything I've ever been taught."

"No," Doctor Gill said, putting out the cigarette she had barely smoked. "I'm not saying to disregard anything. I'm just asking you to open your mind to the possibility of the infinite. There are powers on this earth we can't explain. We know extrasensory perception exists. We don't know how it works. We can't measure it or quantify it, but it's there.

"There are people who 'lay hands.' They'll admit they are only conduits for a higher power, but they can touch a sick person and make them well. Have you ever seen anything like that, Margarite?"

"Yes. I have to admit I have."

"Is there a scientific explanation?"

"No. And like you said, Lansing, things like that fly in the face of logic."

"Sheriff, what I'm trying to say is, instead of limiting yourself to what is probable, allow yourself the luxury of exploring what is possible." Gill noticed the clouded look on Lansing's face. "Why does that bother you?"

"I write tickets for people who drive too fast. I track down bad guys who break into other people's homes. I break up arguments between married couples and fights between drunks.

"I know that when a person gets cut, they bleed. I know that sometimes when a person gets shot, they die. These are all cause-and-effect activities. They're tangible. I understand them. This is what I know.

"Right now, up in San Phillipe, there's something

wandering around the mountains at night killing people."

"Why haven't you gone after it?"

"I thought it was restricted to the Apache reservation. I offered my help but they didn't want it. Now whatever it is has killed a shepherd outside the reservation."

"And you still haven't gone after it."

"Because I don't know what I'm going after. The jaguar idol that Virgil wrote about has to be the emerald I found under my house. A Pueblo man from Pojoaque told me Giancarlo's death was my fault because I found that damned emerald. He said he couldn't help me with the animal in the mountains until I recovered it.

"That's fine. I'd love to recover it. I'd love to get my hands on the man who killed Dr. Giancarlo. But I refuse to believe that a rock can conjure up a demon or a vicious wild beast or anything of the like."

"Then why did you want to talk to me about it?"

"Because you've read the manuscript and you're a scientist. I wanted you to tell me that what I was thinking was impossible."

"And what's that, Sheriff?"

"That if I don't find that damned jaguar emerald, I won't be able to stop that thing in my county."

"Is that what you believe?"

"I don't know. I'd be up there with a hunting party right now if I thought it would do any good. A dozen men from the Jicarilla tribe went up there. I'm talking about the best hunters and trackers in the state. They couldn't get whatever it is and they lost two of their men trying.

"I haven't seen the latest pages from the journal.

What happened with Phillips and the rest of his soldiers?"

Gill lit another cigarette and shook her head. "We don't know. We couldn't get anything out of the next several pages. When we pick up Virgil's story again he's at the siege of Vicksburg under General Grant's command. I'm having one of my students do some cross-referencing with the state archives. Maybe his research can fill in a few of the missing pieces." She noticed Lansing's look of disappointment. "So what are you going to do?"

"I'm going to find the man who killed Elmo Giancarlo and get that emerald back."

"I thought the police already had a suspect."

"It's the wrong man." Lansing thought about explaining further but decided not to. "The Pueblo man I told you about knows something. He knows what's up in those mountains. But he won't help me until I have that stone. I'm going to have to take things one step at a time."

"Is there anything I can do?"

Lansing leaned forward in his seat. "Yes, you can answer a few questions. Do you know if Dr. Giancarlo had any enemies?"

"I know that Baron Vencel and Elmo Giancarlo hated each other's guts. But that won't do you any good."

"Why not?"

"Vencel has an airtight alibi. He's been supervising an archaeological dig up in Chaco Canyon all summer. He didn't get back till yesterday afternoon."

"I suppose there are people who can corroborate where he was."

"If you give me a few minutes, I can get you a list of who was with him. Anything else?"

"Dr. Giancarlo checked the emerald out of the museum the day he was killed. Is something like that unusual?"

"I would say so, yes."

"Why he would do something like that?"

Gill shook her head. "Research, maybe. But the only place he could do detailed analysis would have been in my lab, and he never came down here that I know of."

"Just in case, would you mind asking your students?"

"Sure."

"One more question, for the time being. Do you remember Giancarlo ever mentioning a man by the name of Jonathan Akee?"

Gill thought for a moment. "No. It doesn't sound familiar."

"Well, I guess that's it." Lansing and Margarite stood. He reflected a moment. "I was curious, Dr. Gill. How long do you think it will take to finish with that journal?"

"I don't know."

"If we're going to explore the realm of possibilities, it could be important. Only Virgil Lansing knew why he buried that emerald. Margarite thinks he wrote the journal to explain what we were supposed to do if we did find it."

Gill nodded knowingly. "That's why he wrote that he hoped no one would ever read his words." She looked up at Lansing. "We'll get it done as fast as we can, Sheriff."

"Thanks."

"Just a minute." She rummaged through a desk drawer and pulled out a stack of papers. She quickly thumbed through the stack, finally pulling out a single sheet. "Here's the personnel list for the Chaco dig. Names, local addresses, and phone numbers."

"Thanks. If you can think of anything else"—he jotted down the name of his motel and room number—"you can reach me here. If we're not in, just leave a message at the desk."

49

"WHERE TO NOW?" MARGARITE ASKED AS THEY WALKED
down the hall.

"Since we're here, we might as well start with the
crime scene."

They followed the signs through the corridors until
they found the administrative offices for the Archae-
logy Department. A woman in her early twenties sat
behind the reception desk. She didn't look happy
about having to be there.

"Can I help you?" The question dripped with
disinterest.

"Yes, I'm Sheriff Cliff Lansing." He was dressed in
civilian attire and looked more like a rancher in town
or shopping. He showed her his badge and identification. "I'm working on the Giancarlo murder case. I'd
like to see his office."

"The police have already been through it a hundred times."

"I'm sure they'll be through it a hundred more
times. I just want to see it once."

The receptionist sighed in resignation. "It's around
the corner and two doors down. But it's locked." She

reached into her desk and produced a ring of key
"Here, you'll need this."

"Tough having to come in on weekends," Ma
garite commented.

"Tell me about it." She handed the keys acro
the desk. "Please don't be long. Dr. Vencel said
could leave at two."

Lansing glanced up at the clock. It was twelve
thirty. "It won't take us that much time."

Lansing and Margarite followed the direction
they were given, ending up at a door that was blocke
with yellow crime-scene tape. A DO NOT ENTER sig
was hung on the door. In the small print it claime
the instruction was by order of the Albuquerqu
police.

Lansing unlocked the door and pushed it ope
He stepped under the tape and into the room. Ma
garite followed.

The office was comfortably furnished with a larg
sofa, easy chairs, floor lamps, and Giancarlo's over
large desk. A built-in bookcase made up one wal
Glass-shelved display cases stood along two other
although much of the glass had been smashed. Glas
and broken artifacts still littered the floor. In a cleane
state the room probably looked like a combinatio
study and museum, which it essentially was.

Although the place had been dusted for print
Lansing was careful not to touch anything. H
walked around the side of the desk. On the floo
next to an overturned seat, was the tape outline o
Giancarlo's body. The carpet was stained reddish
brown and the walls were splattered with bloo
almost to the ceiling.

There were also bloodstains on the top of the desk. The stains were smeared, as though something had been dragged through blood. The outline of the body showed a prone position, as if Giancarlo had been laid out intentionally.

"First impression?" Margarite asked.

"Giancarlo didn't put up a struggle."

"It looks to me like there was a big fight," she observed.

"No. All the furniture is still in place. The floor lamps weren't knocked over. Whoever broke those shelves had to step around the sofa to get at them."

He walked over to the broken glass. Taking a handkerchief from his pocket, he examined several shards before picking one up. After looking at it closely he handed it to Margarite. "You can see a light trace of blood on this. A faint splatter pattern. The same instrument that killed Giancarlo was used to break these shelves, after he was dead."

He walked back over to the desk and began looking around. Margarite replaced the sliver of glass on the floor and followed.

"Giancarlo probably knew the person who killed him," Lansing observed. "He was sitting at his desk. I haven't seen photos of the body yet, but my guess is that they'll show his wounds are around his face and upper torso. Detective Gonzalez mentioned something about him being hacked to death.

"They made an inventory of what was missing from this office. I'll bet we'll find a stone ax or hatchet on that list."

Lansing positioned himself next to where Giancarlo would have been sitting. "The assailant came up

close and struck him while he was still in his chai
Giancarlo fell forward on the desk and bled. That
why there are all the stains."

"If he was lying across his desk, why do they hav
the body outlined on the floor?"

"Jonathan Akee came to the office after Gian
carlo was attacked. He saw him on the desk, bleedin
He laid the body on the floor to see if there was an
thing he could do to help. He got blood on his hand
when he moved the body. He touched the wall or th
desk with that bloody hand. That's how his prin
ended up here.

"Realizing Giancarlo was dead, he panicked. H
was sure he would be blamed. That's why he ran."

"Excuse me," a booming voice said from th
hallway door. "This area is off limits, or can't yc
read?"

They both looked toward the voice. A tall, wel
groomed man wearing a suit and tie stood at the doo
just beyond the yellow tape. Tanned, with salt-anc
pepper hair, the intruder looked like Hollywood's ide
of a corporate mogul.

"I'm here investigating the Giancarlo murder
Lansing explained, not the least bit intimidated.

The newcomer seemed to be sizing Lansing u
with an air of disapproval. "And you are?"

Lansing stepped forward, producing his badge an
ID. "Sheriff Cliff Lansing."

"It says here you're from San Phillipe Count
You're a little beyond your jurisdiction, aren't you?"

"Not entirely. I have some vested interest in th
case. A friend of mine has been accused of th
murder, and I don't think he did it."

"I'm sorry to hear that, but you should be going rough proper channels. I can't let every Joe Blow off e street come tramping through here whenever they ant."

"And who are you?" Lansing asked, still not timidated.

"I'm Dr. Baron Vencel, the head of the Archae-ogy Department. This"—he waved his hand in no rticular direction—"is my domain, so to speak, and u are intruding."

"I didn't mean to." Lansing tried to sound a little ologetic. "I'm interested in this case for more than e reason. I took courses under Dr. Giancarlo a long ne ago. We've stayed friends over the years. Need-ss to say, I was a little upset when I heard he was lled." He and Margarite stepped under the crime pe and into the hall, pulling the door closed behind em. "I apologize if we've inconvenienced you."

"No harm done, I suppose." Vencel's face seemed soften a little, reflecting an inner pain. "I under-and how you feel, though. Dr. Giancarlo was a sur-gate father to us all in the department. We're going miss him a lot."

"So you're the man replacing him?" Margarite ked.

"Yes." He turned to her. "I'm sorry. We didn't get chance to introduce ourselves."

"I'm Dr. Margarite Carerra," she said, extending er hand. "I work for the Indian Health Service at a uple of the pueblos."

"Baron Vencel."

Lansing found Vencel's smile to be too warm, as if e stood in front of the mirror and practiced it.

"And let me correct myself. I'm taking ov‹
Elmo's position, but nobody could replace him."

"I take it you two were friends," Lansir‹
observed.

"I considered Elmo Giancarlo my best frien‹
both on a personal level and professionally. Still,
was completely caught off guard when I found o‹
he had personally selected me to replace him ‹
chairman."

"That's a great honor, I'm sure." Lansing nodde‹
"It's kind of funny, us meeting this way. I actual‹
tried to reach you by phone a couple of days ago."

"Oh, that would have been impossible. I wasn‹
even here."

"I know. I was calling your motel over in Cour‹
selor. You must have been in Chaco Canyon at th‹
time."

"Why did you need to speak to me?"

"It was about one of your students. Joel Conra‹
We had found his abandoned truck but there was r‹
sign of him."

"Oh, my God. Has something happened to him‹

"No. As far as I know, he's fine. One of n‹
deputies saw him yesterday. Excuse me for askin‹
though. Didn't you notice he wasn't around?"

"Joel's working on his Ph.D. He's been doing a l‹
of independent research, and I always try to give n‹
students plenty of latitude. It wasn't unusual for hi‹
to take off for two or three days at a time. There w‹
no way I could have known he was in trouble."

"I didn't say he was in any trouble. I just said h‹
was missing."

"Well, you know what I mean." Vencel tried t‹
make the remark seem offhand. "Since you were

friend of Dr. Giancarlo's you should know we're having a memorial service for him tomorrow at the university chapel. At noon. We'd be glad to see you there."

"Thank you. We'll see if we can make it."

50

LANSING PULLED OUT OF THE PARKING SPOT AND BEGAN following the narrow campus street until they reached Yale. A moment later they were on Lomas Boulevard, heading downtown.

"Next stop?" Margarite asked.

"We're making a call at the police department. I want to see how the real professionals handle a murder case."

"What did you think of Dr. Baron Vencel?"

"Either Dr. Gill misjudges character and human relationships worse than anyone else in the world, or Baron Vencel is a liar."

"You mean his remark about what good friends he and Giancarlo were?"

"Yes."

"We're total strangers, Lansing. Maybe he didn't want to hang out his department's dirty laundry for us to see."

"I get the idea that you thought he was pretty good looking."

"I do, but what does that have to do with anything?"

"First impressions. Good-looking guy. Well dressed.

Well spoken. The analogy is 'Good people look good.' It's human nature to believe the inverse. If a person looks good, then he's a good person. Vencel obviously couldn't be a liar because he looked so good."

"Oh, I know. You're jealous. You didn't like the way he smiled at me."

"No, I think Vencel's a liar, no matter how good he looks. And that wasn't a smile he gave you. It was a leer."

"Jealous, jealous, jealous," Margarite sang under her breath as she gazed out the window.

Lansing ignored her prodding for the rest of the drive. He was trying to come up with a plausible excuse for looking at the police evidence.

"As a matter of fact, Detective Gonzalez is in this afternoon," the desk sergeant said. "Just a moment, I'll ring him."

A few minutes later Chet Gonzalez entered the reception area through double glass doors. The look on his face said Lansing wasn't welcome.

"Good to see you again, Chet," Lansing said, pretending they hadn't parted on a bad note. "This is my friend and sometime medical examiner, Dr. Margarite Carerra."

"Pleased to meet you." His handshake was brief and businesslike.

"Same here."

"What are you doing here, Cliff? I thought you had a county to run."

"I've got it well trained. Sometimes it can run itself. I'm here about the Giancarlo case."

"I don't know what for, unless you brought my

suspect along with you." Gonzalez looked behind his visitors. "And it appears you haven't. So there's nothing for us to discuss."

"I'd like to look at your police report and what-ever evidence you've collected."

"You're out of your jurisdiction. This is an Albu-querque police matter."

"I'm not saying it isn't. And I'm not saying you can't do your job. But the stolen emerald belongs to me. It was found on my property. I had only loaned it to the university for their analysis. I would like to get involved with recovering it."

"Go ask the guy who stole it. He's sitting in your jail right now."

"I did ask him. He said it was already missing by the time he got to Giancarlo's office."

"So he admitted to the murder?"

"No. Giancarlo was already dead. Jonathan tried to help him but it was too late. But that's how you got his fingerprints."

"What was he doing there to begin with?"

Lansing shook his head. "Can we go somewhere a little more private?"

Gonzalez studied his old classmate for a moment. "All right. Come back to my office."

Margarite and Lansing followed the detective through a maze of desks and cubicles until they reached a glass-walled office with windows that looked outside. Gonzalez directed them to sit as he closed his door.

"So why was he there?"

"I don't know," Lansing admitted. "He won't tell me. There's a Pueblo Indian by the name of Querino Ortiz who's involved in this. Akee wouldn't tell me a thing until they spoke. After that I got the story I gave you. And from what I can see, it fits."

"It fits what?"

Lansing described his visit to the crime scene and what he had observed: the broken glass, the blood on the desk, the final position of the body. What he had seen matched Jonathan Akee's story.

Gonzalez pulled a folder from his desk drawer and handed it to Lansing. "This is what we have so far. Our boys see things a little differently. We agree that Giancarlo slumped across his desk after he was attacked and killed. The relaxing of his muscles and the force of gravity caused the body to slip to the floor. Nobody had to lay him out.

"It's a moot point about when Akee broke the glass shelves or what he used. He could have worked himself into a frenzy during the murder and started busting up the place."

"If this was just a robbery, why would he do that?"

"You're going to have to ask him."

Lansing glanced through the folder. "No murder weapon recovered. Autopsy says it was an object with a chiseled point, like a hatchet." He thumbed through a few of the pages. "Coincidentally, a prehistoric stone ax is missing from the inventory of Giancarlo's relics in his office."

"I hadn't noticed that," Gonzalez said, honestly surprised. "Maybe we know what to look for now."

"And maybe your perp broke up the display cases so you wouldn't notice what he used to commit the murder. Your report also says there was no indication that the desk had been ransacked."

"Everything was neat and orderly when we looked."

"Wouldn't you think, if this was a random robbery,

that the intruder would have taken everything he could get his hands on? If I was going to kill someone and rob them, I would walk off with as much stuff as I could find."

"Maybe."

"According to your inventory the coin collection in his desk wasn't touched."

"Akee must have figured the emerald was plenty. It was small enough he could put it in his pocket and walk around with no one noticing. I'm sure a coin collection is heavy, bulky, and hard to conceal."

Lansing turned to the back of the folder, where he found several photos. There were six pictures from the crime scene and four of the autopsy. He showed Margarite the autopsy photos. As he had predicted, there were only wounds around the face, neck, and shoulders. The hands and forearms were free from damage, which meant he'd never attempted to protect himself.

One crime-scene photo was a close-up of a fingerprint. The next shot was an expanded view, giving a better perspective of where the print was found. It was on the wall, close to the floorboards. The only way Jonathan could have left it there was if he had been kneeling on the ground, probably next to the body.

Lansing tucked away that bit of information.

"Do you know if Giancarlo had any enemies?" he asked.

"Everybody loved the old man," Gonzalez admitted. "Which makes your Akee that much more of a suspect. As far as I know, they were strangers."

"What's the statistics? Seventy-five percent of all murder victims are killed by someone they know."

"Well, this one falls in that other twenty-five percent."

Lansing could tell the detective already had Akee tried and convicted. All that was left was the sentencing. He stood to leave. "I appreciate your cooperation, Chet."

"Does that mean, come Monday morning, you'll return the favor?"

"I'll do everything you need for me to do."

"That includes handing the Indian over."

"If you think you still want him, sure."

"What is that supposed to mean?"

"It means I have about a day and a half to find the real murderer."

51

LANSING SAT ON THE EDGE OF THE MOTEL BED WITH the roster Dr. Gill had given him. For no particular reason, other than the fact that he was familiar with the name, he started with dialing Joel Conrad's number. A woman's voice answered.

"Yes," Lansing said. "I'd like to speak to Joel Conrad."

"Just a minute."

A few seconds later a man's voice came over the phone. "This is Joel."

"Hi! Listen, I'm Sheriff Cliff Lansing from San Phillipe County. I'm looking into the Elmo Giancarlo murder case. I was wondering if you had a moment to answer one or two questions."

"I don't want to sound suspicious," Conrad said, "but I don't like giving information out over the phone unless I know who I'm talking to."

"Okay," Lansing agreed. "That's fair. Your truck was found abandoned in my county two days ago after you disappeared. You showed up that night at Roberto Sanchez's ranch, a little unannounced, and he shot you. Fortunately, only your scalp was grazed."

"How do you know all this?"

"I got it from my deputy, Gabe Hanna. You met esterday at the Sanchez ranch."

"Okay, Sheriff. I'm convinced. What do you want o know?"

"I just needed to confirm that Dr. Baron Vencel as the director of your archaeological dig in Chaco Canyon this summer."

"Yeah. He was."

"So you can vouch that he was at the motel in Counselor this past Wednesday night."

There was muffled conversation at the other end or a moment, then, "No. I'm afraid I can't do that."

"What do you mean?"

"Vencel took off for Santa Fe that afternoon. He ad to deliver a progress report to the staff at the Museum of the Americas. He spent the night there nd came back Thursday morning."

"You're sure he didn't come back to Counselor."

"His truck wasn't there when I went to bed about en o'clock, and it wasn't there at four the next morning when I got up."

"But you know for a fact that he was in Santa Fe hat night."

"I know that's what he said." There was a touch f disgust in Conrad's voice, as if he didn't trust any-hing Vencel told him.

"I met Dr. Vencel earlier. A very impressive man. have to admit he seemed awfully upset over Gian-arlo's death."

"Ha!" Conrad snorted.

"What do you mean, 'Ha!'?"

"Dr. Giancarlo couldn't stand Vencel and vice ersa."

"Your Doctor Vencel made it sound like they

were the best of friends. In fact, Vencel said he wa
hand picked by Giancarlo to replace him."

"What a damned lie!" Conrad snapped angrily
"Dr. Giancarlo was going to pick his replacement, a
right. But I guarantee you, Vencel would have bee
the last person in the world on that list."

Lansing thought for a moment. This was only t
have been a routine call to touch all the base
Conrad was supposed to have told him that Vence
was at Chaco Canyon the whole time. Vencel woul
have an alibi and Lansing could pursue other lead
Vencel's trip to Santa Fe gummed up the works. No
he had to follow that lead, just to make sure it didn
go anywhere. "Mr. Conrad, I'm only in town for
short time. I don't suppose we could meet somewher
this afternoon. There may be a couple more question
I'd like to ask."

"Sure. Can I bring a friend? She was at the d
with Vencel and me all summer."

"That would be fine."

They agreed to meet at four. Conrad suggested
coffeehouse not far from campus. Since school wouldn
start for another week it wouldn't be too crowded, eve
for a Saturday.

As Lansing hung up the phone, Margarite knocke
at the door between their adjoining rooms, the
pushed it open. She was dressed in a robe and in th
process of towel-drying her hair. "You're still on th
phone?"

He began dialing another number. "I'll be off
a minute." He waited for the connection to g
through. On the other end Deputy Cortez picked u
"Danny, this is Sheriff Lansing. I'm still down
Albuquerque, but I need for you to do me a favor.

want you to call the Museum of the Americas in Santa Fe. I need to confirm that a Dr. Baron Vencel delivered a report to them from Chaco Canyon this past Wednesday. It would have been in the afternoon sometime. When you're done with that, I want you to call up all the motels down there and find out if he stayed at one of them. I know it will take some time, but I figured you needed something to keep you busy. I'll call back later and see what you found out."

"What was that all about?" Margarite asked, stretching out on the bed next to Lansing.

"Just routine police work," Lansing said, lying back on the bed. "Vencel wasn't at his motel Wednesday night."

"Where was he?"

"That's what I'm trying to find out." He gave her a quick kiss on the lips and jumped out of bed.

"Where are you going?" She pouted. "I thought we were supposed to have a quiet afternoon together."

"The only time you're quiet is when you're asleep. And you had no intentions of taking a nap. I know you."

"What are you doing?"

"I'm going to clean up a little. We're meeting Joel Conrad and a friend of his in an hour or so."

"What for?"

"We're going to discuss that new friend of yours, Dr. Vencel. Conrad agrees with Dr. Gill. Vencel and Giancarlo did not get along. At all."

"So what am I supposed to do while you're getting cleaned up?"

"I thought you wanted to make a call."

"Oh." Margarite tapped her temple, as if remembering something. "That's right. I did."

She went back to her room, still drying her hair. As soon as she found her purse, she dug through it until she found a small address book. Sitting on the edge of her bed, she quickly dialed the number she wanted.

"Dulce Hospital."

"Yes. This is Dr. Margarite Carerra. I was wondering if Dr. Velarde was available."

"One moment, please."

It was almost a minute before Velarde answered. "Dr. Carerra. I'm so glad you called. I've been trying to reach you since last night."

"Is something wrong?"

"No, nothing like that. I got the results back from the state crime lab."

"That's wonderful. That's what I was calling about. What did they say?"

"They have a positive ID on the animal fiber found on Matthew Vicinti and the two other men." He paused, as if he was still trying to accept the findings. "They said the fibers came from a *Panthera onca.*"

Margarite made a quick browse through the mental file cabinet where she kept her Latin reference material. *Panthera* referred to "cats." But all the "cats" in North America belonged to the genus *Felis* except for one. "You're telling me they were attacked by a jaguar!"

"A big one. Most likely it's melanistic. They only found black hairs."

"So you're saying there's a big black jaguar running around our mountains."

"I couldn't believe it either. Last night I called your friend in Shiprock, Kimberly Tallmountain. Since she's a biologist I thought she might know about things like this. She wasn't able to tell me anything until she did some calling around. She finally got back with me this afternoon."

"What did she find out?"

"The jaguar was once indigenous to the southwest United States. They ranged from eastern Texas to the Pacific Coast and as far north as the Grand Canyon. Like everything else the white man has touched, it was driven from its native lands or destroyed.

"The last California jaguar was killed in 1860. The last time a jaguar was even seen in the United States was 1971. That was in Arizona somewhere."

"But that was over twenty-five years ago. How did one end up in New Mexico all of a sudden?"

"I don't know," Velarde admitted. "Neither does Kimberly. She did say, though, that jaguars can be dangerous. They have no fear of man. If this one escaped from a zoo or a private game compound, it could be even more aggressive than one raised in the wild. What's worse is this particular animal is probably disoriented and may have been wounded, which will make it that much more dangerous."

"Jeez," Margarite swore under her breath. "Did Kim have any idea what should be done?"

"Short of an organized expedition, there's nothing anyone can do. The jaguar's nocturnal. With all the caves and crevices for it to hide in up there, we'd never find it in the day. And we already know what happens at night. . . . We become the hunted."

"Have you passed this information on to Police Chief Vicinti?"

"Oh, yes."

"Is he organizing anything?"

"No. In fact, no one's seen him since I gave him

the results of the analysis. I'm afraid he's gone after the animal alone."

"That's insane!"

"I think that's just what Chief Vicinti has become since his son was killed. I know Bram. The only way he'll ever return to Dulce is if the animal is dead. Or he's dead."

"What should I tell Sheriff Lansing?"

"Just what I've told you. If he wants help from the reservation, I'm sure the tribal council will cooperate in any way possible."

"Thanks, Juan." She hung up the phone, worried. Knowing what was up in the mountains now, Lansing would go after it. Other men, just as brave and just as knowledgeable, had gone up there and had been killed. She didn't want that happening to him. But there was nothing she could say that would stop him.

Lansing appeared at the door wearing only a towel wrapped around his waist. His hair was still wet from the shower. "Did you make your call?"

"I'll tell you in a minute. You have to do something first."

"What's that?"

She crooked her finger seductively. "Come here . . . and give me that towel."

52

MR. TOAD'S WAS A DEPARTURE FROM THE SOUTH-
western motif most coffee shops and bistros catered to
in Albuquerque. Instead of drawing on the Hispanic
or Native American culture that permeated society
here, it derived its atmosphere from a late Victorian
influence.

The front room resembled a British pub, dark and
musty with the sour smell of stale beer. The back
room was designed to resemble a gentleman's library.
Bookshelves lined the walls from floor to ceiling.
They were filled with real books that the clientele
were encouraged to browse through while they
enjoyed a coffee or light meal. Booths ran along one
wall, each stall separated by six-foot-high partitions
that doubled as the backs of the seats. Wainscot
extended four feet up the walls, topped by Tudor-style
whitewashed stucco. All the wood had been stained a
uniform dark rich brown. The effect was warm, comfortable, and academic.

It took a moment for Lansing's eyes to adjust to
the dimly lit interior as he and Margarite stepped in
off the street. They were in the front room. At the
bar sat a couple, a man and a woman, engaged in

quiet conversation. The man casually glanced at the newcomers, then turned his attention back to his companion.

With no one else in the bar, Lansing escorted Margarite into the study. They stopped in the doorway and looked around. A man got up from one of the booths and walked directly to them.

"Sheriff Lansing?" the man asked.

"Yes."

"I'm Joel Conrad." He extended his hand and they shook.

Lansing was a little surprised at the bandages on Conrad's scalp and along one side of his neck. He tried not to stare. "This is my friend Dr. Carerra."

"Nice to meet you. Would you care to join us?"

"Certainly," Lansing said. "Lead the way."

In the booth they were introduced to Conrad's companion, Renee Garland, a very attractive graduate student with golden hair and a bronze complexion. Lansing always hated dealing with first impressions. If he got them wrong, they were hard to shake off. Renee looked like a beach bunny bimbo, especially when she looked at Conrad. She gave him a fawning, adoring look that made her seem vacuous. He honestly wondered if she could speak in complete sentences.

Margarite flashed him a glance. Lansing suspected she was thinking the same thing.

Once they were seated, a waiter approached. Every one was satisfied with a round of coffee. At least for the moment. There was small talk about the atmosphere of Mr. Toad's and the weather outside until the coffee were delivered. As soon as they were alone again, Conrad changed the subject.

"Just what did you need to talk to me about?"

"How well do you know Baron Vencel?"

Conrad thought about his answer before giving it. "I'll be honest. Anything I tell you is going to be affected by my total dislike for the man. He is a leech and a liar. He has no professional integrity. And he can't be trusted."

"I see," Lansing said, taking a sip from his cup. "Have you known him long, or are these just casual impressions?"

"I took my first course from him eight years ago. I've been on three of his summer excavations. And I've done everything in my academic career to avoid him."

"I can't believe you dislike him that much."

"What do you mean?"

"I had a couple of professors I really disliked when I was in school. I thought they were jerks. It was easy enough to avoid them. I just didn't take any more of their classes. You just spent all summer with a man you seem to hate. Why would you do that?"

"This is not a brag, Sheriff. I am one of the leading experts in the country on Chaco Canyon. I've been climbing up and down those cliffs since I was in high school. I did my master's thesis on the subject. I'm going to do my dissertation on it. Having to work with Baron Vencel this summer was a sacrifice I was willing to make just so I could do my independent research and still make a little money."

"You must have gotten quite a bit done. According to Vencel he gave you all the time off you wanted."

"Like hell!" Conrad fumed. "I missed one day on the dig and he fired me! Thank God it was at the end of the project."

Lansing looked at Margarite. He was beginning to

wonder if anything Vencel said could be trusted. "Just what did Vencel do to turn you against him?"

It was Conrad's turn to look at his companion. He let out a long sigh, then related his confrontation with Vencel over his master's research. "Before that Dr. Giancarlo tolerated him. After the review committee Doc G. wanted him booted off the faculty. But it's awfully hard to get rid of a tenured professor. I think Dr. Giancarlo wanted to make Vencel's life so miserable that he would resign from the university. Vencel's such a slime, though, that he figured out how to stay put without Giancarlo's blessings."

"Tennis with the university president? A little sucking up to the bigwigs at alumni coffees?"

"How'd you hear about those?"

"I guessed about the coffees, but you have an ally in Dr. Gill. She told me about the tennis and racquetball."

"You said you're investigating Dr. Giancarlo's murder. I'd pin it on Vencel in a heartbeat if I didn't know better."

"If you're talking about his night in Santa Fe, I can almost assure you it didn't happen," Lansing said.

"Why do you say that?"

"I had one of my deputies do some checking. Vencel was in Santa Fe all afternoon at the museum. But he never checked into a motel that night."

"Where was he?"

Lansing shrugged. "Not in Santa Fe and not in Counselor, according to you."

"I may have to change that statement."

"You mean he was in the motel that night?"

"No, but he was in town. He followed me into the mountains around four or five in the morning. That's how I got all this." He gestured toward the bandages on his neck, then unbuttoned his shirt. Fresh bandages were wrapped around his shoulder as well. "I had to go into the infirmary this morning and get new dressings. I've started getting an infection."

"When did Vencel do this?"

"Thursday morning. He attacked me when I was in my truck. After knocking me out, he dragged me into the sagebrush and left me for dead."

"You remember seeing him?"

"Not clearly. I saw a movement out of the corner of my eye. When I turned to the window, something came crashing through. I don't remember anything after that."

"I still don't understand why you think it was Vencel."

"Dr. Vencel instructed me to make sure all of our artifacts from the excavation were securely packed," Renee said, speaking for the first time. "He wanted everything tagged, wrapped, and boxed before we finished that night. Thursday night. When I got back to the motel, Dr. Vencel wasn't there."

"What time was that?" Lansing asked, pleasantly surprised his first impressions had been off their mark.

"Around midnight. Maybe a little later. I went to get some ice, and while I was at the machine he pulled in. I thought he might have gone out for a late meal, but he was acting strange. He checked to make sure no one was watching, then sneaked three cardboard boxes from his truck into his room.

"Friday, while they were loading the moving van, I managed to open one of those boxes. They were back in his truck. I pulled out a spiral notebook full of

Joel's research notes. The other boxes must have had the rest of Joel's stuff that had been stolen."

"So you think Vencel was too busy trailing you to be involved with Giancarlo's death?"

Conrad nodded. "History repeats itself. He didn't get away with stealing my thesis material, so he's robbing me of my dissertation material. Unfortunately, this time around, I don't have Dr. Giancarlo for a guardian angel."

"That and Dr. Vencel has put out the word that Joel is persona non grata in the department now," Renee added.

Conrad touched his shoulder and winced.

"Is that bothering you?" Margarite asked.

Conrad nodded. "Quite a bit."

"Here. Let me take a look. I'm a medical doctor."

Lansing slid from the booth to allow her access to Conrad.

Margarite had him unbutton his shirt and slip it off his shoulder. To give her a clear look he removed a leather strap from around his neck and set it on the table.

Margarite carefully pulled back the bandage. Three parallel scratches extended from Conrad's scalp, just behind the left ear, down his shoulder. There were two sets of puncture wounds, just below his collarbone, front and back. The punctures were deep and showed heavy bruising. Puss oozed from the holes.

"I've got news for you Mr. Conrad. I don't think Dr. Vencel did this. You were attacked by an animal."

"An animal? What kind of animal?"

Margarite let out a long breath. "From what I learned this afternoon, I think you were attacked by a jaguar."

"A jaguar!" Conrad and Renee said in unison.

Lansing had been studiously watching Margarite's work, when he allowed his eyes to drift toward the table. They focused on the strap Conrad had taken from around his neck and the peculiar green stone that it ran through.

He picked it up for closer examination. Hideous hollow eyes stared at him from a jade skull. "Where the hell did you get this?"

53

CONRAD WAS TORN BETWEEN MARGARITE'S REVELATION and Lansing's sudden interest in his jade fetish. "You sure it was a jaguar?" he asked, avoiding Lansing for the moment.

"Not absolutely," the doctor admitted. "But I've seen the bodies of four men in the last few days, and they all had similar wounds. Hair analysis positively identifies the predator as a black jaguar."

"Where was this?"

"They were all killed on the western slopes of the Rockies, in San Phillipe County."

"That's where I was attacked," Conrad admitted.

"One of the men killed was Roberto Sanchez's nephew," Lansing added.

"Antonio? I met him." Conrad was shocked at the news. The look of realization spread across his face. "Damn. I could have been killed!"

"You're lucky you weren't," Margarite observed. "Very lucky."

"Excuse me a minute for interrupting," Lansing said, displaying the jade skull in his hand, "but could you tell me where you got this?"

Conrad couldn't understand Lansing's pressing

interest in his tiny idol. "I bought it at a curio shop. I thought it was kind of interesting."

Renee looked at her companion, wondering why he was hiding the truth about where he found it. She thought he couldn't possibly be thinking Lansing was trying to steal his work too. For the moment she decided to keep quiet.

"It's Mayan, isn't it?" Lansing asked, looking at it closely.

"As a matter of fact, it is." Conrad was surprised at Lansing's knowledge.

Margarite had carefully replaced Conrad's bandages, leaving them a little looser to prevent pressure on the wounds. She slid back into her seat, followed by Lansing.

The sheriff seemed almost reluctant to return the jade stone. "You said you're one of the leading experts in the country on Chaco Canyon. I've read a lot of books about the Pueblo people. I'm part Tewa, so I have some curiosity about the subject. Anyway, in what I've read, no one has said much about Mayan influence. A couple of experts have mentioned possible trade, but nothing about a direct impact.

"Do you think that Mayans could have migrated this far north, bringing some of their traditions with them?"

Conrad gave Renee an uncomfortable look. It was a look that didn't escape Lansing's notice.

"Well," Conrad hedged, "anything's possible. But that's kind of an off-the-wall supposition. Why do you ask?"

"This gets back to the Giancarlo case. The police are convinced he was murdered during a robbery."

"I did hear a little about that. I've been out of the

loop for almost three months. I heard that he had an emerald someone had found. It had some carving on it, something like that. He was doing the analysis."

"It didn't just have some carving on it. The stone had been shaped to resemble a jaguar."

"This is kind of weird," Renee commented, "all this talk about jaguars."

"Trust me. It's all coincidence," Lansing said. "But that's getting away from the point. I have a strong suspicion that the jaguar emerald was first found about a hundred and thirty, hundred and forty years ago in an Anasazi burial ground."

"Oh?" Conrad asked, trying not to sound too suspicious. "And just where is this burial ground?"

"I don't have the slightest idea," Lansing admitted. "Somewhere northeast of Chaco Canyon, within a two-day horse ride. In a valley somewhere."

"How did you find out about this?"

"For the moment that doesn't matter." Lansing was willing to keep his own secrets for the time being. "What does matter is that the emerald was mined from someplace in South America. It was probably fashioned by Mayan craftsmen as a religious totem, then was transported north. Somehow it ended up in the hands of the Anasazi."

"You seem to know quite a bit about this emerald."

"I found it on my property, under my house. I'm the one who gave it to Dr. Giancarlo."

"I see," Conrad sneered. "That's your big interest in all this. You want your emerald back. I should have figured something like that was going on."

Margarite looked at Lansing. His stare at Conrad was cold and menacing. She knew, if he wanted to,

Lansing could break the student in half like a match-stick. The look on his face said he was ready to.

"Watch your step, kid," Lansing said icily.

Margarite looked across the table for Conrad's response. If this had been the Old West, Lansing would just have drawn down on his adversary. Conrad visibly gulped.

"Sure. I—I'm sorry."

Lansing paused for a moment to let the tension ease. "Now, then. Could the Mayans have gotten this far north?"

"Yes. I think they did." From his tone Conrad sounded like he was ready to cooperate.

Lansing held up the jade skull. "So where did this really come from?"

"I found it in the mountains. In the valley you just talked about."

"The valley with all the mounds?"

"What do you know about mounds?"

"The valley is supposed to be full of them. Something like a hundred."

"A hundred?" Conrad looked astonished. "I thought maybe fifty at the most."

"You've been there? You didn't count them?"

"It took me three weeks to realize what I had found."

"What do you mean?" Margarite asked.

"The valley's been filled in. At first I thought there might have been a landslide. There are two stone lions at the mouth of the canyon. They were covered with debris. When I found them, only the part of one head was exposed. But as I cleared away the rocks and dirt to expose them, I realized the rubble hadn't come from the valley walls. There was

too much variety in the sediment. The rocks didn't fr
the geology.

"But I figured the lions had been put there for a
reason. I started looking at the valley behind them. I
was broad and flat. Lots of native vegetation. There
were some animal paths. It looked fairly normal, but
knew there was something different about it and
couldn't figure out what.

"It took me almost a month to realize the floor o
that valley was ten to fifteen feet higher than any of the
other canyons or arroyos around there. The other thing
was, most of the other canyons coming down from the
mountains had water erosion down to bedrock. That
erosion was from a time when the weather pattern wa
a lot wetter.

"The canyon I found, the one with the two jaguar:
should have had the same erosion. But it didn't. I
had been filled in after the climate had turned drier. I
had to have been filled in by humans.

"The first question that came to my mind was why

"I started stripping away some of the vegetation
At regular intervals, every twenty or thirty feet, I foun
long, raised humps on the ground. At the most eacl
hump was only two or three inches higher than the sur
rounding earth."

"What were these humps from?" Renee asked, fas
cinated by his story.

"I carefully dug a few exploratory pits and a trench
I only went down about three feet. The humps were th
tops of huge mounds. I'm pretty damned sure they'r
burial mounds. And the tops have to be at least ten fee
above the valley floor.

"If these are the tombs of Chaco Canyon, the firs

ones were put there over a thousand years ago. The last one maybe seven hundred and fifty years ago.

"The earth on the mounds was packed and settled. Someone came in at a much later date and tried to bury the mounds so no one could find them. Over time this new earth settled, exposing the tops of the original mounds. With the plant growth, no one would have ever known. It was purely by luck, and a little guesswork, that I found the stone lions.

"I'll bet people have hiked in and out of that valley for years and never realized what they were walking on."

Renee's eyes were as large as saucers. "Joel, this is going to be one of the greatest archaeological finds of all time!" She put her arms around his neck and gave him a kiss.

"Thanks," he said, wincing from the pain.

"Oh, I'm sorry."

He patted her hand. "You see now why Vencel was after my research. He plans on taking credit."

Lansing nodded, frowning. "And the jade skull. You found that while you were digging?"

"Yes."

Margarite touched Lansing's arm. "Could that be the one Virgil wore?"

"That's what I was thinking. But why would he come back and bury his lucky charm and not the jaguar emerald?"

"I don't know," Margarite admitted. "Maybe he explains in the journal."

"Journal?" Conrad asked. "What are you talking about?"

Lansing glanced at Margarite, a questioning look on his face. Margarite only shrugged. It was up to him.

Lansing looked across the table. "Wait here."

"Where's he going?" Renee asked.

"He has something to show you," Margarite said.

A minute later Lansing returned with a manila folder. It was stuffed with thirty or forty sheets of fax paper. He handed it to Conrad.

"What's this?"

"Just read," Lansing instructed.

The waiter approached. "More coffee?"

"I think I'm ready for a beer," Lansing said. Margarite nodded. She was ready too. "How about you two?"

Conrad shrugged. "Why not?"

"Make it four," Renee said.

"A round of drafts," Lansing said. "And put this all on one bill for me."

The waiter jotted down the order on a pad. "I'll be right back."

54

AS CONRAD FINISHED EACH PAGE, HE WOULD HAND IT to Renee so she could read it. Thirty minutes and two rounds of beer had elapsed before he completed the last sheet. He leaned back in his seat, very contemplative.

Lansing could see the fledgling archaeologist was trying to digest what he had just read. He decided he could wait until Conrad reconciled the new information with what he already knew.

Finally, Conrad leaned forward on his elbows, staring at the center of the table. He didn't bother to look up while he spoke.

"What we call the Mayan Empire started out around 600 B.C.E."

"Excuse my ignorance," Lansing interrupted. "But what happened to plain old B.C.?"

"B.C. isn't politically correct any longer." Conrad gave a brief explanation of why B.C. and A.D. were no longer used as a reference system.

Lansing could only shake his head. "Thanks. Please, go on."

"Let's see." Conrad reviewed what he was going to say again, then, "The Mayan culture started emerging around 600 B.C.E. It had a lot of starts and fits along the way, but it achieved its Golden Era starting about 750 C.E. The Golden Era lasted about a hundred and fifty years.

"You have to understand, the Mayan Empire wasn't like the Roman Empire. It didn't have a central capital or a single ruler. Instead, it was a bunch of city-states that shared a common culture, including language, writing, religion.

"Around 900 C.E. these great city-states, and there were at least a dozen of them, started warring with each other. Some of the cities were abandoned, some of them were destroyed, some were still around when Cortez conquered the Aztecs.

"It's believed a great number of people fled the Yucatán Peninsula during these wars. Some traveled by boat across the Gulf of Mexico and settled in the Mississippi Valley. It's believed they help develop the Mississippi Mound-Building Culture. Some Mayan artifacts from that time have been found as far north as Oklahoma along the Red River.

"Other groups left the peninsula by land. The Hopi Indians have been in Arizona for a thousand years. Coincidentally, their arrival approximates the time that the Mayan city-states were falling apart. Their oral history states that some of their people came from a great city far to the south, but no one's ever identified what city that was. What is important to note is that the second most important clan in the Hopi nation is the Parrot Clan. Where did they get that name? There are no parrots in the southwest United States. None in northern Mexico. The closest place that parrots can be found is the Yucatán Peninsula."

"What about Chaco Canyon?" Renee asked.

"I'm getting to that!" Conrad sounded irritated at

he interruption. "Pre-Pueblos started living in Chaco
Canyon around 2000 B.C.E. They built different kinds
f dwellings, most of them pit houses. These were just
oles in the ground with branches or logs laid across
he top for roofs.

"The tradition of building aboveground, upright
tructures made out of stone, didn't begin until 900 C.E.,
he same time that Mayans were trying to escape their
warring homeland."

"So you're saying the Mayans built the Chaco
Canyon houses?" Lansing asked.

"Not by themselves. I think they brought a tradi-
ion of building in stone that influenced the people
hat were already there. They brought something else
s well."

"What was that?" Margarite was as enthralled
with the history lesson as the others.

Conrad finally looked up. "If you study the people
f the Southwest, you'll find they are comprised of
amily groups called clans. There are dozens of dif-
erent clans: the Corn Clan, the Water Clan, the
arrot Clan, the Bear Clan. Their names are all taken
om elements or animals that have great significance
n their religions or to their very survival.

"There is one animal whose name has never been
aken, as if it was forbidden. It's the one animal that's
ever seen on ceramics. Only once have I ever seen it
n a petroglyph. And when it was drawn, it was com-
letely black."

"What are you talking about?" Renee asked.

"The mountain lion . . . or maybe more correctly,
he jaguar."

"Why is that?" It was Margarite's turn.

"In Mayan religion the Jaguar god was the god of

the underworld. He was the god of night. He was the
god of death.

"It was a tradition the Mayans could have brough
to Chaco Canyon. The two stone lions at the mouth o
the valley aren't lions. They're jaguars. And that wa
their burial valley. The jaguars were placed there t
protect the dead.

"This Major Phillips had his men dig up the bigges
of the mounds. That was probably the tomb of th
Mayan priest-king who came from the Yucatán an
settled in Chaco. When he died he was buried with hi
gold finery and the emerald fetish that symbolized hi
power."

"But what about all of the other mounds?" Lansin,
interrupted.

"The Mayans gave the Pueblos a death cult. Wha
we call a moiety. For two hundred and fifty years it wa
this moiety's responsibility to see that all the dea
were buried in that one valley. That's why we've foun
so few skeletons in Chaco Canyon. But they built
great ceremonial road from the canyon to the valley
Portions of it are still out there. That's how I kne
where to look for the place."

"But the modern Pueblos have no death cult,
Renee observed.

"That's true, but it fits. The Chaco Canyon cul
ture was built around a central religion. Somehow o
other that religion failed. The people abandoned th
canyon and the religion, along with all the tradition
that went with it. The new religion had no use for
death cult. They forgot about it and so did history
Until now."

All four sat in silence for several minutes. Conra
was waiting for a response. The other three were tryin

to absorb the historical panorama he had just spread in front of them.

"It almost sounds too simple," Lansing finally said. "It makes too much sense."

"I know," Conrad agree. "Schliemann had the same problem when he excavated Troy. All he did was take the *Iliad* and follow the map Homer had provided. No one would believe it could be that simple."

Conrad fell silent for a moment, then looked at Lansing. "What's the rest of the story about Virgil Lansing and Major Phillips?"

Lansing shook his head. "I don't know about Phillips. That part of the journal is missing. Virgil lived to the ripe old age of eighty-two. He died around 1903. He's buried on a knoll at my ranch. His grave overlooks the homestead he built."

"Do you think the jade skull he wore around his neck really protected him all of those years?"

"About as much as I believe in the tooth fairy. Why? Do you?"

Conrad shrugged. "I don't know. He survived down on the Yucatán Peninsula. Major Phillips was losing men left and right and he seemed to do just fine.

"This past week four people get killed by some animal. Dr. Carerra says it's a jaguar. She also says it attacked me. But it didn't kill me. The only thing I can see that might have been different is that I was wearing this jade figurine. Just like Virgil Lansing wore.

"In Mayan religion the skull was a symbol of death. It held great power because it was also a symbol of wisdom. The Thirteen Crystal Skulls of the Maya supposedly hold all the knowledge of the cosmos. When all thirteen are finally brought together, the secrets of the universe will be unveiled."

"Mr. Conrad, did you take a lot of classes from Dr. Gill?"

"Sure. Why?"

Lansing shook his head. "It sounds like you both might have fallen out of the same tree when you hit your heads." He looked at Margarite. "And I'm a little confused myself. You say that Mr. Conrad here was attacked by the jaguar up there in the mountains. He was in his truck at the time. Wouldn't that have protected him?"

"Jaguars can get up to three hundred pounds. It could easily have broken the glass and dragged him through the window. Gabe's report said there was blood smeared down the door and a blood trail leading into the sagebrush. The animal obviously dragged him there as well."

"Did your jaguar steal Mr. Conrad's research material?"

"Joel's theory isn't completely invalid. Vencel still could have followed him there. He could have witnessed the attack and stolen the things out of the truck once the jaguar was gone."

"I have to admit that meshes with what Vencel said. Remember, he made a comment about Mr. Conrad being in trouble. Why would he say that unless he knew something had happened to him?

"Of course, that leaves me nowhere, now," Lansing grumbled.

Margarite cocked her head to one side. "What do you mean?"

"I'm no closer now to figuring out who killed Dr. Giancarlo than I was two days ago."

"You know Jonathan didn't do it?"

"That was a given." He looked across the table to

Conrad. "Thanks for your time. I found this afternoon very educational. I'm sorry it didn't get us anywhere." He signaled the waiter for the bill.

"Yeah. Me too," Conrad said.

Lansing gave the waiter a twenty and told him to keep the change. Sliding out of the booth he nodded to Renee. "It was nice meeting you."

"Same here, Sheriff."

While Margarite got up, Lansing produced a business card from his wallet. "I know Dr. Giancarlo's murder is an Albuquerque police matter, but if you remember anything, or hear anything, I certainly would like to know about it." He handed the card to Conrad.

"I was wondering," Conrad asked as he took the card, "could I get a copy of this journal?"

"That's my only one. But you can talk to Dr. Gill. She has everything, including the original. Tell her it's all right with me if she gives you a copy."

"Thanks. It was nice meeting you, Sheriff. And I apologize if I offended you earlier."

Lansing shrugged. "Dr. Giancarlo was my friend and I feel responsible for what happened to him. The only thing that matters to me is getting his killer."

55

MARGARITE WATCHED LANSING ACROSS THE DINNER table. He seemed less than interested in his meal. He would poke at his refried beans for a moment, then shift his attention to a lone piece of rice. A full two minutes elapsed before he would cut a portion of enchilada with his knife and finally eat it. All the time he avoided eye contact.

She knew he was reviewing the thousand avenues that he could follow. She also knew he wouldn't say a word until he was ready.

"I'll talk to Chet tomorrow," Lansing finally said. "I have a few ideas he might try."

Margarite was grateful he was conscious again. "Like what?"

"For starters, get a log of calls from the telephone company. Find out who Giancarlo had been talking to prior to his death. I'll also suggest they check Vencel's residential phone. There's still a chance he was in town Wednesday night. If he was, he might have made a call or two."

"You seem to have it in for Vencel."

"I just don't like being lied to," Lansing admitted.

"And the only truthful thing I heard out of his mouth was the time and place for the memorial service."

"Does that make him a killer?"

"Of course not."

"Then why pursue it?"

"Because I don't have anyone else on my list of suspects."

"But there is one other suspect you can talk to."

"Who?"

"The guy from Pojoaque. Didn't he seem to know an awful lot? I mean, Jonathan wouldn't say a thing until they talked."

Lansing's face brightened. "Damn. I was so wrapped up with him blaming me for what was going on . . ." He took a bite of his meal, thinking intently while he chewed. "The problem is, I've got to come up with something that's going to get his attention."

Lansing worked on his meal for another half-dozen bites, then set down his fork. His face clouded with another thought.

"What's wrong?" Margarite hated it when he slipped in and out of his moods.

"I'm kidding myself about this Giancarlo mess. I'm down here in the big city playing Sherlock Holmes when I've got bigger problems back home."

"You mean the jaguar?"

"Yes, I mean the jaguar. I've had such a damned mind-set about Giancarlo and Jonathan that I've ignored my main responsibility. I'm supposed to serve and protect the people in San Phillipe. If one more person gets killed, it's going to be my fault."

"You can't go after that animal by yourself," Margarite protested.

"No, but I sure as hell can get a hunt organized.

That animal's a threat both to people and livestock. There's not a rancher in the country who won't volunteer to help.

"I can get trackers and bloodhounds from the state police. With enough manpower we can eliminate the problem in a day. Then I can try to help Jonathan. Besides, if he doesn't care enough to tell me what went on, he deserves to sit in jail for a few more days."

"When are you going to do this hunt?"

"We'll start it first thing Monday morning. That'll give me all day tomorrow to set things up."

"What about the memorial service? I thought you wanted to go to it."

"That doesn't eliminate my animal problem, and it won't get me any closer to finding Giancarlo's killer. Besides, the service was just an excuse to poke my nose around here for a while. I've done all the good here I can do."

"So when do we go back?"

"I've had a few beers. I suppose a good night's sleep would be a good idea before we hit the road. We can leave early, if that's all right."

"That's fine. At least I'll have you to myself for a little while."

"Boy are you lucky," Lansing said sarcastically.

Margarite considered a snappy retort but changed her mind. She really was lucky to have him for herself for even a short time.

56

THE LIGHT ON THE MOTEL PHONE WAS BLINKING WHEN they entered the room. Lansing walked over and dialed the operator.

"Yes, this is Cliff Lansing in room two fourteen. Do you have a message for me?"

"Yes, sir," the desk clerk responded.

Lansing copied down the name and number the clerk provided.

"What's going on?" Margarite asked.

"It's a message from Dr. Gill. I guess this is her home number. She wants me to call her."

"I think you have a secret admirer," she kidded. "Leaving messages at your motel."

"That means you'd better watch yourself," he kidded back. "You can be replaced."

Lansing dialed the number he had been given. Dr. Gill picked up at the other end after one ring.

"Dr. Gill, this is Sheriff Lansing."

"Yes, Sheriff. Thank you for returning my call."

"No problem. What's going on?"

"I know you're in a rush for us to finish with the journal. I thought I'd fill you in."

"I'm all ears."

"As far as the manuscript goes, we haven't had a lot of luck. We're back to pulling off scraps of sentences and isolated words, but we haven't come up with enough to tell a story. I told you earlier we picked up his story at Vicksburg. It appears Virgil stayed with Grant for the duration of the war. We found references to the Wilderness Campaign and Grant's march on Richmond. But I can't understand in what capacity that might have been."

"What's the problem? He was an officer in the Army."

"No, he wasn't. Not anymore."

"What are you talking about?"

"Remember, I said one of my students was looking into the state archives to see what he could find? Well, he turned up a lot of information today that fills in some blanks."

"I'm listening."

"Major Phillips and the rest of his troops never made it out of the desert. Only Virgil survived. He told General Carleton that they were attacked each night for two more nights after they left the valley. Major Phillips was the last one killed. After his death the attacks stopped.

"I don't know how familiar you are with General James Carleton, but he is generally considered a black mark in the white man's history books. He was driven by two things, hatred for the Indians, particularly the Navajos, and pure greed. He tried to break every treaty he could lay his hands on and stole everything in sight with impunity. It's been called Carleton's Lost Patrol because everyone pretty much agrees Major Phillips was operating on the general's direct orders.

"Carleton evidently was in a rage over Virgil's report. He didn't believe any of the story. Virgil was brought up on charges of desertion and cowardice in the face of the enemy. He was summarily court-martialed, stripped of his rank, and drummed out of the service.

"From the description in the records Virgil was led to the edge of Santa Fe and turned loose without a horse. His only weapon was his broken saber. Carleton put a price on his head, dead or alive, of a thousand dollars if he was found in New Mexico territory after twenty-four hours."

"Obviously he survived."

"Yes," Gill agreed. "How or why, I suppose we'll never know. The facts are that he was court-martialed in October of 1862 and turned up at the Siege of Vicksburg, which ended July fourth, 1863. That's a six-to-nine-month span where we'll never know what happened."

Lansing had his guesses. In the opening paragraphs of the journal Virgil talked about his friends at Burnt Mesa. There were a half-dozen pueblos north of Santa Fe where he could have been hidden. It was something he might discuss with Gill some other time.

The court-martial, though, was a different matter. No wonder there was no family history about Virgil's past. As much as the trial sounded like a frame-up, it wouldn't be something anyone would brag about.

"Any more good news?" Lansing asked.

"I'm sorry. I just thought you would want to know we were able to fill in the gaps. The other thing to consider is that we've found corroboration from an outside source. We know what Virgil wrote in his journal actually took place."

"Yeah, I guess I never thought of it that way."

"Too bad the outcome couldn't have been more positive."

"Yeah," Lansing agreed. "That too."

"Well, that's all I needed to pass on tonight, although I suppose it could have waited. We could have talked after the memorial service."

"No. It's a good thing we talked tonight. I have to go back first thing in the morning."

"Is there anything wrong?"

"No more than usual. Thank you for all your help, Dr. Gill. I'll appreciate anything else you pass along, good or bad."

"Okay, Sheriff. Good-bye."

Lansing hung up the phone and flopped back on the bed.

"It didn't sound like good news," Margarite said, lying down next to him.

Lansing sighed tiredly. "I'm not sure I would recognize good news even if it came up and bit me on the butt."

"You want to talk about it?"

"Yeah. Why not?"

57

T WAS ONLY NINE O'CLOCK IN THE MORNING WHEN Lansing rolled to a stop in front of the guest house. He and Margarite had hit the road at six, stopped for a leisurely breakfast in Santa Fe around seven, and reached Las Palmas with a full day ahead of them.

Lansing knew he had been quiet most of the morning. He appreciated the fact that Margarite left him alone when he was engrossed in his thoughts.

Margarite got out of the truck cab, pulling her bag from behind the seat. "Lansing, I have to admit, I had a pretty good time."

"How good?"

"On a scale of one to ten, you hit an eight. That's not bad for you. Just once I'd like to go somewhere when you would leave your job at the office." She walked around the truck and put her arms around him.

"If I did that, I think my head would implode."

"I'm a doctor. Trust me. It won't." She gave him a long, lingering kiss.

"What was that for?"

"For showing a girl almost a good time. At least I had you to myself for a change." She gave him a squeeze, then released her grip. "I guess you're heading into the office to set up your big-game safari."

"In a few minutes. I'll check on the animals first. They always get ticked off if I go out of town and don't tell them I'm back."

"Sure, Lansing, sure." She walked over to her truck. "I'm heading back to the Mesa. Give me a call later."

"I'll do that."

"And, Lansing"—she hesitated, not wanting to sound too worried—"if you do go up in the mountains tomorrow, please be careful."

"I'm always careful."

"Well, then, don't change."

Lansing walked into the barn as Margarite pulled away. His horse, Cement Head, greeted him with a scolding whinny.

"How's it going, horse?" He walked up and rubbed the animal's nose. Trying to show off his dissatisfaction, Cement Head gave his master a nip with his lips.

"Oh-h-h. Don't be that way. Why don't we go for a little ride? That's all you need."

Lansing saddled his horse and led him into the ranch yard. "Wait here a minute," he instructed.

A moment later Lansing reappeared carrying a shovel. Cement Head eyed the tool with concern.

"Don't worry, horse. I'm not going to use it on you. At least not this time." He swung himself into the seat, then pulled up the shovel so it lay across the saddle.

Pulling on the reins, he pointed Cement Head toward the bridge behind the ranch buildings and the hills beyond.

58

RAM VICINTI FINISHED FILLING HIS CANTEEN FROM THE trickle of water below the lichen-covered boulder. The sun was already high, but it wasn't quite midday. Once his water supply was replenished, he knelt and washed his face, then cupped his hands to drink again.

He had traveled light since leaving Dulce two nights earlier. Only a sheepskin jacket for the cool nights, a knife, a canteen, and his rifle. He had been raised in the mountains. Food was plentiful. Piñon nuts, rose hips, wild onions, squirrels, rabbits, deer: each day provided another banquet for him to enjoy.

But he was not in the mountains for his enjoyment. He was on a death hunt. And it would be to the death, either his or the jaguar's.

He had quit blaming himself for the death of the two hunters earlier in the week. They were brave men who knew that facing nature meant facing your own death. He now knew, though, that he had to go after the animal himself.

Pinto Velarde, the chief medicine man of the Jicarilla Apache, had blessed him and his weapon. Velarde had also given him a small leather pouch of

hodentin. The mystical herbs would supposedly protec
him on his quest.

Although Vicinti doubted the power of th
hodentin, he dutifully wore the pouch from a stra
hung around his neck. It would have been an insult t
the medicine man if he hadn't taken it. Besides, it wa
wise to wear the pouch just in case it did work.

Vicinti had crept quietly through the mountai
forests, looking for any sign of the jaguar. Jua
Velarde, the new doctor, had said Matthew and th
two hunters had been killed by a jaguar. A blac
jaguar. A creature that could stand in front of you a
night and not be seen. An animal that hid during th
day and was impossible to find.

Vicinti would find it. He knew he would. He ha
sworn on his son's dead body that he would find an
destroy the creature.

During the day he carefully studied every twi
every blade of grass, looking for any sign that th
beast had passed through. If he came to a crevice or
cave, he would start a fire and try to smoke the crea
ture out. At night he would sit silently with his bac
against a tree or a boulder, listening, waiting.

This was now the third day. He had graduall
worked his way from the higher peaks down to th
edge of the tree line. There were several canyons an
valleys that led to the high desert west of the mour
tains. His search in the forests had been fruitles
Maybe there would be tracks down below. He kne
he would be beyond the limits of the reservatior
That was not his concern any longer. The animal ha
to be stopped no matter where it was hiding.

From a ridge Vicinti spotted a broad, flat valle
below him. At first it seemed no more remarkabl

…an any of the others he had seen. Squinting his eyes
… shade against the bright sunlight, he noticed the
…alley floor had been pockmarked with several holes.
…an-made holes.

Out of casual curiosity he descended the steep
…ope to the valley below. As he got closer he discov-
…ed the holes were really pits. Some of them were
…ur and five feet deep. Strewn around the ground,
…ixed with the freshly dug earth, were the skulls and
…ones of humans long dead and forgotten.

Vicinti knelt for a closer examination. Pieces of
…ottery were mingled with the bones. He even spotted
… lone bead of turquoise.

He stood, shaking his head. This was sacred
…ound. It was wrong for living men to be in this
…lace. As he started to turn to examine some of the
…ther pits he heard the unmistakable metallic "click-
…ick" of a round being chambered.

"Hold it right there!" the man bellowed. "Throw
…own your rifle!"

Vicinti carefully tossed his gun a few feet in front
…f him, then raised his hands so they could be seen. "I
…on't want any trouble," he said.

"What are you doing here?" the man with the
…un said.

Vicinti slowly turned. "I'm tracking an animal."
…e completed his turn so he could face his adversary.

"What kind of animal?"

The man had the sun at his back. Vicinti had to
…quint his eyes to identify him. "Sparks?" he asked
…Harvey Sparks? Is that you?" He had known Sparks
…r years. Sometimes the handicrafts from the reserva-
…on drew a better price at the Carson Trading Post

than other places. It was always worth an extra thirty mile drive to find out. He started to drop his hands.

"Keep 'em where I can see 'em."

"It's me! Bram Vicinti. From the reservation."

"Oh," Sparks lowered the gun from his shoulde but the muzzle was still pointed at the Apache. "Wha are you doing here?"

"I told you. I'm tracking an animal. A jaguar. killed my son."

"A jaguar!" Sparks spit out a wad of tobacco. "Yo been in the sun too long, Vicinti. There ain't no jagua around here."

"I'm not here to argue," Vicinti said, dropping h hands completely. "The state crime lab said it was jaguar that killed my son. That's what I'm looking for

"Well, I haven't seen nothing like that aroun here." Sparks kept his gun ready, just in case he had t use it.

Vicinti gestured toward one of the pits. "Th your work?"

"It's none of your business if it is. This isn't c your reservation."

"Yeah, you're right about that. Sorry if I interrupte anything." He carefully turned and slowly picked up h rifle. He wanted Sparks to know his movements wer deliberate and that he meant no harm. "I'll just get n gun and go."

Sparks watched him closely, all the time his fac squeezed tight with a suspicious glare.

There was something about the white man tha didn't look right. There was a wildness in his eyes. craziness. It was a look that said the Apache had bett be careful.

Vicinti cradled the gun across his chest. He wante

it evident that his finger was nowhere near the trigger. He started back up the canyon, retracing his steps.

He kept walking, staring straight ahead. Sparks disappeared from his peripheral vision. What Sparks did was his business. Vicinti wanted the same opportunity. Let him go about his business as well.

Vicinti felt the bullet strike the same moment he heard the rifle explosion. The force of the shot knocked him face first onto the ground. He didn't notice any pain. There was just numbness. He could still breathe, but only in short, quick gasps.

Sparks used his foot to roll the Apache over. "Sorry, Chief. In a day or so I'll find the gold and be out of here. You just had lousy timing. Can't have you running around telling everyone I found Carleton's Lost Patrol, now, can I?"

He picked up Vicinti's feet and started dragging him along the ground. A moment later they were next to one of the pits.

Sparks dropped Vicinti's legs, then pushed his body with the bottom of his foot.

Vicinti was almost grateful for the numbness. He felt nothing when he hit the bottom of the hole. He was suddenly overwhelmed by confusion. Where was he and why was he there?

He closed his eyes, trying to remember. That's when the numbness took over everything.

59

CONRAD LIFTED THE COVER TO THE TELEPHONE JUNC-tion box and began disconnecting wires.

"Now, why would a Ph.D. candidate in archae-ology know anything about house alarms?" Renee asked in a heavy whisper.

"When I was an undergrad my roommate was a double-E major. He earned tuition money by installing systems like this. He taught me a few things, just in case I ever wanted to become a burglar." He disconnected the last two wires in the box. "That should do it."

"So how is disconnecting the phone going to keep the alarm from going off?" Renee followed Conrad from the junction box to the back door.

"Oh, the alarm will go off. We won't hear it, though, because it's a silent alarm system. It sends its signal through the telephone lines to the police sta-tion. But since the telephone lines are disconnected now, no one's going to hear it."

Renee nodded, honestly impressed. She was going to be more impressed if they managed to pull this off.

Conrad walked up to the back door and opened the screen. He tried the doorknob, just in case it was unlocked. It wasn't. He took the pry bar he had brought along and stuck it between the door and the jamb. Just as he was about to force the door open, Renee called to him.

"Psst! Joel! Come here!"

A little put off by the interruption, he walked over to Renee. "What?"

"He left a window open." She pointed at a window five feet above the ground. It was a smaller window, probably to a bathroom.

"I wasted my time with the alarm system," Conrad complained. "He never turned it on."

He reached up and pried the screen off. Using the pry bar as an extension, he pushed the window all the way up.

"Boost me up," Renee instructed. "I'll walk through and let you in."

"You sure about this? As soon as you go through that window, you're an accessory."

"They have to catch us first, don't they?" She gave him a devilish smile. "Come on. Give me a boost."

As soon as Renee was through the window, Conrad replaced the screen. He then hurried back to the junction box.

Renee was waiting impatiently for him at the back door. "Where were you?"

"I reconnected the wires. Maybe we can do this without anyone suspecting we were here."

They stood in the middle of Vencel's study, trying to decide where to begin.

"Do you think he's going to notice we're not at the memorial service?" Renee asked.

"He'll notice you're not there. He probably expects me not to show up anyway."

"Does that mean my career's shot here?"

"I doubt it. But it looks like I'm changing universities. You could always come along with me."

She put her arms around his waist. "Would you want me to?"

He bent down and kissed her. "I'd insist on it."

"Good." She looked around the room. "And if we don't pull this off, do you think they'll let us share the same cell?"

"Think positive, my girl."

Conrad walked over to the desk and started pulling out drawers. Renee went to the two oak file cabinets and began her search. After several wasted minutes Conrad slammed the last of the desk drawers shut.

"Well, there's nothing of mine in here."

"What about the rest of the house?"

"We can take a quick walk-through, but if the stuff is here it's probably in the same boxes you saw. All we need to look for is those boxes."

Vencel had a large, rambling ranch-style house. The three bedrooms were separated from the rest of the rooms by a long hallway. From the immaculate condition of everything, Conrad was convinced he employed a full-time housekeeper. If Vencel had brought home some extraneous boxes, they would have been stuffed into a closet. That's where they concentrated their search.

After fifteen minutes they were about to give up. Nothing even remotely resembling Conrad's research work turned up. Renee was about to suggest they bail out before anyone showed up when Conrad snapped his fingers.

"If I had stolen something and I had a maid, I'd put the goods someplace she never went."

"The garage?"

Conrad smiled. "The garage."

The large, three-car garage was attached to the house. Conrad pushed the door open and turned on the overhead light.

Vencel's red truck sat in the slot farthest from the door. A white Miata convertible was parked in the closest space. The middle slot was empty. Vencel had driven his Town Car to the memorial service.

The first place they both checked was the back of the truck. The bed was empty.

The rest of the garage was equipped with a workbench that ran the half the length of the back wall. The rest of the wall was taken up by storage shelves that reached the ceiling. The shelves were full of boxes.

Conrad gestured toward the shelves. "Let's get busy."

Renee sat on the floor and began pulling out boxes from the bottom. Conrad started halfway up.

Renee discovered her boxes were indeed full of papers, but they were all Vencel's. They were mostly typed in magazine formats. She couldn't help but wonder if anything in there was his original work. She finished one box and started another.

One had nothing but notebooks stuffed full of miscellaneous papers. Another was full of books. Another full of loose paperwork. Nothing appeared to belong to her accomplice.

Conrad was having similar luck, but he was finding mostly junk. A boxful of old tennis shoes. Another full of rags. Two boxes had the remnants of broken radios, tape players, and assorted other electronic gizmos.

Each time they finished a box, they stuffed it back on the shelf where they had found it. After sifting through over thirty boxes they were resigned to the fact that none of Conrad's research material was there. The only things they hadn't gone through were a stack of empty coffee cans on the top shelves. Conrad wasn't going to waste his time with them. They couldn't hold what he had lost.

Just as Conrad was going to suggest that they leave, the garage door started opening. They both ducked down in front of the truck.

The Town Car slowly eased into its parking space. Classical music boomed from the car's interior.

The two would-be burglars scooted to the far side of the truck. The vehicle had a high suspension. Conrad motioned for Renee to lie down and slide underneath. She did as she was told and he followed right behind her.

It was a few seconds before Vencel shut off the engine to his car. He evidently wanted to hear the finish of the orchestral piece he was listening to.

As Vencel got out of his car, the garage door began to close.

Conrad expected that the coast would be clear in a second, but he was wrong. Instead of going into the house, Vencel walked around to the front of the truck. He paused for a moment before the shelves.

Lying on his back, Conrad was positioned perfectly to peek at Vencel's activity.

The professor had removed one of the coffee cans from the rear of the top shelf. He raised the plastic lid, then took out a handful of rags. Peering inside, he seemed satisfied with the contents. He replaced the rags and the lid, then returned the can to its spot on the shelf.

Renee was dying to ask what was going on. All she could see was Vencel's motionless legs less than a yard away.

Vencel finally headed for the house. At the door he stopped again, as if trying to remember something. A moment later he turned off the garage light as he went inside.

The windowless garage was as dark as night. The only light came from the thin crack at the bottom of the outside door.

"How are we going to get out of here?" Renee whispered.

"We'll use the remote from the truck," Conrad said. "I need to see something first."

"What?" Renee asked impatiently.

Conrad ignored the question. He scooted out from beneath the truck and stood. His eyes were gradually adjusting to the dim light. He was beginning to make out general shapes.

He carefully felt his way down the side of the truck until he reached the shelves. He allowed his hand to lightly trace the shelving supports until he reached the top. When he got to the coffee cans he carefully removed the same can Vencel had handled a few minutes earlier.

Renee now stood next to the truck, terrified. She had no idea what Conrad was doing and could care less. All she wanted to do was get out of there.

Carefully setting the can on the workbench, Conrad removed the plastic lid, then the rags. An object at the bottom of the can emitted a pale green glow. He fought to restrain a gasp.

Renee was immediately drawn to the light.

Conrad reached inside and pulled out the object. It was the size of a man's fist, and heavy. The sculpting was magnificent.

Renee couldn't restrain her gasp.

The emerald jaguar seemed alive.

Conrad hurriedly wrapped the idol in one of the rags, then stuffed the rest back into the can. He replaced the lid and returned the can to its former position.

He felt his way down the side of the truck until he reached the driver's door. He reached through the window to make sure the keys were not in the ignition. Finding that they weren't, he opened the door. Suddenly they had plenty of light to see by.

He pulled the sun visor down and found the remote garage-door opener clipped to it. He guided Renee to the front of the garage.

"Hopefully, Vencel is at the far end of the house changing. I'll hit the button. As soon as the door's open enough for us to get out, we'll go."

"Okay."

Conrad pushed the button. When the door was barely a foot off the ground Renee rolled out. Conrad followed her, hitting the button again when he did.

The door stopped.

He hit the button again as he got to his feet.

The door came closed.

He stuffed the remote controller into his back pocket and grabbed Renee's hand. They hurried down the driveway and across the street. Any moment they expected to hear Vencel's booming voice ordering them to halt.

They kept walking at a quick pace until they finally turned the corner. There, they only slowed a

ttle. Renee's Escort waited for them around the next
orner.

Halfway down the block they finally ventured a
ook behind them. There was no pursuit.

They kept their glee to themselves. It wasn't until
hey were in Renee's car and a safe three blocks away
hat they both burst into laughter.

"Vencel, you son of a bitch!" Conrad laughed.
'I've got you now!"

60

LIKE MOST OF THE BLACKJACK DEALERS AT THE
Pojoaque Casino, Querino Ortiz seldom looked up at
his customers. His concentration was total. He had
only been dealing for two years and the game still
hadn't become second nature. Sometimes it was even
a chore to add up the points if more than three cards
had been dealt to a single player.

The pit boss always kept a close eye, especially if
the table was crowded. Ortiz was smart in many
things, but math, even simple math, caused him to
stumble.

"Place your bets." There were four players at the
table. He ran his hand across the felt surface as a
guide, making sure each of the betting circles had
been filled. This was a five-dollar table. Each customer invested the minimum.

As he dealt the cards, Ortiz noticed from the
corner of his eye that a fifth person had joined them.
He sat down at the "third base" position, so he would
receive the last card before the dealer took one.

Ortiz had a six showing. The other players opted
to stay on their first two cards, counting on the dealer
to bust.

Ortiz turned over his down card. It was a four. That gave him a total of ten points. He had to keep dealing until he reached a point count of seventeen or higher, but not greater than twenty-one.

The next card was a three. Then another three. He studied the total for a moment and hesitated giving himself another card.

"You need one more card," a fat white woman sitting across from him instructed. "Hit it!"

Ortiz had found the woman obnoxious from the moment she sat down. Yes, he would turn over another card. He knew what he was doing.

He flipped over a five.

"Busted," he said.

He reached into his tray to pull out a handful of five-dollar chips to pay off the players. The pit boss quickly intervened, pointing to Ortiz's hand.

"Six and four is ten," the pit boss whispered in his ear. "Three and three makes it sixteen. Five makes it twenty-one. Collect their money."

Without a word Ortiz turned the players' cards over. No one came close to beating him. He scooped up the cards and the money.

"I've had enough of this!" the fat woman complained. She grabbed the few chips still in front of her, almost falling out of her seat as she got up.

Ortiz didn't notice. He still hadn't bothered to look up at his customers.

"Place your bets." He ran his hand across the felt, making sure the bets were up. He hesitated when he got to the third base position. He was expecting to see a red five-dollar chip. Instead, there was a rock. A green rock.

"It has to be a . . ." Ortiz was going to say "chip"

until he realized what he was looking at. A tiny jade skull stared at him from the betting circle. Ortiz immediately looked up at the bettor. Sheriff Lansing stared grimly at him from across the felt.

"Wh-where did you get this?" Ortiz asked, visibly shaken.

"We need to talk," Lansing said quietly.

Ortiz hesitated, then called the pit boss over. Lansing quickly removed the jade stone from the table as they talked.

When they were finished, Ortiz turned back to Lansing. "I go on break in five minutes. Meet me behind the casino."

Lansing got up from the table and left without another word.

It was late afternoon. The one-story casino/restaurant faced the west, casting a long, cool shadow behind it. Lansing stood in the shade, patiently waiting for the dealer.

Ortiz opened the door, saying something to someone inside as he did. He allowed the door to close behind him as he approached. "May I see it?" he asked.

Lansing reached in his shirt pocket and produced the skull, handing it to the Pueblo.

Ortiz studied it closely, turning it over and over, as if looking for a flaw. He reluctantly handed it back to the lawman. "Where did you get this?"

"Right now that's none of your business. It's time you started answering some questions."

"Have you found the emerald jaguar?"

"No."

"I cannot help you, then." He turned to go inside.

"I know about the moiety," Lansing said. "I know bout the tombs in the mountains."

Ortiz stopped and turned around. "What do you now?"

"I know the jaguar idol came from a grave up here in the mountains. It was dug up over a hundred ears ago. It was hidden under my house by my great-reat-grandfather."

"It was stolen by him."

"No. Others took it. But they were killed. I don't now why he hid it. Maybe so more people wouldn't ie."

Ortiz stared at the white man. Whatever he knew e would keep to himself.

"Jonathan won't tell me why he went to Gian-arlo's office. He won't tell me anything unless you ive the word. My guess is you sent him there."

The red man shrugged. "There is no proof."

"I have enough proof to get a warrant for your rrest. You and Jonathan can keep your little secret rom now until doomsday for all I care. The Albu-uerque police think there's enough evidence to con-ict Akee. I think there's enough to cite you as an ccomplice."

"There are things more important in this world han the white man's laws."

"You can be a martyr if you want." Lansing ighed. "But I already know why you went to Gian-arlo's office." Ortiz just stared in response. "You went here to get the emerald back. You believe it belongs o your moiety and that you have sole rights to it."

"You know nothing about our people or our ocieties."

"I know that once, a long, long time ago, your death moiety was very powerful. It was before the people migrated to Pojoaque and Burnt Mesa and San Ildefonso. You had the ultimate responsibility to usher souls from this world to the next.

"You conducted great processions, carrying bodies to the canyon of the tombs. Your power was supreme because everyone had to finally come to you before they could be resurrected into the next life."

Ortiz remained impassive.

Another worker, dressed in a casino uniform, walked past them to the back door. Lansing remained silent as she went by. Though Ortiz said nothing, the sheriff knew he must be close to the truth, otherwise the Pueblo would have walked away.

"I thought that when the people left Chaco Canyon, they had abandoned the old ways. But the moiety still survived. You were just a shadow of your old society. The people no longer needed you. The new religion said no to your death cult."

"We still existed, but how would you know?" Ortiz asked, a touch of defiance in his voice.

"The valley. The canyon of the tombs. Someone spent a lot of time trying to hide it. It probably took years to haul in enough dirt and gravel to fill in that entire valley floor."

Ortiz studied the white man for a long, silent moment. "Eight years," Ortiz finally confirmed. "Our society is small. It took them almost eight years to hide the tombs."

A woman opened the back door and called, "Querino, your break is over."

Ortiz looked at Lansing. "Wait." The Pueblo went inside. He was gone for less than two minutes. When

e emerged, he was no longer wearing his vest and
ow tie. "Do you have a car?"

"I'm in my truck," Lansing said.

"We drive for now."

"Where?"

"Away from here."

Ortiz instructed Lansing to drive toward Los
lamos. Ten minutes later they came to the parking
rea for Tsankawi, the unrestored Pueblo ruins over-
ooking the Rio Grande Valley. They pulled off and
ot out. For a Sunday afternoon there were few cars
here.

Ortiz led the way up the steep path to the rim of
he mesa. He turned off the hiking path and climbed
igher until they had reached the top. He stood and
arveyed the vast expanse of the canyons and valleys
elow.

Lansing followed his gaze, appreciating the mag-
ificent view. He knew why Virgil Lansing had
ettled in this land. It was rugged and beautiful. It was
land that God had taken extra pains in con-
ructing. It was one of those places on earth that
uly touched the soul.

Ortiz sat on the ground, cross-legged. "I know
om your voice you judge our moiety. But you do not
nderstand."

He talked slowly and deliberately, staring into the
pen spaces below him. Ortiz was ready to speak the
uth as he understood it. Lansing sat quietly on a
ock a few feet away, ready to listen.

"We are the Moiety of the Jaguar. Once we truly
ere important. We were created by the Wise One
ho came from the south. He brought with him pow-
rful magic and strange gods that were new to us.

Although we learned much from his wisdom, he held the people in fear. The most powerful god he brought was the Jaguar God, the god of death and the night. He could call it forth whenever he wanted by use of the glowing stone, a stone fashioned in the form of the god. It would kill, at his bidding, anyone who broke his commandments.

"When the Wise One died he was buried in a great earthen tomb of his design. Along with him was buried all the gold and jewels that he had worn in life. The Jaguar God was buried with him too.

"Two Stone Jaguars were carved to watch over the holy place.

"But the Jaguar was still held in great fear. For that reason we buried our dead as the Wise One had instructed.

"When the people left Chaco, a new way began. The Kachina People taught us a new life, free of evil and fear. There was no more need to worship the Jaguar God. But the moiety stayed, not to follow the ways of the Jaguar, but to protect the people from his evil.

"As long as the glowing stone remained buried, so would the God. When the pony soldiers came that day so long ago, they awakened the Jaguar God and he destroyed them. The moiety gathered all that the soldiers had taken and returned it to the valley. The glowing jaguar was not found. It was thought that it had not been discovered and was still buried in the valley.

"Then the newspapers said you found a strange stone of green under your house. It was carved in the likeness of the mountain lion. Our moiety gathered to discuss if this was the Jaguar God that we guarded

THE DARK CANYON   335

against. We did not know for sure until the first sheep were killed. Then I saw in a dream a shepherd boy dying. I knew then it was true. It was the Jaguar God.

"It was our responsibility to return the stone to the ground. It had been our moiety's reason for existing all these centuries, to protect the world from the Death God.

"Jonathan was chosen to go to Giancarlo. We know the greed of all white men. He was to offer two hundred thousand dollars for the return of the stone so that we could destroy the Jaguar.

"But now the stone is gone and the Jaguar God is free to roam and kill as it chooses. It cannot be stopped."

61

LANSING STARED AT THE EXPANSE OF THE RIO GRANDE Valley below him. Ortiz had been quiet now for several minutes. It was up to the lawman to decide what to do with the information. The historical accounts he had no problem believing. Everything Ortiz had said fit comfortably with what Lansing already knew.

The metaphysical aspects he had a harder time dealing with.

He pulled the jade skull from his pocket. "What is the significance of this?"

"It is a talisman. It protects the wearer from the powers of the Jaguar God when he walks the earth." As if to make a point Ortiz reached beneath his shirt and pulled out a leather string. From it hung a skull identical to the one Lansing held. "Along with the Jaguar it is a symbol of our moiety."

Lansing stood. "I'm going into those mountains tomorrow morning with a hundred volunteers and state policemen. We're going to scour every inch of that territory until we find the jaguar and destroy it. God or not. I think you'll find out that it can be stopped."

Ortiz smiled. "He will not be there. The night is

his realm. He walks in the darkness and only in the darkness can he be destroyed, if he can be destroyed at all."

Lansing shook his head. "Come on. I'll drive you back to Pojoaque."

Ortiz shook his head, looking older and more tired than when he had first climbed to the top of the mesa. "I will stay here. It has been a long time since I last talked with the stars."

Lansing tried to think of something to change the man's mind, but came up with nothing appropriate. He turned and headed down the mesa to where he had parked.

62

Renee would sit quietly and try to read a magazine or a book for a while, then start pacing back and
forth in front of the phone. Periodically she would
pick up the receiver to make sure the phone was still
in operating order. Conrad had said that he would call
her and tell her what she needed to do. But that had
been nearly two hours earlier.

She reviewed over and over again their conversation after sneaking out of Vencel's house:

"Do we go to the police now?" she asked.

Conrad thought for a moment. "What if they
don't believe us? I mean, we could say we found it at
his place and he could claim he never saw it before in
his life."

"You don't mean we have to put it back!"

"That's the same song, different verse. He could
say he didn't know anything about the emerald. The
only reason why we knew about it is because we put it
there.

"We're talking about a university department
head. A highly respected man, at least to anyone
who doesn't know him. It would be his word against
ours."

"Yeah but we didn't have anything to gain by murdering Giancarlo!"

"Only the emerald. I think the police would consider that motivation enough."

"What are we going to do, Joel?"

"Let me think."

Several minutes elapsed while Conrad tried to formulate a plan. "When Vencel discovers that we have the stone, he'll know that we figured out he killed Dr. Giancarlo. We've got to get him to come after the emerald."

"Won't he think it's a trap?"

"Maybe not. I can tell him that I'll give him back the emerald if he returns all of my research material. I'll tell him I only want a chance to get my dissertation finished. The emerald doesn't matter. Giancarlo doesn't matter. All I want is my shot at immortality."

"Do you think he would believe that?"

"That's the only thing he would believe. That's how his psyche works. He can understand a person's motives if they are self-centered and self-serving. Anything else would be beyond his comprehension."

"Where are you going to meet?"

"Someplace neutral. Someplace where he thinks he's safe."

"His office?"

"No. No place around here. Someplace where he'll think the police can't get to him."

"Where's that?"

Conrad pondered the question for a few moments. "I'll tell you later."

He never did tell her where the rendezvous would take place. Around three o'clock Conrad left the apartment, taking with him a jacket, the jaguar emerald, and a tape recorder. Renee was to stay there and wait for his call. He would tell her what to do.

At five o'clock the phone finally rang.

"Hello," Renee said desperately.

"It's me," Conrad said from the other end.

"Where are you?"

"I'm in Cuba."

Renee knew he wasn't talking about the country. It was first town you came to after leaving the Jémez Pueblo. "What are you doing up there?"

"I just talked to Vencel. He's going to meet me."

"Where?"

"At the Canyon of the Jaguars."

"Does he know where it is?"

"He's got all my maps. He won't have any trouble finding it."

"But why are you all the way up there now? It will be four hours before he can get there."

"I didn't want to run into him on the drive up here. Besides, I wanted to get a head start so we can be ready for him."

"What do you mean 'we'?"

"I want you to call Sheriff Lansing and have him meet me there." He gave her the number to call from the business card Lansing had supplied.

"Does he know where you'll be?"

"He'll be able to find it. Tell him to use a San Phillipe property map. The canyon is located at grid point C-fifty-seven. It's about a thirty-minute walk from the nearest road. You got that?"

"Grid point C-fifty-seven. Thirty-minute walk from the nearest road." She wrote down the information on a pad next to the phone. "Got it.

"When should I tell him to meet you there?"

"Tell him to get there as soon as possible."

"Okay. I will. And, Joel. Please be careful."

"I will."

Conrad hung up at the other end. A moment after the click came the dial tone.

Renee stared at the receiver for a second. She wished she could be with Joel. Maybe she could drive up there after she contacted Lansing. Then she remembered, she had no idea where this place was.

She hung up the phone, then picked it up again, dialing the number Conrad had provided.

"San Phillipe Sheriff's Department. Deputy Cortez. Can I help you?"

"Yes," Renee said. "I'd like to speak to Sheriff Lansing."

"I'm sorry, ma'am. He's not in. Is there something I can do?"

"No, I—I need to speak to Sheriff Lansing. This is important."

"I'm sorry. He drove out of the county this afternoon. Would you like to leave a message?"

"Yes . . . I mean, no. I need to talk. . . ." She couldn't decide if she should leave a message or have him call her back. "Yes, I'll leave a message."

"All right. What is your name?"

"My name's Renee Garland."

"And where are you calling from?"

"I'm in Albuquerque."

"Do you have a number there where you can be reached?"

She gave him Conrad's phone number.

"All right. What did you need to tell the sheriff?"

"Tell him he has to meet Joel Conrad at the Canyon of the Jaguars as soon as possible." She said the words so fast even she couldn't understand them.

"Slow down, man," Deputy Cortez said. "I didn't get a word of that."

Renee took a deep breath. "Tell Sheriff Lansing to meet Joel Conrad at the Canyon of the Jaguars. It has to be as soon as possible."

"Excuse me, ma'am. Who's Joel Conrad?"

"Sheriff Lansing knows him," she snapped impatiently. "They met yesterday."

"All right. All right. Just calm down. They're supposed to meet where?"

"At the Canyon of the Jaguars."

"I'm not familiar with that place."

"Sheriff Lansing knows about it. On the San Phillipe County property map, it's located at grid point C-fifty-seven."

"Okay. County map. C-fifty-seven. Now, when is he supposed to meet Mr. Conrad?"

"The sheriff has to get up there as soon as possible."

"And what is all this in regards to?"

Renee was at her wits' end. What did it matter what it was about? She didn't want to waste twenty minutes explaining who Vencel was and why they were trying to trap him. "Tell him it has to do with Dr. Giancarlo's murder."

"Excuse me, ma'am. Are you telling me you're trying to report a murder?"

"No, no, no!" Renee had reached her breaking point. "The murder happened last week. Sheriff Lansing knows about it. Just give him my message! Please! A soon as possible. If he has any questions, have him call me!"

She slammed the receiver down, before she really blew her stack.

Someone knocked at the apartment door. Exasperated over her conversation, Renee stomped across the room, not conscious of her actions. She turned the knob, still fuming.

The door suddenly swung open, pushed with so much force, she was knocked to the ground. Vencel stepped into the room and slammed the door shut. He held a pistol in one hand. He used the other to drag Renee to her feet.

"All right. Where is the bastard?"

"Wh-who?" Renee whimpered.

"This is Conrad's apartment. Who do you think I'm talking about?"

"He's not here."

Vencel began a quick search, dragging the girl along with him. Satisfied Conrad wasn't there, he pushed her onto the sofa.

"You surprise me, Miss Garland. I thought you had better sense that this."

"I don't know what you're talking about."

"Oh, yes, you do. Where is he?"

"I have no idea. Joel took off earlier today. Around noon. He told me to stay here. He said he'd be back later. I haven't seen him since."

Vencel eyed the grad student. The look on his face said that he almost believed her. He casually surveyed the room as if looking for something that would dispute her claim. His eyes finally focused on the notepad next to the phone. He walked over and picked it up.

"San Phillipe County? Grid point C-fifty-seven?" He held up the pad. "Does this mean anything to you?"

She shook her head. "I've never seen it before."

Vencel tossed the pad aside and smiled. "Miss Garland, I've been reading your daily reports all summer. Don't you think I know what your handwriting looks like by now?"

Renee jumped from the sofa and tried to make a run for the door. Vencel grabbed her by her shirt collar and tossed her to the ground. As she tried to get up, he backhanded her.

She crumpled to the floor, sobbing. "What do you want?"

"You know exactly where Mr. Conrad is, don't you?" There was no response. "DON'T YOU!" he screamed.

She nodded meekly, afraid to look up.

"Has he really gone up to that canyon?"

She nodded again.

He picked her up by her hair and dragged her into the kitchen, pushing her to the floor once again. He rummaged through three drawers until he found what he wanted.

Setting his gun out of reach he knelt in front of her and began wrapping her wrists together with duct tape. Once they were secure, he tore off a strip and covered her mouth with it.

"I know you're dying to know what's going on, so I'll tell you. We're taking a little drive into the mountains. I'm going to keep that meeting with Mr. Conrad and I'm going to get my emerald back. He can go to hell if he thinks he's getting that research mate-

ial. I have something much better to trade with
now."

He stood. "I'm afraid you'll have to wait here a
moment while I bring my truck around. We don't
want to alarm the neighbors, now, do we?"

IT HAD BEEN A LONG DAY FOR LANSING. AFTER TH
early-morning drive from Albuquerque and after Mar
garite had left, he had ridden up to his great-great
grandfather's burial spot. Only two people had been
laid to rest on the homestead, Virgil and his wife
Kele. They lay side by side, guarding the ranch they
had built from scratch.

Lansing had stared at the simple tombstone for a
long time before he stuck the shovel into the ground
He kept telling himself this wasn't desecration. Virgil
was just helping him solve a problem he was facing.

The earth was soft and pliable. The top of the
coffin was fortunately only four feet from the surface
It took almost no time at all to clear away the dir
from the lid.

Using the shovel blade, he pried the top open.

There, staring up at Lancing through hollow
sockets, was Virgil, a man he had come to know and
like. It was hard to believe their lives were separated
by nearly a century.

Bits and pieces of cloth still clung to the bones i
places. The cloth was dark blue. Metal buttons, black
ened and tarnished with time, were spaced at regula

ntervals. Epaulets rotted on the shoulders. It took
Lansing a moment to realize his great-great-grandfather
had chosen to be buried in his military uniform.

One arm was laid across the chest. The other rested
at his side. The bony fingers were wrapped around the
hilt of a saber. An officer's saber that had been broken
in half.

Suddenly Lansing felt great pride in his ancestor.
Here was a man who had been wrongly accused and
convicted of a crime he didn't commit. Yet, when he
died, he chose to be buried with the symbol of his dis-
grace. Defiant. Knowing till the end he had done no
wrong.

There came a stir of wind that lightly caressed his
face. In a way, Lansing felt Virgil knew his thoughts
and appreciated his sentiments.

The sheriff cleared his throat, embarrassed by his
sentimentality. He had not dug up the old man's grave
just so they could meet. He knelt and looked closely
around Virgil's neck. His guess had been right. The
jade skull that had played such an important role in
Virgil's life had been buried with him.

Lansing carefully picked it out of the coffin.

"I'm not stealing it, Grandpa. I just want to
borrow it for a while. I think you know why."

Lansing and Deputy Cortez had spent four hours on the
phone making arrangements for the dragnet they were
going to set out in the morning. Every rancher in the
county volunteered to join in the hunt. The highway
patrol promised ten men and two bloodhounds.

Once all those arrangements had been made,
Lansing was ready to confront Ortiz. It was the jade

skull from Virgil's grave that Lansing had laid on the
blackjack table.

After leaving Tsankawi Mesa, Lansing didn't feel like
hurrying home. He took a leisurely drive over to
Espanola for a quiet steak dinner. As he ate, he
wished Margarite were sitting across the table from
him. He enjoyed her company. But he was also a man
who enjoyed his solitude. These were feelings that
tore him apart sometimes, and he knew he avoided
facing them whenever they arose. Like that very
moment. He pushed the thoughts from his mind and
began reading the paper while the waitress brought
him an after-dinner coffee.

It was seven o'clock when Lansing opened the door to
the guest house. He had been up since five-thirty but
didn't feel the least bit tired. He turned on the radio
then noticed the message light was blinking on his
answering machine.

"Sheriff, this is Danny Cortez. Could you give the
office a call when you get in? I have a message here for
you from a Renee Garland in Albuquerque. She says
it has to do with a Dr. Giancarlo. It's five-ten now. I'll
be on until eight."

Lansing pressed the "cancel" button on the
recorder, then dialed his office.

"San Phillipe Sheriff's Office. Deputy Cortez."

"Yeah, Danny. Sheriff Lansing. What's this message you have?"

Cortez related all the information Renee had given
him. "Do you know what this is all about?"

"I have a pretty good idea. Who do we have out n patrol?"

"Deputy Hanna called in from Dulce about twenty ninutes ago. He's heading back to base for shift hange."

"Radio him and tell him to forget about shift hange. Send him up to that canyon. I may need some ackup."

"Yes, sir. Is that where you're going now?"

"Yes."

He hung up the phone and dialed Conrad's umber, just to see if Renee had more complete infor- nation. After six rings he hung up. Obviously no one as around.

He trotted out to his patrol Jeep, cursing himself nat he had taken his private truck that afternoon. He uickly backed it up to his horse trailer and con- ected the hitch.

Five minutes later he had Cement Head saddled nd ready to go. He could cover the distance from the oad to the canyon in half the time on horseback.

64

CONRAD HAD PARKED HIS TRUCK AS CLOSE TO TH valley as possible. It was only six-thirty when h arrived. He was sure Lansing would be there by seve at the latest. When the sheriff arrived, they woul hide the patrol vehicle so Vencel would think onl Conrad was up there.

Seven o'clock passed, then eight. The sun ha already drifted below the western mountains whe Conrad's watch read eight-thirty.

Lansing wasn't going to show. But Vencel was.

Conrad couldn't wait by his truck any longe Grabbing a flashlight from his glove compartment, h started up the path that led to his valley.

He had been along the path dozens of times. As game to kill time he had picked out markers along th way that told him how much farther he had to g Somehow it seemed to ease the monotony of the wall

On this particular hike there was plenty to kee his mind occupied. What was he going to do whe Vencel arrived? Obviously he wasn't going to arres the man. But he could get him to talk. That was th purpose of the tape recorder. And he knew Venc loved to talk. Especially when the subject was himsel

Conrad mentally noted he had just passed the fifteen-minute marker. He was halfway to the canyon. From this vantage point he could still see his truck. In another five minutes he would round a boulder and lose sight of the desert below. He looked behind him. There was no sign of Vencel or Lansing.

The twilight was quickly disappearing and the stars were popping out by the hundreds. There was a new moon, so the night was only going to get darker.

He thought about turning on his flashlight, but he didn't want the beam seen from below. Besides, he was confident he could find his way in the dark.

He passed the boulder that marked his last checkpoint. He was only five minutes from the stone jaguars.

As he approached the two effigies, the sound came rumbling down the canyon like low thunder. Conrad was confused. There wasn't a cloud in the sky.

The noise came again, louder, more guttural.

Conrad look up at the valley ahead of him. In the distance the beam of a flashlight bounced erratically. He could hear the muffled sound of running feet and a man gasping for breath.

The roar shattered the night, reverberating off the canyon walls. A second later a man screamed, a piercing, blood-chilling scream.

The beam of the flashlight disappeared as the night air filled with the vicious sounds of an enraged animal.

Conrad stood frozen, knowing if he dared move, he might be next.

65

LANSING PULLED HIS JEEP TO A STOP AND JUMPED OUT
There were already two trucks parked along the sid
of the road. He ran over and checked the hoods. The
older truck with the camper top was cold. The new
red truck was still hot. It had been there only a brie
time, though Lansing couldn't tell how brief.

He backed Cement Head out of the trailer, ther
went back to his Jeep. He grabbed his jacket and slippe
it on. He then pulled out a box of shotgun shells from
beneath his seat and stuffed his pockets full.

Grabbing his scattergun from its mount on th
console, he crammed as many shells into the gun as i
would hold. Slipping it into the rifle holster next t
the saddle, he swung onto his mount.

The normally cantankerous horse obeyed imme
diately, as if he sensed his master's concern. He se
out at a quick trot and they were soon covering a lo
of ground.

Vencel held a flashlight in one hand and his gun i
the other. He pushed Renee ahead of him as h
searched the slopes above him for the mysteriou

valley Conrad had discovered. Renee could only whimper in protest. Her hands were still bound with tape, as was her mouth. Occasionally, Vencel would push too hard and she would trip and fall. Soon her legs were bruised and bleeding from the treatment.

Had it not been for the fact that he had seen Conrad's truck, Vencel would have thought he was on a wild goose chase.

They rounded a boulder and he flashed his light ahead. Just yards away the beam caught the unmistakable shape of a jaguar's head carved out of stone.

Vencel started chuckling to himself. "A find of a lifetime," he said. "And it's going to be mine."

He continued pushing Renee until they were past the stone sentries and standing on the floor of the valley. Vencel tried to scan his surroundings with his flashlight, but the beam was getting weak. He could only light up objects within five or six feet.

He continued farther into the valley. "Conrad! You hear me? It's Vencel."

He stopped and listened for a response, but none came. He pushed Renee ahead. "I know you're up here! I saw your truck back there. I'm here to make our trade!"

Renee tried to stay ahead of Vencel's push. Just a few feet ahead of him she tripped over something on the ground. Vencel flashed the light on the object. Renee began screaming as desperately as possible with her mouth taped shut.

Lying next to her, eyes wide with insanity and terror, was the body of Harvey Sparks. His throat and chest had been ripped open. The fresh blood still glistened in the dim beam of the flashlight.

"So you and Harvey were in this together?" Conrad shouted.

Vencel wheeled around, his gun ready. Conrad was nowhere to be seen. His voice seemed to just bounce off the high valley walls. "Did you do this?" Vencel screamed.

"No. I didn't have to."

"Where are you, you son of a bitch?"

"Answer my question. What were you and Harvey up to?"

Vencel wheeled around again, firing his gun twice into the darkness.

"Not even close, Vencel! Answer me or you'll never see that emerald again."

"I hired Sparks to keep an eye on you. When he saw that brass button, he knew you had found something. That's when he followed you into the mountains." Vencel slowly turned. He listened for even the slightest sound.

"So he's the one who knocked me out and stole my research stuff."

Vencel fired again.

"You missed," Conrad taunted.

"He didn't attack you. You weren't anywhere around your truck when he found it."

The night filled with silence. "So while Harvey was chasing me around, you were busy killing Giancarlo."

"The old bastard had pushed me as far as he was going to push. I found out in Santa Fe that afternoon that Giancarlo had picked a replacement. The curator from the Museum of the Americas. I went to Albuquerque to plead my case. He wasn't going to shut me out. Not after all I had done for that department."

"So you killed him."

"It was an accident." Vencel wheeled around and ~~~red again, hitting nothing.

"Where did Sparks fit in this? What did he want?"

"He wanted Carleton's gold. That's all he's ever ~~~anted. He's been crawling around this desert for ~~~rty years looking for it. He figured you had found it. ~~~guarantee, he was a willing partner." Vencel looked ~~~round the steep walls. "All right, Conrad. You know ~~~he whole story. It's time to trade. I want that emerald."

"Sorry, Vencel. You've already given me every- ~~~hing I wanted. I've got your confession on tape." ~~~rom his position behind a protective boulder Conrad ~~~it "rewind" on his tape, then "play."

The faint but clear voice of Baron Vencel came ~~~hrough the speaker. "He's been crawling around this ~~~esert for forty years looking for it. He figured you found ~~~. I guarantee, he was a willing partner." Conrad hit the ~~~top button.

"Nice try, Conrad. Now that's two things you're ~~~oing to hand over to me."

"Why would I do that?"

"I don't know where you're hiding, but you'd ~~~etter take a look down here."

Vencel pulled Renee to her feet and ripped the tape ~~~rom her mouth. He held the flashlight in front of her ~~~ace so it could be seen clearly, then turned her so she ~~~ould be viewed from wherever Conrad was hidden.

Conrad peeked over the boulder. "You bastard," ~~~e whispered under his breath. He called out loud, ~Renee, are you all right?"

Vencel shook her so she would respond.

"Y-yes." She sobbed.

Conrad had no idea how many more bullets Vencel ~~~ad. He had to take a chance that he was almost empty.

Reaching in his pocket, he pulled out the emerald, still wrapped in a rag. When he exposed it, the mystical light glowed almost bright enough to read by.

"It's here, Vencel!" Conrad yelled. He set the glowing idol on top of the boulder and then began running.

Vencel whipped around and began firing at the sound of the footsteps. He stopped as soon as he saw the idol, glowing seductively on top of the boulder. He pushed Renee aside and began stumbling toward the emerald.

He suddenly froze when he heard the deep, thundering growl of the beast.

Lansing had no idea how much farther he needed to go. There were no lights or sounds in front of him. Then came two reports from a pistol. Despite the echoes he knew the sound originated somewhere ahead of him.

He spurred Cement Head into a gallop. Both horse and master trusted each other, even in this untrod territory. Another shot rang out, this time closer.

In the distance came the muted yells of men. Two men. Lansing slowed his mount, seeking a direction. One more pistol report echoed through the canyon just above them.

Lansing pointed his mount toward the sound. A million stars poured only the faintest light into the valley as they entered. Dark shades moved against shadows.

A man yelled something and Lansing looked toward the sound. A pale green light appeared in the darkness. Someone started firing a pistol, the shot spewing like a Roman candle.

The fading beam of a dying flashlight bounced cross the valley floor in front of him. Lansing didn't now if he was looking at friend or foe.

The thunderous roar ripped through the night.

Lansing wasn't prepared for it. Neither was the orse.

Cement Head reared in terror.

Lansing grabbed for his shotgun as he fell from the addle. He hit the ground hard as the earth trembled rom another roar.

A woman's voice started calling out to Conrad.

A man in the darkness began to scream in horror. The scream mingled with more pistol shots and the nrelenting thunder of the beast.

Vencel tried to run, throwing his flashlight to one ide. A searing pain shot down his spine when razor laws dug into his back.

He fell to the ground, twisting so he could face is adversary. The great cat seemed to weigh a thou-and pounds as it pounced on his chest. The green yes, mere slits of rage, glowed from within.

With every ounce of strength he could muster, Vencel shoved the pistol against the animal's rib cage nd began firing.

The black terror screamed in outrage. In one quick move it clamped its jaws on the frail throat of he man beneath him and tore the life away.

As soon as Vencel shoved her aside, Renee started alling out to Conrad. She tried desperately to get to

her feet. The roar of the animal so close by terrified
her. Fear almost froze her to her spot.

"Conrad!" She sobbed. "Conrad! Help me!"

Lansing jumped to his feet. He knew he couldn't help
the man being attacked. He ran in the direction of
Renee's pleading yells.

He was almost surprised at how much he could
see with only the stars for light. As he closed on
Renee's voice, he could make out her form against the
darker ground.

He knelt at her side. "Miss Garland! It's Sheriff
Lansing!"

"Oh, my God. Thank you." She tried to grab him
but her hands were still bound.

"Hold still," he ordered. He set down his shotgun
and pulled out his knife. In one quick motion he cut
through the tape, freeing her.

Behind them Vencel's struggle was over. An omi-
nous growl was now turned in their direction. Lansing
could see the black shape as it crept closer.

The first gunshots brought Bram Vicinti to consciousness. His eyes had been closed for so long, the stars
were almost blinding. It took a moment for them to
adjust to such brightness.

He tried to remember where he was. His last
thoughts had been about the jaguar. He was in the
mountains. He was stalking the creature. It was now
night. He must have fallen asleep.

He started to get up but his body wouldn't respond.
He could move his hands. He could feel that his body

was there. But when he touched it, it was like touching someone else.

The memory of the morning came flooding back. Harvey Sparks. He was walking away from Harvey Sparks. Then he heard a gunshot.

The realization was crushing. Harvey had shot him in the back. He couldn't feel his body because his spinal column had been severed. He was a cripple.

He heard more shots and men yelling.

He remembered his mission. He was out to kill the jaguar.

He looked around. He was in a hole of some sort. Yes, Harvey had been digging up graves. He was now in one of them.

Vicinti could move his arms. If he could find something to help pull him up . . .

Sparks had blessedly thrown his rifle next to him.

Pushing himself onto his stomach, Vicinti leaned the rifle against the wall of the grave. Putting fist over fist he managed to gradually drag himself up and forward.

The night was filled with the roar of the jaguar. The beast was out there, Vicinti thought. Just within his reach.

He had pulled himself up enough so that he could grasp the top of the grave. He chinned himself to ground level, finally heaving himself up on his elbows.

Clinging to his perch with one arm, he retrieved the rifle that had gotten him out of the hole. He set it in a position where he could fire it and surveyed the situation.

Not twenty feet away a man and a woman knelt beside each other. To his right the black beast from hell was creeping toward them.

Vicinti brought the rifle to his shoulder. It took all his strength to hold his grip on the edge of the hole and take aim.

Just as the jaguar was about to pounce, he fired.

The animal wheeled around toward the new threat. In three quick bounds it closed the ground between it and Vicinti.

Vicinti's efforts to chamber a second round were useless. He couldn't keep his grip and handle the weapon at the same time. As he started to slip back into the hole, the beast was on him.

The jaguar grabbed the Apache by the nape of his neck and dragged him from the grave. Vicinti was almost beyond pain now. His dying thought was that he had kept his word: It would be the beast or him.

Lansing had no idea where the shot came from, but he was grateful for the reprieve. He pulled Renee to her feet the same moment that Conrad came running up.

"Renee, are you all right?"

She managed to wheeze a yes.

Lansing reached into his pocket and pulled out a small, square object. He shoved it into Renee's hand.

"What is this?"

"Never mind," Lansing yelled. "Get out of here! Both of you."

"What about you?" Conrad protested.

"Shut up and run!" Lansing pushed them toward the mouth of the canyon.

As Conrad and Renee stumbled toward safety, Lansing wheeled around to face the jaguar. For the moment Vicinti's limp body had the animal's attention.

To Lansing's left, still on top of the boulder, sat the emerald totem, glowing like an eerie beacon.

Lansing sprinted toward the stone.

As if sensing a threat the jaguar ripped the night with its blasting roar. It broke into a run, after a final quarry.

Lansing heard the vegetation and gravel being crushed beneath the animal's weight. The emerald was still out of reach when he twisted around.

The jaguar was in midair, about to land on him, when Lansing pumped two quick shots into the animal's chest.

The force of the blasts sent the beast tumbling backward. The explosions of the shotgun, mingled with the monster's last roar, reverberated through the canyon.

It was several seconds before silence filled the darkness.

For Lansing it was over. He took a few careful steps toward the dark form. The jaguar lay motionless. Hollow, gurgling sounds came from deep within the creature's chest, its death rattle.

Lansing turned once more toward the boulder. The emerald seemed to blaze brighter than ever. As he approached, he stooped and picked up a rock the size of a small melon.

But he found himself hesitating when he reached the boulder. The emerald was beautiful, its internal light almost mesmerizing. And it was valuable. The Pueblos had offered a small fortune for its return.

Did he have the right?

If it was his to sell, was it his to destroy?

This intricate piece of art had caused so much pain and suffering. But it was a stone and nothing more.

His gaze locked on the face of the stone effigy. The teeth were bared in a perpetual snarl and the eyes flashed in eternal warning. He felt the rock he had picked up begin to slip from his fingers.

From behind him came the warning growl.

Lansing pivoted around as the jaguar raised its head. The monster turned its gaze on the human. The green eyes, as if lit from within, blazed with hatred. Never once diverting its glare, the great cat got to its feet once more. Crouched and ready to spring, it shattered the night again with its tremendous roar.

Lansing turned to the gleaming emerald. He raised the rock above his head and brought it crashing down on the jaguar effigy once. Twice. A third time.

Each strike shattered the idol more and more. Yet the slivers and chips still glowed the eerie green.

The jaguar let out a scream of pain and anger as it leapt through the air.

Lansing dove to one side as the beast crashed against the boulder.

Angered even more at his prey's agility, the great cat turned for the final blow. This puny human would be destroyed.

Lansing stood his ground, pumping round after round at the charging beast. With one final effort the jaguar sprung at him. The roar was deafening.

Lansing felt himself lifted off his feet as if caught by a wall of wind. The fetid stench of death enveloped him as he was tossed in the maelstrom like a tumbleweed.

He slammed hard onto the ground, the wind knocked from his lungs. He fought hard to catch his breath as he struggled to get to his feet, bracing himself for the great cat's final strike.

It never came.

The canyon filled with silence as thick as the night. Somewhere in the vast darkness lay the beast.

Stunned from the creature's last blow, it took Lansing a minute to realize it wouldn't attack again. He had finally killed it.

Exhausted, bruised, and still dazed, Lansing picked up his hat and shotgun and stumbled toward the mouth of the canyon.

Behind him, on top of the boulder, the glowing fragments of the ancient emerald grew dimmer and dimmer until they faded into a final darkness.

The Jaguar God was dead.

66

LANSING APPROACHED THE KNOT OF PARKED VEHICLES just as Gabe Hanna pulled in. Conrad was the first to see him.

"Sheriff! You're alive!"

"Yeah," he said tiredly.

"The jaguar?"

"It's dead."

Gabe jumped out of his patrol Jeep and came running up. "I got here as fast as I could, Sheriff."

"Don't worry about it. It's over." He glanced around. "Anyone seen my horse?"

"He's behind your trailer," Renee said. "He was there when we got here."

"That figures." He grunted. "The coward."

"Is there anything I need to do?" Gabe asked.

Lansing shook his head. "There's nothing anyone can do till morning." He looked at Conrad and Renee. "I know it's late, but I need for you two to follow us into town. I have to find out what happened up there tonight."

"Sure thing, Sheriff," Conrad said.

*　　*　　*

It was four A.M. before Lansing finished with their statements. He made arrangements for them at the Thunderchief Motel, an offer neither one could refuse.

Gabe waited patiently in case Lansing needed anything. Once Conrad and Renee were taken care of, the sheriff gave him a list of instructions.

The hunting expedition would need to be called off. Gabe would have to make the apologies to the volunteers and the highway patrol. He would also have to make arrangements for a recovery team. There were at least two bodies to be retrieved. Conrad had found the corpse of a first victim before Vencel and Renee arrived.

"I'll need for you to take them to the same spot you found us parked earlier tonight."

"What about you, Sheriff?"

"Don't worry, I'll meet you there. I'm going to head back up there now. See what kind of mess we're looking at."

"But it's still dark."

"It'll be daylight soon enough."

Lansing had no idea why he felt compelled to go back alone. It made no sense. But he knew he had to.

The last stars of the night were fading as he directed Cement Head past the two stone sentinels and into the canyon. Despite the growing dawn the broad floor was still bathed in the shadows of the mountains to the east.

Cement Head hesitated slightly, remembering the terror from the night before. A few sniffs of the air, though, seemed to reassure him that the danger was gone.

Lansing found Vencel's body near the center of the canyon. As in the descriptions of the other victims his throat had been torn away, his chest ripped open. A dozen yards farther down the canyon he saw the second body. Conrad would later identify the man as Harvey Sparks, owner of the Carson Trading Post over in San Juan County. He, too, had fallen prey to the Jaguar God.

Getting down from his horse, Lansing made another grisly discovery in one of the holes Sparks had dug. It was the mutilated body of Bram Vicinti. Next to the Apache lay his rifle.

Lansing thought back to the chaos of the previous night. Someone had shot at the jaguar as he shoved the two college students toward safety. The shot could only have come from Vicinti.

Lansing and the Apache police chief had never been on the best of terms. And even though there was nothing Lansing could have done, he knew Vicinti's death would bother him for a long time to come.

As he got out of the hole, he noticed the boulder where he had smashed the emerald. When he approached, he could see there was little left of the figurine. Barely a chip remained large enough to fit into the smallest setting for a ring.

He brushed the remnants of the effigy onto the canyon floor and ground them into the sand. But the swell of relief he felt over that action came crashing down on him in a wave of horror and doubt.

Strewn across the ground were the dozen spent

shotgun shells from the night before. But at the spot where he knew he had left the carcass of the jaguar there wasn't even a stain of dried blood.

Save for the carnage across the valley floor, it was as if the Jaguar God had never existed.

67

WHERE THE ANIMAL HAD COME FROM NO ONE KNEW FOR sure. No zoos, carnivals, or circuses had reported any escapes. As an endangered species, it couldn't be raised on a hunting preserve. That it had traveled almost two thousand miles from its haunts in southern Mexico was the only rational explanation, as preposterous as it sounded.

Despite the theories it was nearly two weeks before the furor died around Las Palmas. Ranchers had to be satisfied with Lansing's explanation that the jaguar had crawled off somewhere to die. Secretly, though, Lansing had his own doubts. Nothing should have survived, even for a few minutes, after the dozen shots he had pumped from his weapon. But he had no other explanation.

With no more reports of missing livestock coming in, the locals finally accepted the fact that the jaguar incident had come to a close. Even Lansing finally quit holding his breath.

In Albuquerque, Chet Gonzalez was only partially pleased that he could close the book on the Giancarlo case. That meant he had to admit he was wrong about Jonathan Akee and the true motive for the murder.

For his part Akee was glad to get out of jail. Lansing never pushed for an arraignment on the domestic abuse charges. All he asked for was a promise that Akee would never strike his wife again . . . and stay off the booze.

It was also around the two-week point that Lansing got a couple of visitors from the University of New Mexico, Joel Conrad and Renee Garland. He hadn't talked to either one since Vencel's body was brought down from the canyon.

When they arrived he was still fighting his budget battle with the county commissioners, though he was confident he would lose. He was grateful for the interruption.

When they came into office he offered them seats.

"We can only stay for a few minutes," Conrad said. "We have to get back to campus."

"Just passing through?"

"Sort of," Renee said, reaching into her pocket. "This is yours." She handed Lansing the jade skull he had shoved into her hand that night in the canyon. "Do you mind if I ask, why did you give that to me?"

"I didn't want to see you get killed. I thought you should take it, just in case it worked."

"Are you going to wear it?" Renee asked, smiling. "Just in case it works."

Lansing studied the object for a moment, then shook his head. "No. I borrowed it from someone. I have to give it back." He unbuttoned his shirt pocket and dropped it inside, then looked at Conrad. "So, how's your dissertation going?"

The Ph.D. candidate shrugged. "I'm looking for a topic right now."

"A topic?" Lansing raised his eyebrows, surprised

at the news. "After your great discovery I thought you have everything all laid out."

"When we got back to Albuquerque I spent a couple of days thinking about everything that happened up there in the mountains. Then I looked up the Pueblo man from Pojoaque you told us about, Querino Ortiz." He gestured toward Renee. "The three of us had a long talk. I guess I'm starting to realize I'm not nearly as smart as I thought I was."

Lansing was intrigued. "What do you mean?"

"He means that maybe the tombs of Chaco Canyon should stay a mystery for a little bit longer," Renee said, taking Conrad's hand in hers.

Conrad looked Lansing squarely in the eyes. "Would you have a problem with that?"

Lansing shook his head. "Not at all. Can I ask why?"

"Maybe I'm starting to learn there are sacred places in this world and that there could be a reason why they exist. I know what I saw and heard up there that night. I could dig up every Native American grave in New Mexico and still not come up with a rational explanation for what happened.

"As Dr. Gill likes to say, open yourself to the improbable and the infinite is at your fingertips."

"But you found that canyon up there," Lansing pointed out. "Don't you think someone else will?"

"Probably," Conrad admitted. "But maybe not for another hundred and fifty years or so. We're on our way back from there. With the help of Mr. Ortiz we filled in the holes Harvey Sparks left behind and buried the stone lions again."

"Put everything back the way it was, huh?"

"Well," Conrad said, sheepishly, "not everything."

He reached under his shirt and pulled out the jade skull that had saved his life.

Lansing nodded. He understood.

As they got up to leave, Conrad snapped his fingers, remembering something. "I'm sorry. I almost forgot. Dr. Gill asked me give this to you." He pulled an envelope from his back pocket and handed it to the sheriff.

Once he was alone again, Lansing opened the envelope. It contained two sheets of paper. The first was a note from Dr. Gill.

Dear Sheriff Lansing,

Congratulations on solving Dr. Giancarlo's murder. Our entire department is grateful.

I know I'm late getting this to you, but things have been a little chaotic. I've been appointed chairwoman of the department and I'm having to learn a whole new set of responsibilities. Attached you will find the closing paragraphs of Virgil's journal. I'm so very sorry we couldn't have provided a complete document. Thank you for sharing his incredible life with us.

Lansing had to admit he was pleased with Doctor Gill's appointment. If anyone could fill Giancarlo's shoes, he figured she could.

He turned to the second page.

JOURNAL OF VIRGIL LANSING (CONT.)

My resolve had been complete. Upon my return to New Mexico, before I entertained any personal projects, I would return the emerald jaguar to its rightful place of rest. I found it still hidden where I had placed it the morning after Phillips had been killed. The valley, I knew, would be only two days away.

Where I made my mistake, however, I do not know. I traveled up and down the canyons and arroyos for three weeks, looking for the sacred tombs. They were nowhere to be found. It was as if the Anasazi gods had scooped them up and placed them far beyond the reach of plundering white men.

I do know, with the emerald unearthed, that the Jaguar God walks. Every night during my search I could feel him watching. Only the Mayan charm that hung from my neck protected me.

More than once I have considered destroying the jaguar image. But that is not my right. And if I did, would it destroy Him or free Him to walk forever? That is for a wiser man to decide.

And so it is my decision to return the ancient relic to the ground and let the God of Night sleep. I hope whoever reads these words accepts my story as truth. Marvel and wonder at the craftsmanship and beauty of the jaguar for a moment, then return Him to the earth. He belongs to another time and another people who no longer exist.

Lansing read the final paragraphs a dozen times. He couldn't help but wonder, if he had seen those pages first, would he have smashed the stone to dust? Then again, if he hadn't destroyed the emerald, could he have stopped the beast?

And the ultimate question yet remained: Did the Jaguar God still walk the night, guarding its dark canyon?

Match wits with the best-selling
MYSTERY WRITERS
in the business!